RAVES FOR DEBORAH BEDFORD'S NOVELS

CHICKADEE

"Well-crafted, powerful drama guaranteed to touch your heart . . . a moving and eloquent novel."

—*Romantic Times*

"Her love for the country is obvious in every description of scenery and seasonal change. . . . the slow pace of an isolated country town is described to perfection."

—*I'll Take Romance*

A CHILD'S PROMISE

"Deborah Bedford provides her fans with a fabulous relationship novel that will entertain from start to finish. A top-rate release by one of tomorrow's superstars."

—*Affaire de Coeur*

"Well written . . . enjoyable."

Critiques

"Kudos to M

lezvous

Books by Deborah Bedford

A Child's Promise
Chickadee
Timberline

Published by HarperPaperbacks

TIMBERLINE

Deborah Bedford

HarperPaperbacks
A Division of HarperCollins*Publishers*

This is a work of fiction. The characters, incidents, and dialogues are products of the author's imagination and are not to be construed as real. Any resemblance to actual events or persons, living or dead, is entirely coincidental.

HarperPaperbacks *A Division of* HarperCollins*Publishers*
10 East 53rd Street, New York, N.Y. 10022

Cover illustration by Jim Griffin

First printing: April 1996

Printed in the United States of America

❖ 10 9 8 7 6 5 4 3 2 1

To two special women in my life who have opened doors and helped my spirit to fly free: my editor, Carolyn Marino, and my agent, Irene Goodman. You are precious gifts in my life, from my Father, who excels at precious gifts. Thank you both, for believing.

To Duane Shillinger, warden at the Wyoming State Penitentiary, and to Mark Setright, prison historian in Rawlins. Without your assistance, Ben Pershall might never have escaped from prison and this tale might never have begun.

To the students in Mrs. Anderson and Mrs. Cuilla's fourth/fifth-grade combo class at Colter Elementary School. Your joy in your own stories makes me come to my own work reborn. Thank you for reminding me to write with the faith of a child.

In you, I seek
a finer place,
a message,
freedom call of grace.
In you, I know
sure solitude,
a blessing
where heartbreak once moved.
In you, I run
away to hide,
and find the
truth and trust inside.
No battle won,
no fortress gained
without the
hope of love reclaimed,
I come to you
at timberline,
and make the
sanctuary mine.

—*db*

TIMBERLINE

Prologue

When Thomas Tobias Woodburn's first original screenplay showed at the Spud Drive-In, half the residents of Star Valley caravaned across Teton Pass to see the movie.

The day the story of Thomas Woodburn's marriage to actress Jillian Dobbs hit the cover of *People* magazine, Sarah Hayden, owner of Hayden's General Store down by the waterwheel, ordered five dozen extra copies to keep from selling out before the end of the week.

But for Oscar night—this night—Dora Tygum, owner of the Caddisfly Inn, rented a big-screen Sony and invited everybody in Star Valley to the party.

"Just imagine it. Little Thom Woodburn," they all said.

"Haven't seen so many folks gathered in one place since the one-fly fishing contest on Caddisfly Creek last fall." Judd Stanford, who'd come straight from his law offices in Afton to attend the occasion, reached across three people and nabbed a cheese finger sandwich as it passed on a tray.

"Would've thought Rebecca Woodburn would be here." Prentiss Smith conveyed a plate of onion rings to the next table. "You'd think, with Thomas being her brother and all—"

The presenter on the television screen leaned into the microphone and announced the night's nominees for best feature documentary. "Don't imagine Rebecca cares to sit around and ogle over her brother the way the rest of us do," Doc Bressler said. "She watched him grow outta diapers, after all. Besides, she keeps to herself. It's been five months since I've seen her down in Star Valley for anything. What with all those elk to feed, and nobody to take care of that huge acreage but herself."

"Strange bird, that Rebecca Woodburn," Charlie Egan said. "I heard she wasn't even willing to leave the land long enough to go to Thomas's wedding."

Margaret Cox joined heads with the rest of them. "I heard that Rebecca Woodburn wasn't invited to her brother's wedding."

"That's ridiculous, craziest thing I've ever heard."

"Guess Thomas didn't invite her because she's got an aversion to weddings," Jake Haux interjected. "After all, she didn't even show up for her own."

"A man can't well compete with all those acres," Mona Teetsel announced wisely. Then, as if in perfect orchestration with Mona's comment, the heavy pine door swung open and, along with the spring Wyoming wind, in blew Cyrus Cotten, his wife, one two-year-old, a second baby slung in a hamper, and a third on the way. "Well," Mona said, lowering her voice. "Little things turn to big things in a small town. Can't even talk about a man without having him walk in the door."

Abby Owen, the pastor's wife from Morning Star Baptist Church, touched Mona's hand as she walked by. "I suppose it would've been awful to take care of all the babies Cyrus wanted, and eleven hundred head of elk besides."

"Oh, good heavens, Abby," Maudie Perkins said, laughing, as Kimmy Jo, the waitress, brought them a tray of fresh-fried mushrooms and a bowl of ranch dressing so they could dip. "What's more important, anyway? That wretched elk herd has been surviving without anyone's help for the past two hundred years."

"I don't suppose Rebecca sees it the same way you do."

"It'd be different, you know, if we were talking about land that belonged to the Woodburns. But we're not. That place went to the government the day Lucille Woodburn died. There's no legacy there."

"Perhaps there is, though," Abby said gently, ever the one to stand up for the valley's lost sheep. "Perhaps there's a legacy somewhere and you just don't see it."

On the big-screen television, Johnny Depp and Annabella Sciorra stepped to the podium and focused on the TelePrompTer. Depp began. "Nominees for best original screenplay are—"

Sciorra proceeded. "*Spirit Dance*, written by Thomas Tobias Woodburn—"

"*Casual Affair*, written by—" Depp read the next nominee, Sciorra the next, Depp the next, Sciorra the next, until they'd finished. But in Star Valley, Wyoming, the other movies didn't matter—nothing in Hollywood mattered, only their favorite son, Thom Woodburn, who'd sat at one of these very cafe tables when he'd been a boy, unscrewing salt-shaker lids and being made to sit still by his grandpa.

"Look what he's made of himself," Prentiss Smith said in reverence. "How many people are watching this? Seems like everybody in America is hearing his name."

"Funny, that. Funny how his name is heard all over America and that sister of his never comes down to the valley for anything. Funny how two kids can grow up together and one turn out so different from the other."

"Yep, it's funny all right. Funny as anything."

"What if he doesn't win?"

"He'll win. He married Jillian Dobbs, didn't he. I've known this about him a long time. Everything he does is blessed, foredestined. He's riding high."

On screen, the actress fumbled with the signet on the envelope for an inordinate amount of time. In Dora Tygum's Caddisfly Inn, in Star Valley, Wyoming, thirty hearts silently urged her to hurry. *Open it. Tell us! Please make Thom the winner.*

At last, at last, she flipped open the envelope. "And the Oscar goes to—" She stopped, smiled directly into the camera, handed the small note to the actor at her side. "Here, I'll let you do this."

"The Oscar goes to," Depp said, "*Spirit Dance* by Thomas Tobias Woodburn."

In the orchestra pit, musicians raised their instruments for a rousing rendition of *Spirit Dance's* title song. The cameras panned the audience until they found him, the lanky dark-haired fellow wearing the rented Armani tuxedo and the western four-in-hand tie, rising from the seat while everyone nearby reached to be a part of Thom's victory, all of them patting his back or kissing him or shaking his hand.

"Where's Jillian Dobbs?" Maudie Perkins asked from her table at Dora's Caddisfly Inn. "All those dressed-up people jumping on him, and I don't see his wife."

"She's gotta be there somewhere, doesn't she?" Becky Farrell asked.

"Well, I'll be damned," said Lester Burgess. "There he is on national television and he's wearing Howdy's old Sunday-go-to-meetin' tie."

Thomas came onto the stage at the Dorothy Chandler Pavilion alone, finally breaking free of the people who surrounded him, springing up the steps, his legs akimbo, his smile a Wyoming mile wide, as he reached out with both hands for the Oscar and held it high so the camera could see. The camera focused on Thomas Woodburn's extraordinary rawboned face as the writer stood in perfect silence for some time, fingering the treasure laid so neatly within his grasp. Timidly, awkwardly, as if all manner of things might be broken by words he'd chosen to say, he at last announced:

"Don't figure I'd be standing in this place if not for my grandma, Lucille. Once, when I was young, she sat me on a downturned bucket in the feed stall and said: 'I'm giving you the facts of life right here. Today. So get ready.' I figured she was gonna tell me about sex, which I already knew about, so I could feel my ears gettin' all warm. I just sat there waiting and, instead, she says, 'Don't let what people say around this place fool you, boy. It isn't easy to change what you believe or don't believe. Your whole life, you're gonna be wondering if you just switched what you believed in, if things would get easier. But it won't work that way. Even if you *wanna* change, you can't make yourself do it. Something's got to come along in your heart and set you free. That's what living with this elk herd has taught me.'

"'That isn't what it's taught you,' I said, thinking I knew everything. 'It's taught you to hang the broom high on the house, else the elk'll eat the broom straws right off the handle.'

"'That, too,' she said then. 'That, too.' And three years later, when she died, we found out she'd signed an agreement with the federal government to make the land a refuge. The land didn't pass into our hands, like I'd always thought it would. Lucille didn't leave anything for me to do but grow up and write screen-plays. So here I am."

He toasted the camera with the golden statue, toasted the millions of people who sat watching from behind it. And that was that. He turned to leave the spotlight as the applause began hesitantly, then swelled to full volume. No flowery mentions of the producer and the director. No thanks to the financiers and the production company that had optioned the script. No use of the platform to fight for causes he might well have believed in, the homeless in L.A. or AIDS victims or the multinational soldiers who'd invaded Haiti. No reference to the talented actors and actresses, the ones who'd made *Spirit Dance* come alive. No glowing remarks about the female lead, Jillian Dobbs, the shining Hollywood star who just happened to also be his storybook-marriage wife.

1

In the library at the Wyoming State Penitentiary, Corrections Officer Fred Pickins turned off the television and issued the order. "Gentlemen. We have ten minutes before moving to the shower room. Let's secure this area."

"Come on, Pickins," someone said. "This is the Academy Awards. We watch the whole dadburn thing and you make us leave before best actress."

"Shut up, Copeland. You talk outta turn, I'll write you up faster'n a cat fries on live wire. You wanna watch TV on your own time, you shouldn't've gotten incarcerated. You damn well'd better step in line. Any more voice and everybody gets early lock-up."

Don't know why 'ol Pickins lies and calls us "gentlemen," Ben Pershall reflected with disdain. We're nothing but trained rabid dogs in a hellhole. Trained rabid dogs.

Still, for good reason tonight, more than other nights, his dog idea brought him irascible pleasure. Enjoy it now, he reminded himself. By this time tomorrow, he'd be long gone.

Pickins planted his feet apart, a sure sign he was about to give another order. "As of this minute," he warned, "you're out of assigned area. Shower room. Let's go! Now!"

Ben stood straight as a sight on a warden's rifle, arms at his sides, staring at nothing as he waited to be moved to the shower room. Twice a week this perdition came, the thumping fights from group stall, the blood, and sometimes even the bodies. "You wanna die?" an inmate asked Ben once when he'd first come to C Block. "This is the surest place. More inmates are killed in the showers than by lethal injection."

"That's good to know."

"Turner smuggled his tooling needle from hobby craft. Stabbed Wilford fifteen times before guards got 'em apart."

"Adds whole new meaning to the words 'shower with a friend.'"

"Only problem is, you've gotta shower with who they tell you to shower with. Most times it's your enemy."

One after another, with Fred Pickins and another roving officer guarding them, the prisoners left the library and trudged across the complex, floodlights aimed with grating accuracy into their eyes. Ben Pershall followed. He'd spent what seemed a lifetime memorizing this place, numbering the steps from one assigned area to another, dreaming of the day he'd be released with each glimpse of shamelessly wide sky.

In the shower he made through the motions, feeling emptied out and superstitious, the way a soldier felt when called to his last battle before returning home. Twice the corrections officer came into the huge ten-head stall, shoving inmates back against the walls and confiscating shims of metal. Blood ran into the drain with the water, eddying ominously on the tiles before it dashed away.

"You know how I feel about do-gooders, Pershall? I hate 'em." Mance Copeland, stark naked and wet, stood from the bench and obstructed Ben's exit. "What's more, I don't much like the way you keep to yourself these days. Don't much like the way you'll never meet my eyes."

Ben couldn't resist. "Guess I don't figure your eyes are worth meeting."

Mance Copeland advanced, his immense hands raised and clenched into misshapen knots. Ben stepped past, turning his back in faith the way he'd never turned it in the joint before.

Ben Pershall's rejection of conflict had nothing to do with giving in. Anything but. He choked it back. He couldn't afford isolation or flatbottom for twenty-four hours. Not tonight. Beneath it all, he stayed charged with outrage. And in turning away he fought the only way, the strongest way, he knew to fight. Silence. Incommunicado.

When Mance jumped him from behind, Ben fell to the floor, yanking his attacker onto the floor with him.

Once during a hunters' course, he'd learned to fend off a bear by rolling into the fetal position. He did so now, gripping the soap in his hand. No matter the cost, he'd hang on to it. In hours, after lights went out, this soap would prove his salvation.

"We got a fight in here!" somebody yelled.

"Damn. I hate a tourist," Mance muttered from above him. He kept hammering, hammering, with steely fists. "Think they've gotta announce it to everybody." And he was right. The word always got around fast.

Ben's fetal position didn't work. But if he fought back, the warden'd throw him in close maximum for twenty-four hours. Twenty-four strategic hours. Dear sweet heaven, he couldn't afford this.

In one sickening rush, he realized the blood dancing with water across the tile was his own. As he lay with the soap tight against his belly, he heard the sound of strikes he didn't feel, skin beating skin, deliverance.

"Get off the floor, Pershall!" the guard bellowed at him, toeing him with one boot. "Get your ass in line." He gestured with his drawn gun. "What's in your hand?"

"My soap," Ben said, standing slowly. The smell of many men in one place, the mildew and the urine, made his eyes water. He thought of the sky again, vast blue, brilliant nothingness. Seemed they let prisoners see the sky, like a giant flag of freedom, just to make them miserable. No bars. No boundaries. "Nothing but my soap."

"Let's see it."

Ben opened his fist. He'd squeezed the white bar so hard, he'd left finger impressions. Words stamped into it said "U.S. government issue. All-Purpose Soap."

"Get your towel and underwear."

"Yes"—Ben didn't meet his eyes, either; meeting eyes wasn't something he liked to do anymore—"sir." He took his place in line. He dried off and scrubbed blood off the cut on his jaw with his U.S. government-issue towel; he pulled on one pair of prison-made jockey shorts. As he followed the others back to Block C, he felt transfigured by time, the passing of each hour bringing him closer to the cold, full moon that would offer its blazing guidance across the sage.

Once in his cell, Ben stood over the sink and examined his face in the steel mirror. He wondered, after all this time, if his wife still wanted him.

What will Wyllis think when she sees me? What will she say when she touches my face?

In the reflection he saw a man he wasn't certain he knew. He recognized the thick, straight nose, the intelligent eyes. He didn't recognize the lines drawn by hardness and grief, or the skin gone sickeningly white like a fish belly. Sweet heaven, he didn't even know the color of his hair anymore; he hadn't seen it in daylight in five years. It lay chopped in uneven tufts upon his head, not much different from alfalfa stubble left in the fields after harvest.

He'd lost so much. So much. And all for what?

Please, God, he prayed. *Please help her see who I can be instead of who I've become.*

Ben opened his footlocker and took quick stock of the items he'd need after lights went out along the corridor. Soap. Black shoe polish. Three layers of clothing. MacLeans toothpaste. Threads he'd pilfered from working in the prison woolen mill.

He was ready to go.

After the Sixty-eighth Annual Academy Awards went off the air, the residents of Star Valley, Wyoming, scraped back their chairs, stretched, donned coats and mittens, bade their good-byes to Dora Tygum and Kimmy Jo.

"You'd've thought he'd talk about something *big*," Etna Bressler said. "You'd've thought he'd talk about something different from what we always talk about in Star Valley."

"Just because an incident occurs in a close-by place doesn't mean it has no consequence," chided her husband.

"But to discuss Lucille Woodburn and sex in the same breath on national television! Poor woman is probably rolling over in her grave."

"You wanna go up there and see, Etna? I'll drive you up for a look at her fancy granite stone. If Lucille's rolling over, you'll be able to see the earth move."

"Good heavens, Doc." Etna called him Doc, too, just like everyone else for forty miles around. "In your line of work, you mustn't make jokes about the dead."

"Don't see why," Doc said, winking across the room at W. D. Owen and Abby. "If Lucille's up there rolling over, I'd best find out about it. You know, for my medical records and all."

"I still can't figure out why Thomas Woodburn never mentioned his wife, Jillian, through all this," Maudie Perkins said.

Prentiss Smith tipped his Stetson to everyone as he held open the door. "Good-bye, everyone. Good night."

"Doesn't anyone else think it's strange?" Maudie asked again as the whole group headed out into the parking lot, lit only by the coursing of the stars and gentle fluorescence from Dora's full-pane front window. "Didn't anybody else notice what happened?"

"No," Carol Mortimer said as she climbed into her own car. "I didn't notice anything unusual. Don't know what you're so worked up about, Maudie."

"Thomas could've talked about so *many* things when he got that Oscar in his hands. Why do you suppose he talked about this place? And people we know? I'm a bit disappointed. I expected more of a show than that. Don't you realize, any of you? During the entire evening, he never once mentioned his wife."

On any given day, the prison bells rang for a count six times, four at scheduled intervals and two at unscheduled ones. The fourth bell came tonight at 9:12 P.M., eighteen minutes before the inmates were scheduled to be in their beds. After the count, Ben lay on his cot in electric wakefulness, thinking, Gotta run. Gotta run. Gotta run.

Ben hadn't slept in a year. He didn't sleep now. He waited, lying there, staring at the springs beneath the empty bunk above him. He heard the guard in the cage leafing through pages of a book.

In the rigid schedule of this place, the sheer honored timelessness of controlled life in prison, Ben's body had developed a clock that defied science, a homing sense that matched the sense of any animal in the wild. He'd read in the prison library about elk that traveled miles from the high rocks down into the valleys on an historic schedule, the young ones following an older cow, one that had made the journey for years and sensed the way.

He liked that story about elk. Every time the boredom got unendurable, every time he got sick of standing around or playing jailhouse rummy or picking paint off the bars, he read that book again. He drew strength from thinking about it as he lay waiting, considering the human fact of nature within him while, for so long, he'd been locked away in this brick and metal fortress of man.

As midnight passed, the guard cage became silent. Pages no longer turned. From other cells came the reassuring, gentle measure of slumber.

Ben rose and dressed. He smeared his face with black shoe polish. He scratched the soap, keeping just enough of it beneath the fingernails on his right hand.

He covered one length of woolen thread with MacLeans. He moved close to the bars and checked the length of the hallway, both right and left. Nothing.

These next moments would be crucial, life or death, freedom or defeat. If a watchman came or the fifth bell clamored, he'd be caught and punished. This was it. Once he got out of the slammer, once he did what he had to do on the outside, he intended never to let them find him.

He reached to the top of the johnson bar as he'd done so many times before, braced two fingers against the metal, and set to work. He worked the thread against what looked like solid steel, cutting into the soap and shoe polish he'd used last week to patch and cover his work.

Twenty seconds, thirty, and a piece of the bar dropped into his hand.

Ever since he'd started thinking about Billy, he'd known this day was coming. For weeks, months, he'd focused solely on slicing through the bar with nothing more than thread and abrasive toothpaste, desperate to get out yet not thinking of freedom. Last week, when the johnson bar had first fallen into two pieces, he'd felt odd and disoriented, as if the liberty at hand were of such substance, so elaborate and promising, he wasn't certain he dared accept it. For so long he'd stayed centered on the possibility of cutting the bar, that possibility only, and now he felt at loose ends.

After a day of agonizing thought, he'd penned a cryptic letter to Wyllis, told her in codes where to meet him and what to bring. If only they'd worked out some escape message long ago, if only they'd discussed it back when she'd come to visit every chance she could, before they'd realized how much they'd lost, when each still had hope. But then they couldn't've known, either one of them, that it would come to this.

"Get the money out of savings," he'd written, "and take Demi to visit my mother. My mother will turn 79 at 1 A.M. next Friday." Then he'd added more. "Every time I visited Mother's house, I loved to stand outside the fence on the northwest section of the pasture, watching that old cutting horse named 'Wire,' the one that never let Mother saddle him once she'd put on the blanket. Do you remember?"

So the convoluted missive went. Wyllis couldn't confuse his words. His mother'd died years ago, and before he'd been arrested, they'd never had anything closely resembling savings. He had no doubt but that the letter would be opened by the time it reached its destination. The warden never let a letter go out of this place without checking its contents. Wyllis would understand, and she'd come. Knowing she'd be there, he'd felt relieved again, protected.

The cells in Block C stood back to back, separated by a vast network of vents, pipes, and crawl spaces. Ben pulled the severed johnson bar across the top width of the cell door, opened the door, stepped out. Freedom. Breathless and agonizing freedom. He couldn't turn back from it. In one fluid movement he licked the soap beneath his nails, replaced the bar, patched it with wet soap, used shoe polish from his face to cover the damage. He checked the corridor again. Still nothing.

He removed a vent cover and slithered inside.

Ben propelled himself forward with his arms, moving through a honeycomb of spaces. His heart pushed against his chest in great relentless heaves, compact energy set into motion with nowhere to expend. He crept carefully to the rhythm of her name, and it sounded, in his head, as if he crept through tall grass. Wyllis. Wyllis. Wyllis.

Twice he almost lost his pants. Sweet heaven, what he'd give for his old belt right now. That'd been the first thing they'd taken away from him when they'd brought him in. The warden didn't like new prisoners trying to off themselves.

From along the shaft he saw first hints of light, manmade and piercing, not the warm, natural moonglow he'd yearned for, but the ever-present, ever-hated spotlight of the penitentiary yard. Ben doubled his legs beneath him, inched forward.

Strange, this honor among thieves. A man likely to kill you in the showers would share with you his entire store of wisdom when it came to planning and instrumenting escape. The inmates collected lore, treasured it, and traded it away much like a child would treasure and trade stones. Ben knew the myriad stories, complete tales of the tunnel networks, the vents, the guard schedules in the two massive cement towers. He found himself now moving toward the outer perimeter of the building, facing northeast toward a tower, a chain-link fence with deadly curls of concertina wire and razor ribbon, and a Wyoming fortress of winter-gray sagebrush, snow, and ancient rock outcroppings that stretched on for at least three miles toward town.

For one moment, one moment only, Ben considered the possibility of Wyllis not arriving to free him.

He'd be dragged back alone, put into maximum security, made to rectify his mad, solitary bolt to liberty. He took one full, purifying breath. This foreordained moment brought him to a place inside himself where he felt masterful, everything he'd thought of, every dream he'd dreamed, multiplied. He slithered forward through mud and muck and water, water that splashed up in his face and smelled rank as a sewer. He didn't care. He mustered his certainty. He knew she'd be there. Wyllis would be waiting.

By the time he got to the end of the vent, he'd crept two hundred yards, two hundred yards, the length that some men ran in long races. But he never thought of it that way as he moved. He measured it in his soul, with the continuous scraping of his palms and his knees, centimeter by excruciating centimeter. And as the end of the vent with its network of metal loomed in his face, the promise of freedom loomed, too, signaled by the gentle light that blanketed the prison yard after the spotlight passed over, the living, warm moonglow he'd so longed for.

The excitement overcame him suddenly. He thought his heart might break free and pound clear up out of his chest. With two hands, he tried the vent cover. It gave. Carefully—oh, so carefully!—he pressed it outward, cringing at the grating sound the metal made against rock. Another inch. Another. If a screw saw him now, he'd be shot on sight. He exposed his hands, his arms. His elbows. The top of his head.

The vent cover rested in his hands. He was out. He scrambled to his feet, replaced the cover, rested pressed against the prison wall. The concrete beneath his back felt cold as death.

His breath rasped against the silence in the yard. The spotlight kept at its continuous circles, illuminating distinct low shadows and the vague smoke-gray sage. Just past the third post from the corner on the high fence, in a blind point to the guards where neither spotlight reached, he saw movement.

Someone waited there.

The spotlight beam passed him once. Twice. He closed his eyes, counted the beats it took to pass and come back with the synchronized pummeling of his pulse.

Each time it passed him, he thought, Now I need to run. But he had to be ready, had to know that when he made his first forward motion across the grounds, there could be no turning back. The spotlight passed him again, but he held back. Now. *Now.*

The beam crossed his face, blinding him momentarily. But his legs had already begun to move. Ben ran.

He ran with his face up, embracing the air, his muscles pumping with every ounce of his strength. He ran far and fast, not listening for the gunshot that would kill him, only thinking he must get away from the stench, from the insufferable body smells of many men in one place. He stopped himself with the fence, his fingers looping desperately through the chain link.

She stood by the post, outside the curls of razor ribbon, and when he arrived, he could tell she had already been working for hours. He said, "You've come."

She whispered, "I've brought everything."

For the moment Ben held his aplomb, wishing to God he could see her, hating the coils of glistening cutlery that spilled out savagely across the ground and separated them. "Imagine," he whispered back. "Back there, against the wall, I thought for a minute you wouldn't."

She hesitated for too long, he thought. "Why would you think that?"

"Asking you to help bust me out like this. I've put us both in danger, asking this of you."

She set to work, turning away from him as if she didn't want him to make her out. "I've used wire cutters all the way to the fence. I know you meant to climb over, but it might be best if you tried going underneath."

"How long've you been here?"

"Since nightfall," she told him humbly. "I've dug a hole. Big enough for you to crawl through." The atmosphere was breathless, as if nature understood this noteworthiness, two souls in darkness on either side of a fence. The weather hovered clear as crystal and below zero; air crackled as it froze in their nostrils. She handed the wire cutters through a chain link to him. "Here. You'd best get started on your side."

Ben took them, no small task as he straddled one enormous strand of concertina wire. The wire cleanly sliced the leg of his trousers, then sliced deeper, bringing blood. "They always take a bell count during the night. If it rings while we're still here, I want you to run."

"I will," she said.

He began to dissect the spools of razor ribbon, finding the stuff served its purpose aggravatingly well. With every sever he completed, the lines stretched to take more space, like an accordion expanding to play.

"Hurry."

"This could take forever."

"It mustn't. If you'd had that long, you could've stayed in jail."

He didn't talk after that, he only worked his side of the fence. "Think I've got this," he said at last. "I'm bettin' I can make it through."

She'd laid blankets over the disarray so he could crawl across without being gashed by barbs and spikes and honed metal edges. He wormed his way beneath the barrier, setting gravel and dirt to motion around him, feeling the knifing cuts despite his three layers of clothing and the blankets along the ground. He reached up first thing on the other side and grasped her hand. "Wyllis. Oh, Wyllis."

She said nothing.

He stood and dusted off his shredded britches, doing something, anything, so his mind could fathom this freedom. Nothing hemmed him in. He wanted to scream from sheer joy. Outside. He stood on the *outside*.

Everything seemed different suddenly, the star-filled night, the sky, the landscape so vast that it set him ill at ease. He felt like a child spinning with his arms spread to take it in, wanting the dizziness the movement brought him yet knowing it could make him stumble. The air felt different here, as if it had something to give him, a promise to keep, as if it had been cleansed by rain.

Ben turned to the woman at his side. "Did you park the car at Rip Griffin's?" That was the Texaco truck stop, the closest building but still a mile away.

She nodded, yes.

Ben looked down at her for the first time. For the first time he saw her face. He stared, disbelieving.

"You've cut your face," she said. "It's bleeding."

The girl he saw was someone he hadn't expected, someone he wasn't certain he knew, with bold brown eyes and a face luminous with hope. Her hesitant smile might've belonged to Wyllis twenty years ago. "Dad?"

He stood caught, perilously stranded between what he'd imagined and what stood before him. "Dear sweet heaven," he whispered. "Demi?" He hadn't seen her since she was nine years old.

She'd taken her hand away. She looked now as if she were afraid to touch him. "Do you mind so much?"

"Where is your mother?"

Demi said nothing.

"Wyllis didn't come," he answered himself. "Wyllis didn't come."

"No," she said. "Momma didn't come. But I did."

The tower light swung toward them, skimming the sage. Ben made no attempt to duck or run. He stood his ground, aching to see all he'd missed, measuring in his heart the years his daughter had grown without him, measuring the cost because Wyllis hadn't come.

"I'm helping get you out of this place. That's what matters, isn't it?"

He said, "I've been locked in the joint for five years, with nothing to see but a square foot of sky from a barred-up window. Maybe I forgot what matters."

She spoke as if she were the parent and he the child. "We have to run, Dad. Much longer and they'll see us."

"Okay. Okay." Her words jolted him to reality. Together they ran across the high barrens, their arms full with the tools and the blankets she'd brought with them. They faltered over rocks. When the light chased them, they pitched forward and lay with their faces against the snow. They topped a rise, and the town of Rawlins spread out before them, glimmering like moving water on the still, black prairie.

Demi tottered, clutching her breadbasket. "Car's just down there." To the west, the monstrous highway sign at Rip Griffin's scrolled its message: "Fill Your Tank Here. Unleaded. Diesel. Hot Coffee and Huckleberry Pie. Give Yourself a Break."

Before them stretched a sea of frozen sagebrush. He'd hoped, planned this, for so many months. Every yard now, every step through the sage, came tainted with the colors of that hope. They ran farther, not talking until Demi pointed out the old gold Le Sabre in the parking lot and they clambered inside. "We gave ourselves a break all right," she said, gasping, slamming the door proudly. "A jail break."

He gazed out the frosted window, realizing that after all these months, after being so desperate, he'd won his freedom only to be lost. If Wyllis had come, he'd've wanted her to take him to the house first before he set out to Hanna Coal, to make amends for Billy. He'd've wanted her to let him sit on the hearth and watch flames roil in the stove, his feet propped on the nickel trimmings until his toes got so hot that he had to move them. He'd've asked her to bake him a ham the way she'd baked a ham every Christmas, with crosshatches in the fat and cloves and honey-browned skin that crackled as the fork's prongs pierced it. He'd've touched her face, wanting her, not letting her finish in the kitchen.

Crazy to think about baking ham and making love. He'd so long dreamed of home, of resting within that gentle place of protection, as careless and sure as a child drifting warmly away at cradlesong. The minute he showed up missing for a count, they'd have the house surrounded.

"Which way should we go, Dad?" She had the engine running on the Le Sabre. She tossed him a map, already unfolded so it covered his knees. "I thought we might do this." She pointed across the front seat. "Over the mountains and up north into Canada. They'll never be able to find us if we make it that far."

"We can't go to Canada, Demi."

"Okay. How about south into Mexico?"

"No," he said. "Not Mexico, either."

"But you won't be safe until you leave the country," she said.

"I know that." He stared at her, feeling horribly sad. He'd lost track of so many years. "How old are you, anyway?"

"Fourteen."

"How old do you have to be to drive this car?"

"Old enough to know how."

"That isn't what I mean."

"I don't see as we have any choice."

He turned away from her, looking out the window. "It's against the law for you to be driving."

Demi put the Buick into second gear, lurching them west toward Rock Springs. They had to go somewhere, she'd decided. "We've just broken you out of jail, and me *driving* is against the law?"

She sped up on the highway entry ramp. An eighteen-wheeler raced past with a *whoosh* of icy air. For a moment he closed his eyes, unable to comprehend the speed.

How fast things move, he thought. His past five years, his prison time, had been timeless, slow. Ben scratched a circle on the icy window, then conceded.

"I've forgotten what matters. I've already told you that." He shook out the map and held it with both hands.

2

Highway 191 between Rock Springs and Pinedale isn't much of a highway at all, a two-lane stretch of road that bisects a sea of windswept sage, snow drifts, and solitary bands of antelope. Every so often, the sage had been worn away to ruts and a dirt track started across into nowhere. Folks took to those tracks when they wanted to feel limitless and free, mostly to hunt sage grouse or chiselers, or to four-wheel, or just to spend the night where the morning stars hung golden and steady in a canopy laid out over their heads.

"I'm glad we're headed north. This is good," Demi said, her face a stranger's face, illuminated only by the green, tractable lighting from the dashboard. "There's nothing out here. You could see a sheriff stopping people for miles."

"Let's hope so."

Just after three-thirty in the morning, they passed through a wide spot in the road called Farson. Demi reached for the radio. "You think they've found you missing yet? We could listen to the news and find out."

He reached out, stayed her hand. "No. Don't turn it on. Don't want to know. I'd rather just talk to you."

"Okay."

They drove in silence, the land stretching away past empty watercourses and an occasional somber ranch house squatting low, its roof burdened with snow. He could see the terrain changing, the moon-silvered sagelands giving sway to the first distant, noble rises of the Wind River Range. Now that he'd told her he wanted to talk, he couldn't think of anything to say.

"Well?" she prompted.

What've you been doing since you were nine years old? It suddenly seemed like such a preposterous thing to ask. He'd missed over a third of her life. Then, all at once, a memory came into his head that he'd long forgotten. It might as well have been yesterday. "You know what I just thought of? The day you built your first snowman. You remember that?"

She shook her head, halfway smiling. "Nope."

"You wanted to start out with this big, hard chunk of ice, and I kept telling you, 'Look here, Demi. The smallest snowball you start with, the better off you'll be.' You were five years old and you put your hands on your hips and said, 'That's dumb. How can something that starts small turn out bigger than something that started big in the first place?'"

"Even now," she said, "that seems like a good question."

"I said, 'You can't guess the ending of something by how it begins. From humble beginnings sometimes comes the greatest things, the things that are most powerful at the end. People try to judge beforehand when they shouldn't.'"

"I know that," she said, "and I'm thankful for it. What if I'd known, that day building the snowman, that you'd be going off to jail? It would've scared me. It scares me still. A good beginning with a bad ending."

"It works the other way around, Demi, as well."

"Does it? I was in the fourth grade and I needed you and they came to the parade and took you to that place and we could only come see you on Sundays."

"Just look at us now," he said. "Look what we've done together." Although he hadn't planned it this way at all.

"This is different, though," she said. "This isn't an ending."

After a long time he said, "For some things, maybe there are no endings. Especially when you're doing something you have to do."

"You know, that's always what Momma said, too. 'Ben had to do what he had to do.' If she said it once, she said it a thousand times."

That's always what Momma said, too. Demi's words echoed in Ben's head. He'd seen Wyllis at visitation only three weeks ago. She'd come to the window, pressed her nose against it, laid her fingers high against the glass as if to reach him.

He stared out the car window now, remembering the panel of glass always between them. Outside, darkness rolled past in soft waves over sage and snow. "Why didn't she come, Demi? Will you tell me that much?"

Demi replied, "We'll be in mountains by sunrise. Maybe we *could* go to Canada. We could be there by tomorrow at nightfall, if you'd let us try it."

"No Canada," he said. Then he added, his voice soft, "All I really wanted was to go home. We'll hide out somewhere for a few days. Then we'll go back to Hanna. I've got to get back to Hanna."

Now it was Demi's turn to become very, very quiet. After a long time she said, "Going home wouldn't've worked."

"Why not?"

"It's just that Momma doesn't—" She stopped.

"What? She doesn't what?"

"Dad. There are things you have to know. Things that won't be easy."

He laid one hand on his daughter's arm. "Tell me about your mother. Do it now. Before we go farther."

Demi took a deep breath, didn't look across the seat at him. "She's doing okay. For probably the first time since I can remember, she's really doing okay." She took another breath and clenched the steering wheel. She glanced over at her father's face, an inquiring, frightened look that he answered with the most reassuring nod he could muster. "I guess you remember Pete Giddy, don't you?" she asked.

"Of course I remember him. I've known him all my life."

"He's been coming around a lot, helping her do things. He's been hauling and splitting Momma's firewood ever since I can remember. And he put a new roof on the house last April."

Pete Giddy? Not Pete Giddy. Ben wanted to discuss anything to keep from acknowledging the presence of a different man in Wyllis's life. He asked about the roof instead. "Was it leaking?"

"Like a sieve. When the snow started to melt, water came down like rain all over the sofa."

"Pete Giddy was in my third-grade class. And fourth. And fifth. That man worked the mines at Hanna Coal right beside me."

"That's sort of what started it," Demi told him. "The miners all walked out at Hanna Coal this past fall. Said they wouldn't go back until the company put pillars and steel plates where they were blasting."

"Can't say I blame 'em for standing up for that. Something like that could mean their lives."

"Wasn't the best for Pete Giddy, though. He lost his toe in the labor dispute."

"They had fights over it?"

"No. Nothing like that. They were standing around the front office discussing how to get hot chocolate out of the machine when Buster Hendrix dropped his maul on Pete's foot. Took four men to carry him out and get him to the hospital in Laramie. Hanna Coal started a whole new safety policy the next week. Everybody went back to work except Pete Giddy."

"I see."

"He had to move out of employee housing. Momma figured, after he'd been the one to put the new roof over our heads, that it didn't seem right for him to have no roof at all."

"I see."

"Guess it just gets so people start needing each other for everyday things worse than they need the people they loved and couldn't get to. That's what happened with Momma and Pete, I think."

"Of course," he said, feeling detached and empty. "Makes perfect sense. She began to need him. Of course that happens to a woman."

But he fought now to save himself, to forcibly pull his mind from the pain, from the betrayal. His thoughts raced to disjointed themes, ridiculous and irrelevant. He wondered whether Copeland had skinned his knuckles when he'd belted him in the shower room. He wondered whether the johnson bar had fallen away when they'd opened the door to search his cell. He wondered whether he'd live to see the light of day.

The lean cottonwoods that loomed in the headlights, the cross-barred goshawk that swooped along the road in its hunt, all seemed more real to him suddenly than Wyllis, the woman he'd loved, the woman who'd come to need someone else.

"I heard Momma in the shower one night last week, crying to beat the band. She'd gotten your letter, that funny one you wrote about taking me to Grandma's. I said, 'Momma. What's wrong?' She said, 'I waited until Pete went to bed to read this. Pete and your daddy have always been good friends, you know. Grade-school friends.' 'What does this letter mean?' I asked after I read it. 'I can't visit Grandma on her birthday. She's dead.'"

"Yes," Ben said, trying to stop Demi from telling the rest, knowing the story's conclusion, not now needing to hear. "She is."

But his daughter kept right on going. "'It means your daddy thinks he's gonna break out of that place and come out like nothing wrong ever happened,' Momma told me. 'Just like that. This Friday. After all these years. After deciding what he did so long ago. And now I've gotta decide, too, whether to go all the way back or all the way forward.'"

"That's the way she's always been," he said quietly. "When she has to decide, she picks to go forward." Then, as if the words themselves conjured action on the road ahead, red lights began to play with eerie precision upon the winter landscape. "Demi?"

"I see it."

"You figure that officer's caught somebody speeding?"

"Could be. Could be a roadblock, too."

"They'll have had the bell count at the pen by now. They know I'm missing."

"What should I do?"

He thought for a moment, searching the roadside, searching for breaks in the drift fence. Funny, but he didn't care so much for himself and for escaping anymore. He cared for his daughter, the child who'd believed in him and who'd come to the state pen with blankets and wire cutters. Despite everything, he knew he must keep Demi safe.

"Cut the lights," he told her. "Now."

She didn't question him. She hit the knob. Darkness closed around them like something living. For long seconds they drove in blindness, not able to see. She pressed the brakes once, held them down hard. "It's black as pitch out here. We'll go off the road."

He grabbed the dashboard, too, waiting for the Buick to run off the shoulder and hit gravel. But when they came to a stop and began to make out the road, Ben found they were still on it, pulled halfway into the oncoming lane, dead center on the pavement.

"Take your foot off the brakes," he instructed her. "Don't want 'em to see taillights, either. Just let the car creep along by itself."

"What're we gonna do after we creep along?" she asked, her voice feeble, all confidence gone. "We'll be caught up with 'em in a minute. What'll a sheriff think when he sees a Le Sabre going along with lights out. He'll be suspicious for sure."

"He won't see us, that's what." Ben's eyes had adjusted slowly to darkness. As Demi inched the car forward, the dimness had brightened. The air became soft blue in the moonlight. A mantle of gentle-star gold lay evenly over everything, like dust. "We'll turn off someplace."

"Where?"

"At one of those infernal four-wheel-drive roads that crisscross this country. There," he said, pointing in victory. "There's one right there."

"The historical marker?"

"Yeah."

A Wyoming State Highway sign appeared to their left. Demi didn't brake. She let the old car roll to an easy stop.

"Let me read it," Ben said. "If this is what I think it is, we're in business."

He could barely make out the words. But the few he could read in the dim light told him just exactly what he needed to know. "Oregon Trail—Lander Cut-Off," it read. "In 1843 to 1845, hundreds of travelers passed this way. . . "

"Bingo," said Ben. "We've found it."

"Found what? A history lesson?"

"You're the one talking about pulling off into the sage flats and following ruts. This is the only set of ruts I know that might get us somewhere."

Down the highway a short distance, the ominous red lights kept at their startling revolutions. Demi steered the Le Sabre around the cheerful wooden sign that probably a million summer travelers had stopped to read breathlessly with their children. The old Buick began to bounce along open territory, ground that hadn't seen wheels cutting into it for well over a hundred years. "Hope we don't find any fences out here."

"We'll drive through the fences. Barbed wire hasn't stopped us yet."

Demi bit her bottom lip as the car edged over rocks and stumps and chiseler holes. "When can I turn the lights on?"

"Not for a while." Ben checked out the rearview mirror. "Not until we get over a ridge or something. Not until we're sure he's gone on and isn't following us."

As they drove, picking up speed as Demi became accustomed to the jolts on the wagon trail and the gentle starlight, Ben couldn't leave off his elevated sense of detachment and sadness. In view of that sadness, everything around him seemed frightening, unfinished. "I should find a place to drop you off," he said to Demi. "Or you should take the car and I could catch a ride. You oughtta go home to your mother. You could tell her I've made it out okay."

"She'd be glad to know that. But I'm sure she's heard it already on the news. She'd be listening for it."

"You need to go home."

"Nope. Won't go home. I've waited five years to spend time with you. Momma knew, when she chose Pete Giddy, that she chose against me, too. You're my dad," she said, suddenly quieter. "I'm not giving up on you."

"You could take the car back to . . ." He hesitated, suddenly realizing that he knew so little about them anymore, he didn't even know where this particular Buick Le Sabre had come from. "The car is your mother's, isn't it?"

Demi shook her head. "Momma's old car never would've made it this far. This one belongs to Pete."

"Damn." Ben struck the dashboard with one fist and would've been more colorful with his speech if he hadn't been riding beside his daughter. With Demi at his side, he'd squelched the prison talk real fast. "You mean to say I've made a getaway in Pete Giddy's car?"

"They both figured it was the least they could do, given the circumstances."

"All this," he said again as if he couldn't believe it. "All this and I'm in Pete Giddy's car."

Ben had no idea how long they'd been off the highway. He glanced back once, ready to advise Demi to turn on the headlights so they could pick up speed and make time. Instead, when he looked back, he saw an ominous glow behind them. Certainly they'd come farther off the roadway than that. Certainly no one else could have business on the Oregon Trail in the middle of Wyoming in the middle of the night. "There's somebody back there," he said without emotion.

"Can't be," Demi said. "We've gone five miles."

"Check it. Tell me what you think."

She watched in the rearview mirror. He saw her face as she comprehended it. "They're following us, aren't they?"

"Yes."

"We haven't fooled them."

"Can't imagine how they saw us abandon the road. I suppose, if they were looking, they might've seen tire tracks in the snow."

"Tire tracks. Who'd've thought of that?" Demi's words came in terse, frightened gasps.

"Let me out of the car," he said, grappling with the door handle. "Let me out right here. You go on somewhere safe."

"I won't do that. I helped you escape, remember? I'm an accomplice or something, right?"

For the life of him just then, he couldn't judge her reasoning. He couldn't tell her whether she was right or wrong. "Scoot over, Demi."

"You haven't driven for five years."

"Driving isn't something easily forgotten."

Behind them, the glow on the high land seemed even brighter. She braked for the first time in miles, put the car into park, moved over so he could have the wheel. "What now?" she asked as soon as they'd traded places.

"This is Pete Giddy's car," he said, looking intent in a way that made her love him. "I'm gonna turn the headlights on." As he said it, he did so. "And now I'm gonna drive like hell."

They entered a margin of aspen, smooth white trunks gleaming. As Ben gunned the engine and went to dodge trees, he could tell the trail was climbing. "Don't have much power going uphill."

"They'll catch up with us, won't they?"

"Don't know." He didn't want to scare her. But he *did* know. At this rate, barring a miracle, there'd be hell to pay before they reached safety. Long before.

Looking back, he could see a faint pink flicker across the sage and ice. The officer had turned on pursuit lights.

"This thing have seat belts?" he asked through gritted teeth.

"Used to. Think they're stuck in the seat somewhere."

"Damn."

"Just drive, Dad."

"Don't wanna get you hurt."

The road turned, made a hairpin switchback into heavy lodgepole forest. Ben knew that for the moment they'd disappeared from view to those behind in the chase. The Buick fishtailed around a turn. Ben grappled with the wheel for control.

When they crested the first rise, the heavy wood seemed to fall away again, left them vulnerable and evident upon high tableland that stretched out in every direction like eternity. He drove much too fast. His eyes darted from the trees to the trail to the mirror and back again.

He could see the state trooper's car closing, its red and blue signals piercing in staccato rhythm as it blazed systematically through the timber. The road swerved sharply to the right and Ben veered, toppling Demi. She straightened herself wordlessly and reached for anything to hang on to. She gripped the door handle.

Miracles come in many ways, shapes, and forms. As Ben saw his daughter's small, broad hand clinging to the knob, an idea began to grow. The rutted trail switched abruptly back to the left.

They had no time to lose, no indulgence of a second chance. To survive they'd have to plan it, understand it, implement it, on first try. And Ben had no clue where the wilderness path would offer up its own promise.

He glanced in the mirror again. They didn't have much time. Practically none. He floored it.

A rock bulleted up and took out his left headlight. Glass splintered everywhere.

"Dad," Demi said, whispering. "I'm sorry."

"For what?" he asked, sweating it. "Breaking me outta the slammer?"

"No," she said. "Sorry that Momma didn't come. Sorry that I'm scared."

"Don't be sorry for things you can't help," he said. "I learned that a long time ago."

The moon went behind a cloud.

"I have a plan," he said, knowing he had to hurry with it. "We're going to get out of this." He glanced across the front seat at her, his heart still breaking because Wyllis hadn't come. "It's good to be with you. We aren't givin' up now."

"Tell me."

"You tell me first," he said, giving her a sad smile. "Is Pete Giddy attached to this car?"

"As attached as anybody who's driven something for" —she stopped to count— "nine years."

"I suppose he expects us to return it."

"I figure he does, eventually. But if we end up in Canada—"

"Cut the talk about Canada," he said. "I've told you three times that we aren't going to go to Canada."

"But we—"

"I'm going back to Hanna. But we aren't returning this car." It was unkind, but he took pleasure in that. Let Pete Giddy and Wyllis Pershall explain it to the insurance agent, the state troopers, and the county sheriff. He turned on the dome light and almost lost control again. "We've gotta keep this guy far enough behind us so he'll catch up right when we want him. Look at the map, will you? Find the road."

"This isn't a road."

"It's on the map. See—" He'd already studied it. He pointed to the legend, to the faint mark of *x*'s, *o*'s, and dashes that indicated "Historic Trails." "Tell me how far we have to go before we meet up with the river."

She peered at the map, squinting her eyes. "Is it called Caddisfly Creek?"

"That's the one."

"Hard to figure, Dad. Maybe three miles."

He glanced from the road to the mirror and back again. "You have to trust me on this, Demi," he said. "Do you trust me?"

"I've always trusted you. Ever since I was little." And she said the rest of it very quietly. "Even after they took you away."

"The tire tracks we laid did us in once," he said. "This time they're going to save us."

"How?"

"When the time comes, I'm driving us into the river. If we stay a few seconds ahead, we'll be able to get out of the car without them seeing. It'll look like an accident. If I can get the car stuck in deep enough, it'll take hours, maybe days, for them to figure out if we were trapped in the car or if we've gotten away."

The land continued its steady rise. Ben guessed they were high, somewhere close to timberline. He ran fingers around the circumference of the wheel, feeling certain, limitless, as if the very change of the land from free, wide sageland to the towering majesty of these mountains introduced him to something within himself, something new and vast and magnified, something he could give himself to, something that would give itself back in return. "Roll the window down an inch," he instructed her. "Maybe we can hear the creek."

They listened. "I might hear water rushing," she said. "Don't know. Could be the wind. Don't think we should do it yet."

"Soon, though. When the time comes, move over beside me. I'll help you. We'll both get out this door."

"Will we sink?" she asked. "Will the car go underwater?"

"That's outta our hands. No telling what'll happen. We've got to stay ready for anything."

As abruptly as the trail began its ascent, they found themselves moving down again into a promontory of blue spruce and pine. As the moon began to ease its way from behind the cloud, Ben saw what he'd searched for: a ribbon of moving water burnished silver below him in the fresh-found glow. "There it is, Demi," he whispered. "That's Caddisfly Creek."

"I'm hanging on," she said, scooting beside him and taking his elbow. "I'm ready."

Ben glanced in the rearview mirror one last time. Not a minute to spare. Their pursuers followed seconds behind them.

Their trail began to cross a snow-washed gully. Ben floored the pedal one last time, then garishly laid on the brakes. The Buick swerved in a semicircle, then began to sideslip down the ravine. The front left fender bounced fiercely off a boulder. It set the vehicle rolling backward precariously. One window shattered.

"Hold on." He gripped Demi's hand. "Hold on."

He felt her fingers tighten around his.

3

The Le Sabre careered into the hollow, crunching huge lumps of ice as it slammed down the hillside. The left rear bumper glanced off yet another rock and lifted the back axle off the ground. The car pivoted. For long, paralyzing seconds, the wheels, all four of them, hung airborne.

It'd been years, maybe when he'd been a boy, since Ben had thought to pray. "Damn thing's gonna flip," he whispered, still clinging to his daughter. "Dear God, help us."

One front tire sideswiped a huge fir tree, splintering the trunk and setting the limbs jostling eerily up, down, up, down. The fir began to fall, the riven wood moaning as it cracked apart and gave way. The tree plummeted.

Boughs flailed in every direction. The huge, shattered trunk landed in a straight line toward the creek.

The Buick hit ground, guided by the fragmented, fallen wood, and backed straight into the rushing water.

The current rose quickly to the chrome trim and beyond. "We've gotta get out of here *fast*." He reached for the door handle.

Demi didn't answer.

"Demi?" Ben grabbed the collar of her coat and pulled her toward him. As her head slumped onto his shoulder, he saw the gash on her temple. A purple knot swelled on her forehead.

He shoved the door open with his foot. Frigid water raced in, so cold it took his breath. The current roiled past him toward the valley, sucking him away from the car.

With great difficulty, he yanked Demi across the front seat and gathered her into his arms. He had no idea what she'd hit. The mirror, maybe, or the dashboard, as they'd come down.

"Demi?" he said again as he pulled her close, but even if she'd been able to hear him, the roar of Caddisfly Creek would've tossed his voice adrift.

With all his strength, he leaned against the door and managed to latch it. He heard the highway patrol car skid to a halt above them.

He battled his way across the deepest part of the river. Three times he blundered against the slimy rocks beneath his feet. Three times he nearly missed his footing in the water. He readjusted his daughter in his arms, balancing her knees with her shoulders, giving his all to ferry her to the far shore.

Seconds ticked agonizingly by. Caddisfly Creek churned downhill, swirling past him with futile force. As he struggled to keep his equilibrium, Ben knew the same futility of the river as it ever coursed downstream, ever flowed into the sea. He felt as if life swept him along in the same way, powerful and relentless.

Can it be worth it now? he wondered. Can it be?

It seemed an eternity before his knee struck solid ground and he sloshed up onto the embankment. Despite his burden, he moved deftly through the darkness, shoving his way through the scrub brush and willows that lined the creek.

He'd come far enough from the murmuring water to hear what they said high above. Here, it scarcely met the volume of a cradlesong. "Damn fool. Runnin' wild across all of Wyoming, runnin' wild across one of these old grass-grown wagon trails, and he loses it on an easy turn like this one. Must've been a hell of a plunge into the river."

"That's a crying shame, isn't it?"

"Door's not opened. Think they're still tryin' ta get out?"

"There's no telling."

"Can't be much air space in there."

"Nope. Can't be. Not much. But some."

"You reckon they made it out to shore? Maybe he and the girl set this up. Maybe they tried to get us off track or something."

"Jason, nobody'd be fool enough to drive off the side of the cliff like that. Then, to escape from the car, too. He'd have to walk on water or something."

"I know several hardened criminals who think they can walk on water."

"This one's hardened enough to think it."

"You're right about that."

Ben knelt encircled in a copse of winter-red willow, his breath coming in short, desperate chuffs. His prison-issue pants began to turn to ice around his knees. Like a brutal whip, the air lashed at him. He bundled Demi into his arms, encompassing her with his meager body warmth. What he'd give for a dry blanket now.

"Demi," he whispered. "Demi? Can you hear me?"

She opened her eyes. "Mmmm-m-m," she moaned. "Dad, I'm . . . f-f-freezing. . . ."

Ben needed to find help quickly. Even without the grave knock to Demi's head, hypothermia would take its deadly course upon both of them within the hour. So far, he'd played the odds and he'd won. But wet clothing heightened their chances of ruin. Despite the map and its guidance, Ben had no idea how remote this place was or how readily someone nearby would help them.

The officers spoke again, their voices ringing in the clear frost air. "We'll have to pull the car out to make sure."

"Passed into jurisdiction of Lincoln County some three miles ago," one of the officers announced on the road above. "Best call down to Afton and get the sheriff up here."

"You gonna climb down and secure the scene before he gets here?"

"Won't be much I can do. Measure the slide marks, maybe. Looks like he took out quite a tree."

"It's colder out here than an Eskimo's nose."

"Nope. It's colder than that. It's colder than Sue Emily when I come home fifty bucks poorer on poker night."

"You talk about your own wife, Jarvis. Don't know anything about that kind of thing—" One officer started laughing, then the other. "I'm gettin' in where it's warm. Can't wait to hear what these Lincoln County boys say when you tell 'em they've got an escaped convict trapped up here. Trapped in Caddisfly Creek in a car, no less."

One door slammed, then another.

Ben saw his chance and took it. "We're moving," he said to Demi. "I'm gettin' you someplace where you can thaw out."

"G-g-ggood."

"Hang on to my shoulders."

She clung to him as he struggled to traverse the hill without being seen, his every step sinking deep into the snow, down well beyond his calves. During any given moment, the troopers could look up from their radioing and see him. Ben sloughed through the snow in zigzags, seeking every shelter, hurrying upward from clumps of low-lying willow to stands of green pine wood.

His lungs raged for air. He forged on, gasping with each step, feeling every pump of blood as it pulsed deliciously through his heart. High overhead, he heard the thin, chittering call of an eagle, out to make its first wheeling flight in advance of the sun.

"Dad," Demi whispered.

"We're almost there," he lied, holding her with strong, sure hands.

The mountain sloped boldly upward, a vast angular sweep before him that went for half a mile or so. He had nothing to do except climb, so climb he did, scrabbling his way along a bare ridge where his footing was better. Eventually, after he'd ascended what he guessed was a good quarter mile, Ben found a snow-filled gorge slashed into the mountain, one that led away from the rocky face and took him past gnarled, scrawny timber, up onto the tundra.

He shouldered his daughter higher, knowing he didn't dare pause in this journey. He traipsed down the other side. Rocks rolled out from beneath his feet, and several times he stumbled. After a time he came again to the shelter of the trees.

Ben saw a sight below that intrigued and somehow welcomed him, something he'd read about but had never seen, an elk herd stringing restlessly along, pawing through the snow below him in a cirque cleared among the spruce and pine and fir.

The night sky began to fade before him. He turned away from the paling east and waited. The meadow lay silver bright, silent, poised for morning, its edges still overlaid with the dark tracery of moon shadows from the trees. On the north edge of the snowfield stood a gathered array of barns, roofs snow covered, their entrances tracked by sleigh runners. And in the midst of this sat the house of his salvation, the oddest log accommodation he'd ever seen. Several sides of it seemed to lean; it looked as if it'd been built during many different times by many different hands.

At each of its corners, logs plaited together like fingers in a child's game. A warped walk, two planks wide and swept clean of all but a hint of snow, led from the back stoop to a dilapidated outhouse in the lee of the building. Smoke drifted indolently from the chimney.

"D-D-Daddy," Demi whispered. "My f-f-feet."

"I figure they'll help us here," he said, although he didn't know anything of the kind. "You can warm your feet. There's already a fire going even though the sun isn't up."

She hung on to him, dazed and shivering. "W-w-what place?" she asked. "Where have we come?"

"There's elk down here," he said. "And a house. That's all I know. The elk are all over. Just look at them."

But he realized she hadn't heard him. She'd dropped back to unconsciousness, her head nestled against his neck.

"Demi." He reached over with his other hand and shook her. "Demi."

No answer.

"Damn it, girl," he said. "Why do you have to trust me so much? Just drift off on me like I can take care of everything."

Ben began to hike down toward the house. But he stopped when he saw the lantern go out in one of the windows. He heard the door creak open, saw a dark figure make its way to the barn.

He couldn't go in just yet. He had to wait until the coast was clear, until he could catch the house's occupants unaware. His freedom, and Demi's life, depended on it.

Damn it again. He'd pulled off incredible feats. He'd escaped from the Wyoming State Pen, for God's sake. He'd come into freedom just as he'd wanted it, unscathed. But as he waited here, hiding in the willows as the sun rose, he'd never felt so helpless in his life.

Each sunrise, morning overcame Star Valley in degrees, settling first in feeble pink paint strokes along the high rocks. As it heightened, rays ran in solemn resplendence down crevasses and couloirs, leaving the lowlands to languor in hoarfrost and shadow. This morning, as all mornings, Rebecca Storey Woodburn tied her heavy wool hat over her ears and tugged hide work gloves past her wrists. She started to work in the barn even before the sun began to edge the roof of the ancient log house.

Mabel and Coney, the Belgian draft horses that pulled the government feeding sleighs, nickered inside their stalls as she made ready to grain them. "You're never patient this time of day, are you?" she asked fondly as Coney butted up against her with his immense muzzle. "Calm down. You'll get fed in a minute. Seems like that's all anybody cares about on this mountain anymore. Eating." She dumped a serving of oats into each bin, then loaded the sleigh with hay and alfalfa pellets while the horses devoured their fill.

The harnessing went quickly. She adjusted bits in their mouths, fit the brow and crown bands over their ears. She buckled the huge collars and back bands that would protect Mabel and Coney from the heavy load they bore, fastened the martingale to each collar. Long ago, when she'd been no taller than a horse's gaskin herself, she'd watched her grandfather follow this very sequence, grappling the horses to the wooden sleigh with the doubletree crossbar, taking lines in hand and urging the huge team forward. Except in his day, Howdy Woodburn'd been doing his best to hay cattle, not wildlife.

"Okay, you two. Let's get on out there." Rebecca raised the lines and cracked them evenly over the horses' rumps. The sleigh set forth, its weathered wood groaning as the contraption lurched forward, chains jangling, onto the snow.

By now sunshine spilled across the width of the high meadow, flooding the uplands, gilding the wind-fallowed snowfield with folds of light, sheening against the rises like gathers on a taffeta skirt. Even now, from this far up the draw, she could hear sounds of the animals, the bulls' restless wanderings, the cows' distant mewlings as they rose from hollows where they'd slept.

Rebecca Storey Woodburn was a woman who knew the elk, knew and revered the assembled herd as she'd revere a loving, sacred spirit. For a week now the animals had been dispersing during the daytime, the bulls mounting on hind legs to flail at one another with their hooves, the cows tramping through ice to forage on winter-cured grasses beside the headwaters of Caddisfly Creek. She sensed, because they sensed, the first true stirring of springtime on the mountain.

She'd feed today in four long sections of the field, keeping the elk as isolated from one another as possible in this time when their defenses had ebbed to their lowest, when disease or loss of energy could mean a life. As the sleigh's runners cut narrow tracks through the ice, she eased Mabel and Coney into a slow walk and climbed to the back, stripping open a hay bale with her pocket knife. She pitched the first bale and was going after another when she saw Abby Owen's Toyota Land Cruiser turn in across the front cattleguard and head toward the house.

Visitors to this place came few and far between. Not many dared pass the official brown-and-white Wyoming Fish and Game Department sign at the gate:

TIMBERLINE BIG GAME WINTER FEED AREA.
NO UNAUTHORIZED HUMAN PRESENCE
FROM JANUARY 1ST THROUGH APRIL 30TH.
UNDER PENALTY OF THE LAW.

Rebecca pitched the second bale, climbed to the front of the sleigh, headed the horses around. "Abby?!" she hollered through cupped hands, hoping the sound would carry. "I'm out this way. Already feeding for the day." But she needn't have worried. She saw Abby stepping onto cross-country skis, gathering poles, then striding toward her.

"Hallooo," the woman shouted back, raising one ski pole in greeting. "Don't let me stop you from working.

I've never thrown hay bales, but I figure I could help if need be."

"Company on this place is a decent reason for stopping," Rebecca said, apologizing. "But I can't quit for long. Don't want too many elk ranging in this direction. Guess I'll stop for a minute, though, until they all see this hay over here and decide to follow."

"I almost stopped off at the house. But then I figured you'd already be out here. Came by to tell you how we missed seeing you at the Caddisfly Inn last night. Party would've been better if you'd've decided to come down."

"You were good to mail that letter and invite me," Rebecca said. "Nobody else would've done it." She didn't say "But you're the preacher's wife, Abby Owen. You always invite everybody to everything. It's your calling."

"Others might've done it, too, if you had a phone. Folks're a lot better picking up a receiver than they are picking up pen and paper anymore."

"Don't figure anybody missed me much last night. Saw all the headlights going home on the highway. Looked to be quite a crowd." In truth Rebecca had put out the lantern early and watched at the window, knowing the stream of lights signaled an exodus from the cafe. She'd seen Mr. and Mrs. Lester Burgess turn in at the Pronghorn Motel. She'd observed Doc and Etna Bressler going straight south on Highway 89 toward Afton. She'd noticed W. D. and Abby Owen veering in to park beside the parsonage at Morning Star Baptist Church. She'd even beheld Cyrus Cotten and his massive family headed north toward Palisades, following the state road to Cyrus's cottage, the small bungalow with the garden he'd tilled for his wife the year they'd married, the garden for zucchini, radishes, and snow peas, where, in summer now, only dandelions and thistles grew.

"Of course there was a crowd," Abby told her. "Always is, when anybody in this valley has a chance to poke his nose into somebody else's business." Abby reached up, touched Rebecca's arm. "He won the Oscar, you know."

Rebecca Woodburn stared out over the sweeping expanse of ice, the broadness of the land as perfectly formed and hardened by wind as pottery would be formed by fingers. She held to the lines for control of the horses, her weather-stained face raised with yearning toward the horizon, her one dark braid hanging down her back from beneath her woolen cap. "I knew he'd win it."

"You did?"

"I know a great many things, being here alone with only the quiet to tell me." She also knew last night had been the first time, the only time, her brother'd been offered an award for something solely, completely, his own doing.

"Thomas looked mighty good on television."

"I imagine he did," she said, "all decked out in his tuxedo like an arctic penguin."

"Never quite seen him so fancy myself," Abby said, chuckling. "Not even when Lucille made him wash up and come to church that Easter the furnace went out and all the lilies froze on the altar."

Abby's story reminded her of something dear. "I'll bet he wore his hair slicked back just as smooth and sheeny as hair on a wet muskrat's behind."

"Well, now that you describe it that way. . . yes, he did."

"Howdy used to spit-comb it that way every time the school photographer came over from Riverton." Where were those old grade-school pictures, anyway? She supposed she'd packed them away into a box of old things and shoved them into the attic. And suddenly, at the thought of it, Rebecca longed for the sight of her brother, not the remembrance of a grinning photograph or the span of a camera, but the blood and flesh of the man. "Maybe I'll dig through and bring out one of 'em," she said, her dark eyes trained again on something far in the distance. "If not one of those, than something . . . "

"Pictures of you two together?"

"Back when Howdy ran cattle on this ranch, we tried to saddle an elk once. Damn fool thing oughtta've known better than to wander up past the barn. Lucille took pictures of *that*. Only thing I've got more recent are those photographs from *People* magazine the day he married Jillian Dobbs." A breeze sprang from the east, bringing with it the ponderous smell of winter-frost pine. From across the windswept meadow, bulls and cows began to amble toward the sleigh. The sun had climbed into the sky, casting bronze wrinkles of light across the horses' flanks. "I'd best get 'em going," Rebecca said. "We'll have the whole elk herd over here if I'm not careful."

"Does Thomas ever write to you, Rebecca? Does he ever talk of coming home?"

"No," Rebecca said with profound gravity. "He never does."

Ben watched the visitor climb into her Toyota Land Cruiser and drive off. *Now.* He willed his legs to move. *Go now.*

He felt hollow, as if the magnitude of what he must do swelled larger than anything his own soul could comprehend and, therefore, left him containing nothing. He had no choice but to force his way in, to make somebody help Demi.

Ben shouldered his daughter and ran toward the house.

He'd tell them he had a gun, that he was a desperate criminal, that he'd shoot them if they didn't let him warm his girl. But the residence, when he entered it, stood quiet, empty as a shrine. The stove waited with its door accordioned open, wood ablaze and crackling upon its iron grate.

Ben glanced about awkwardly, looking mean, waiting for someone to accost him about entering uninvited. But no one came.

In the liquid glow from the flames, he laid Demi upon the big rug in the center of the room. He peeled off her frozen coat. "D-D-Daddy," she whimpered again.

"Sh-h-hh," he said, stroking her hair, hoping she could sleep and yet, after the injury to her head, not knowing if she should. He rose, stood, glanced around again. He felt jaded and in suspense. Heaven only knew when someone would appear and confront him. Yet he was desperate, and in that desperation came his sense of providence, an uncomfortable certainty that propelled him onward.

Above the door hung a Ruger lever-action rifle, its walnut stock crosshatched, its sighting rib and barrel freshly blued and gleaming.

He needed to find something to wash Demi's face, anything to clean away the blood so he could inspect her forehead. He found a damp cloth flopped over the side of the kitchen sink. Gently he cleansed his daughter's skin as she slept. The bruise continued to swell. She'd taken a bad hit. She needed a doctor.

He held the rag across his knees for the longest time, staring down at Demi's face in wonder and in sorrow. Then, as the sun came up, he took the thing back to the kitchen and replaced it at the sink. While he was up, he walked to the door and lifted the Ruger lever-action off its hook. He checked the chamber, found it loaded. A carton of ammunition sat on the floor. He helped himself, shoving the extras inside his pockets. Satisfied, Ben carried the rifle with him and sat down, feet by the fire, to wait.

The snow shone with fiery reflections now that the field had succumbed to full sun. Rebecca finished feeding the elk in good time, stringing hay along in small piles at pasture's edge. The sky shone so full-bodied and blue, she felt as if she could reach up and grasp on to it, could dangle herself from it.

She let the horses have their head as she neared the west fork of Caddisfly Creek. They'd be thirsty after their morning's work, and today, as all days, she sought the fellowship of the river.

The horses' hooves cracked through ice at water's edge. Mabel and Coney snorted robustly as the stream plied their noses. "Go on," she said, not needing to tell them yet telling them anyway. "Drink all you want, you two. River won't run out today, anyway."

She dropped the reins and fell quiet as she watched the current roil past. Winter-cured wheatgrass hung in clumps from the stream bank, seed pods swaying beneath their glass coating of ice. Ever so often one would dip low, setting off a whisper against the water. Upstream, two mergansers saw her and flew, their wings beating rapid whistles as they mounted the air.

Here—in this place—Rebecca never felt alone. At creek's edge she stood in the company of an old friend, someone she trusted, someone in whom she could confide. She remained there, watching silently and feeling embraced, until the horses became restless. She drove them back to the barn, her face upturned to the sun.

It was past noon by the time she made her way to the house. She stomped up the porch steps, knocked the snow from her boots, flung back the door. The fire in the woodstove had long since gone to coals. Precious seconds ticked by before her eyes adjusted to the shadows in the hallway.

"Stop," he commanded, stumbling up from the chair where he'd waited. He pointed the Ruger at her. "Don't come too close."

Rebecca followed her first instinct. Without turning, she grabbed for the rifle on horseshoe pegs above the door. Her fist came up empty.

"It isn't there," he said.

Even as he spoke the words, she recognized her own rifle in his hands, aimed at her. For a full minute she said nothing. "I can see that."

He gestured with the barrel. "Get in here. Come away from the door."

She didn't budge. She'd lived alone in the wilderness long enough to know not to show fear. She didn't show it now, even though it overtook her, this hard, sharp constriction in her throat. "Who are you?" she asked. "What are you doing in my house?"

"I didn't tell you to ask questions." He cocked the rifle brutally. "I told you to *move*."

Rebecca took one step, two, in the direction he'd pointed.

"Keep going."

"Where is it you want me to go?"

"Toward the hearth, I suppose. Now. Sit down."

For the first time, she saw the girl lying out along the floor. Without thinking of his reaction, Rebecca quickly knelt beside her. "What's wrong? What did you *do* to her?"

"I said," he ordered, "sit down."

Rebecca stood from the floor and went to sit on the edge of the parlor chair. She stared at him. She had no doubt but that he would kill her. "She's hurt."

"I know that." He sat down, too, the rifle barrel still trained on her.

She hated the look of him. His face shone as pasty and white as a dull spoon. His colorless hair stood up in clipped, uneven clumps all over his head. He seemed as if he'd come from somewhere underground or someplace far away. And in his eyes burned something she hadn't come close to before, a shocking pain-seared desperation that made her afraid to breathe.

"No one but me is supposed to be on this land until the end of April. You'll agitate the elk."

She could tell by the twitch of his mouth that, for some reason, he thought this funny.

"You have no right to—"

His humor ran out fast. "Shut up." He jabbed the gun at her head.

She bit her bottom lip so hard, she tasted blood. She searched her mind for any means of escape. Too late, she realized why he'd been amused. In her anger, she'd informed him quite easily that she'd be alone on the place until spring. Now he could have his way confidently. He could kill her and nobody'd find the body until Eastertime.

From the floor, the girl moaned and rolled to one side, her dusky blond hair fanning away from her face. Rebecca saw the bruise. She gripped the arms of the chair, made as if to stand. "Did you hit her?"

He hesitated almost imperceptibly. "So what if I did?"

She didn't answer him. Instead she rose slowly, not caring so much anymore about his threats. The child needed a doctor. She could see that from all the way across the room. "I want to help her. Please."

"Go ahead, then," he said, and as he gestured toward the youngster, she almost thought he seemed proud of something. "Do what you can. I won't stop you."

Rebecca stooped low beside the girl, brushed the hair away from her forehead. "I don't suppose you'd let me call Doc Bressler."

"No. No doctors. You've gotta figure out how to help her on your own."

"You're cruel."

"Better not talk about what you don't know, lady. Sometimes people have no choice but to be cruel."

"She ought not to be on this cold floor." He stood halfway, as if to help her. That's when she saw the black numbers stamped across the pocket of his shirt. A convict! "I don't need your help," she said. "I'll do it myself."

Rebecca'd grown up on this land, hefting hay bales and harnessing horses. She lifted the girl with little trouble and carried her to the four-poster in the downstairs bedroom. He followed her, the gun poised.

I'll escape, she thought again. What I need is a distraction. But she couldn't think of anything that would serve as such, and she couldn't run away right now, not while this youngster lay needing her. She turned to go back into the hallway and upstairs.

"Where are you going?" he growled.

"To get my first-aid supplies."

"I'll get them," he said. "Where are they?"

"You don't trust me? You think I'm going to climb out of a window up there? There's no place for me to go but the roof. And it's ridden with snow."

"Where are the supplies?"

"In the chest beneath the washstand in my room. There's a wicker box."

"You'd best show me," he said.

They left the girl alone and he stalked up behind her, always two steps below, always with the gun in her back, as they proceeded.

Not many people had entered here, not since Lucille Woodburn had died. When Rebecca'd been a girl, she and Thom had lived in the room downstairs where their patient slept now. She walked straight to the washstand, retrieved the wicker box, and turned to him. "It was my grandmother's room," she said succinctly, as if to remind him how badly he was intruding. "Now it's mine." Rebecca pulled a flannel nightgown from a drawer in her bureau. She tramped out and didn't look back. She heard him behind her on the stairwell.

Carefully she examined the girl's head. As she did, she realized he'd already cleaned it. "I don't know," she said finally, as he stood waiting in the door. "I don't find any evidence of a fracture. But she's disoriented, and that's scary. I wouldn't rule out a mild concussion. Especially with the way she's drifting in and out of consciousness. She'd be better off if I could take her to a physician."

"I can't let you do that," he said.

"They'd find you, wouldn't they?" she asked, trying to catch him off guard. "They'd carry you back to prison."

He glared at her from behind green eyes the color of bottle glass. His silence was affirmation enough.

"You could go," Rebecca suggested smartly. "I could get help for her and you could be on your way. You could leave us alone. Right now."

She had no idea how tantalizing those words sounded to him. "It isn't as easy as all that," he said gruffly. The truth be known, he hadn't the strength or the means to go farther, at least not yet. And Demi'd be in trouble, once they figured out who she was and started asking questions. "Where's your television?" he asked instead. "I need to see what's happening."

"I don't have one."

"You don't have a TV?"

"That's right. You heard me the first time."

"Okay," he said, realizing he'd have to settle for second best. "A radio, then. Where's your radio?"

She sat on the side of the bed and began the delicate job of bandaging. "Don't have one of those, either. Certainly you don't think I could pick up any sort of a signal this high in the mountains." As she spoke, Rebecca inadvertently touched the wound on the girl's forehead.

The teenager whimpered and moved away.

"Easy, little one." Rebecca whispered it in the same voice she used with the elk, when all the world stood green and newborn and she found calves curled upon themselves, their noses to the ground and motionless, hidden in the willow brush. With stalwart hands, Rebecca began to strip off the child's wet clothing. She stopped, turned to the man waiting beside the door. "You wait in the hall. I'm going to undress her."

To her surprise, he didn't argue. He backed away to give them privacy. Eventually, as she unfastened buttons and zippers and cloth, he spoke. "I didn't do that, you know."

"Didn't do what?"

"I didn't hit her."

Rebecca wasn't inclined to believe him. An escaped convict had nothing to lose except his freedom and his life. "After holding a gun on me in my own house, you think you owe me some explanation? Don't bother."

He said, "I wouldn't have her hurt for all the world."

Rebecca looked into his face for a moment, uncertain of the torturous expression she saw in his eyes. She turned away, removed each piece of clothing, and checked thoroughly for other injuries. At last, satisfied, she lowered the flannel nightgown around the girl's neck, fastened it with pearl buttons at the throat, tucked it down into the bed around the girl's spindly legs. "I'm finished now."

He stepped back inside, breathing easier for some reason. "Good."

"I had a telephone once," she said to him, jabbering on to calm her own nerves. "Had an antenna tower installed so I could call down to town if need be. But while that antenna was up, an osprey nested there every spring. She fished in the creek. Every time she landed in her nest with a trout in her beak, she cut me off. I decided, after a while, talking to people just wasn't worth the trouble."

"You're going to make up for it now, are you," he asked, "chattering like this to me?"

"I was just explaining to you about the telephone."

For a moment she glared at him. Then, suddenly, with a cold heart, she realized that once again she'd told him more than she ought to have told him. This place had no telephone. As surely as she'd cut herself off from the world, the situation served as a shield for him. She had no way to call for help without leaving the land.

"I don't like you," Rebecca said. "I don't like you running away from something you did and using my house as a shelter. I don't like you threatening my life with my own gun. I talk because talking makes me forget you're here." There. Quite a speech. She vowed not to say anything else for a good, long while. She stood from the bedside, deciding she'd do well to find something for the girl to eat.

He'd been leaning against the wall. Now he straightened nonchalantly, as if he hadn't heard a word she'd said, and repositioned the gun. "Where are you going?"

"I'm going to the kitchen."

"Why?"

She gave him a cold, even glare, willing herself to stay calm. "Thought I'd get the poor child something. After that injury, she needs her strength."

She paced up the hallway into the kitchen. He followed her, watching her every move. On the bottom shelf of the refrigerator she found what she sought, the dilapidated aluminum kettle she'd tucked away yesterday, still full of vegetable soup. She carried it across the room to place it on the stove. He matched her step for step.

"Do you mind not following me around like that? You make it difficult to do anything."

In the light streaming from the window, she could see that his hair resembled the musty tumble of straw she remembered from when she'd been a girl, playing in Howdy's haymow. "Now. I won't follow you anymore. I'm going to sit right here." He scooted the rickety pine chair away from the table and straddled the seat. "I can see things well enough from here, I suppose." He laid the Ruger across both knees. "There."

Staying as far away from him as possible, Rebecca lit the stove, turned up the flame, and put the soup on to simmer. She reached high into the cabinet for a crockery bowl. She opened a drawer in the sideboard and pulled out two napkins instead of one. She folded the extra, put it back, her hands quaking.

There's a knife in that drawer, she thought. I could turn around and jab him with it, and then I could run away. But how far across the pasture could she run before he shot her? Could she reach the somber woods that edged the meadow?

She laid out the napkin and bowl on a wooden tray. She opened the drawer again. There lay the knife, its serrated edge designed specifically to cut meats. She turned her back to him, presenting her very straight, thick braid and her very straight, steel-post spine.

"What're you doing now?" he asked.

"Getting a spoon," she lied. Her fist closed around the knife's worn handle.

The good Lord knew she hadn't the slightest idea how to stab a man. Perhaps if she imagined the thing, envisioned her movements and made them foreknowledge, she stood to overcome him. She'd leap toward the table. Before he could rise from the chair or raise the rifle, she'd come down fast upon him, holding the knife high, where a ray of sunlight would flash upon it. She'd pound the blade down upon him with both fists, praying she'd hit flesh.

"Well, hurry with it," he goaded her from the chair.

"I can't—"

Many times during her adolescence, Rebecca'd quartered a doe or a buck with her grandfather, Howdy. She knew the challenge of axing through bone and sinew, knew the sweet, sickening scent of warm blood.

Because she knew these things, she knew the odds against her now. Hammering into this man's uppermost regions with a serrated kitchen knife would be as futile as pounding into Wyoming soil. The blade might just as well bend or arc, deflecting off his collarbone and slitting a clean, inauspicious gash down the sleeve of his standard-issue jail shirt.

She removed the spoon from the sideboard, steadied herself. She wouldn't go after him just yet. She'd be crazy to risk her first chance on something she could spoil, something that might set him even more on his guard. Yes, she'd wait. And in the waiting, she'd set him off balance, unwittingly at ease. She shoved the knife bar behind Lucille's linens, which still waited, primly starched and pressed, for the next immense family occasion. She took a spoon.

"I don't like that," he said. "You mustn't think of ways to get away."

The spoon she'd taken clattered onto the cabinet. "I wasn't thinking anything of the sort."

"Really? I warn you. Don't do anything that would make me have to hurt you."

"I don't know why you think I'm trying to come up with something." She readied the bowl upon the tray, and this time, new anger made the movement of her hands unfaltering. Ah, anger felt good. She welcomed anything, espoused anything, besides this wealth of fear jangling about in her insides. "You're awfully good at holding people prisoner. You must do it often. You assume you know everything that's going on in my head."

"Don't I?"

"Of course not." She lifted the ladle off the hook behind the sink and, with it, walked across to the stove. She gazed into the warm, onion-scented liquid, felt steam caress her face. She stared into the pot and saw sudden possibility. In her anger, she began to smell victory. The soup!

All she needed, all she hoped for, was to get the gun off the floor before he did. Long ago, Howdy'd taught her to hunt. She knew how to balance the too long, too heavy gun, how to spread her knees and take position, with one eye squinted so she could see properly along the sight rib. She knew how to stand firm against the recoil, how to anticipate the rifle's sharp report.

She turned the burner up even higher. The broth churned viciously inside the kettle, the potatoes and carrots and peas rising to the surface with merry abandon. Rebecca rested the ladle on the counter. She picked up two hot pads and gripped the handles of the pot.

Father forgive me, she mouthed to herself, *for what I'm about to do to this man.*

With kettle in hand, she reeled toward him, her braid flailing out from her shoulders like the rope that towed skiers up Ferry's Hill. She saw him react, saw him see her intention, saw him begin to rise from the chair with the same beautiful, slow fluidity as a mountain lion when it first arises from its crouch in a tree.

Rebecca flung the boiling soup directly into his face.

"G—damn it!" he bellowed, jumping toward her and clawing at his eyes. "What the f—?" The soup soaked into his shirt, scalding his shoulders. The gun clanked onto the floor.

She didn't give him the opportunity to gain purchase. She raced toward the table, skidding on the wet floor, grabbing for the Ruger.

Even with the hot broth torturing his skin, he anticipated her move. He went for her, knocking her off balance and onto the floor. He captured her, holding her down with his full weight. "Crazy woman," he said. "You thought you could get away with this? You thought you could get the gun?"

She stared at him, her eyes unflinching, snake's eyes. Her hand inched up, toward the rifle.

He stopped her halfway, as she stretched for the stock that lay within certain reach. "Well, you were wrong." He lay over her hard, his torso unyielding and unbroken, like rock. He seized the hand with which she reached, ground his fingers into her wrists. "You don't know who you're dealing with, sister. You don't know what I've had to become in prison, in order to survive."

She twisted beneath him, did her darnedest to wrest away. "Let me go."

"No way." When he stood, he yanked her up with him. He spun her to face him, twisted one arm behind the small of her back so she couldn't attain leverage.

As he'd struggled to get away from the searing liquid, he'd done away with a number of buttons on his shirt. His skin shone red and wet, lanced where blisters would rise. Rebecca could see his pulse beating just below his breastbone, a steady throb that bespoke its merciless rhythm of anger.

She stared long into his pale, outraged eyes. "I want you out of my house," she hissed through her teeth. "I cannot bear this anymore."

With everything else, an onion hung from his hair. Carrots nested in the folds of his sleeves. "You will bear this," he returned. Peas lay all about them on the floor. "You will, and I will. Because neither of us has any other choice, do we? The least you can do is make it a little easier."

"Make it *easier?* When you take my freedom at gunpoint, keep me from the animals, hold me against my will? You want me to make this *easier?*"

"Don't match yourself against me," he said, hanging on to her with one fist, kneeling to retrieve the gun with the other. "You will lose every time."

Darkness came upon the high land, upon the scree of open rock that guarded the Timberline feeding grounds, upon the surrounding somber forests. Some nights in this place, Rebecca thought the starlight so personal, so rich and within grasp. But tonight she found it pale, thin, unfulfilling.

She kept gazing out the blue stained-glass window at the tangle of trunks and branches far off in the moonlight, doing anything, everything, to keep from climbing into that bed. He sat on the floor at the foot of it, the Ruger lever-action rifle laid evenly across his knees. His eyes never left her.

She pressed her nose against the pane like a child, pretending not to notice him or care. Strange what tricks the night played, the light being dark, the dark being light. Snow-ridden branches made each evergreen seem a white apparition against a black sky, like a photographer's negative, white on black instead of black on white, outside the realm of the expected.

"You've gotta give up and sleep sometime," he said. "You can't stand there all night."

"Perhaps I can," she answered back, willing her legs not to melt beneath her.

His eyes, when she turned to them, were like green lake ice—icy, hard. "You want to try? I'm game. You stand looking out windows all night. I'll keep the gun aimed at you. We'll see who gives up first. Let me give you one hint, though. It won't be me."

"Why do you say that?"

"Because I don't sleep at night anyway. Because I have better things to do." He leveled his gaze on her. "I haven't slept for five years."

If she'd felt fear pangs before, now she felt her

insides being burned out. She felt as if he'd pulled the ground out from under her. He sat in her bedroom and she didn't even know his name. She didn't know what he'd done to the girl who lay sleeping in the room below. And she was suddenly scared to death that he might harm her, too. "I won't be able to sleep in front of you. I'll lay there all night, thinking. Might as well do all my thinking here."

"That's fine. It's up to you."

"I'll stare at the ceiling, thinking how I wish I could get away from you."

"That's fine. It's up to you."

"Can't you say something more intelligent than 'That's fine, it's up to you'?"

He rolled to one buttock as if to rise, then seemed to decide better of it. "You're nuts, lady. Crazier than some people I knew in the state joint."

The man had soup stains all over his shirt. Its collar veed open at the neck, revealing red, blistered skin. For a moment, as she looked at him, she was almost sorry. Sorry! I wouldn't be sorry, she thought, if I'd've gotten away. I wouldn't be sorry if I'd've hitchhiked on the highway and gone for help. I'd be alone and he'd be behind bars again.

She hated being unsuccessful. Even more, she hated facing the *humanity* of him, the burned chest, the exhausted eyes. "Don't know why you sit there complaining about not getting sleep. You could've had plenty if you'd stayed where you belong."

"You know why I said you're nuts?" he asked. "I said you're nuts because you think I like being here. You think I get a charge out of sitting on your hard floor, lookin' at dust under your bed?"

"I'll get you blankets and you can sleep, too." Nice, harsh sheetless blankets. It was all she'd be willing to do, and everything, to woo him to sleep, away from guarding her. "Seems a man would have to *get a charge* out of this, in order to do it."

"This isn't a child's game," he said.

When she'd been a child, she'd played a game called Take the Key with her brother, Thom. They'd made it up in the forest one day; they'd been playing in a thicket of willows with two kids from town. And Rebecca knew she could conjure up their names still, that now they'd be grown, people she knew down in town who had never gone away.

The round had started as London Bridge, something everybody knew. They sang, and their voices echoed through the spruce and fir and willow like voices of lost friends, out searching. "London Bridge is falling down, falling down, falling down . . . "

Actually, she had to smile to herself this night. She never should've said she'd made this game up with Thom. Indeed, she'd made it up *because* of Thom.

When the part came where they sang "Take the key and lock him up, lock him up, lock him up," they'd captured him with their clasped hands, their thrashing arms, and pounded him back and forth among them, loving the power.

"Stop!" he'd cried. "You're doing it to me too hard. It's just a song."

"This is how it's supposed to be!" she'd shrieked. "This is more fun. It isn't supposed to be easy at all."

"It's easy for you," he bellowed as he jostled back and forth. "It's always easy for you, Becca."

When it came time for the verse to be over, they didn't stop. They kept going and going and going until, finally, he fell to the ground, dizzy, scratched up with brambles, and crying.

"We won!" the singers shouted, raising fists and jumping around.

"We're going at it again," Thom said, not to be defeated, climbing back up and grabbing Rebecca's coat sleeve. His tears had left white tracks in the dust on his face. "Now it's my turn. Take the key! Take the key!"

They'd come back to the house—this house—with britches all torn and scratches that needed to be treated with iodine. "For heaven's sake," Lucille had scolded them. "You've gotta learn how to get on in this part of the country. You look like you've been assaulted by a bear. You mustn't be such a fright to your old grandmother."

As always, mention of a possible bear served to curtail their vast, newfound feelings of freedom. But not so much as to keep Thom from howling earnestly, "We're assaulted all right. We're assaulted by each other."

She smiled.

"What're you thinking about?" asked the man on the floor with a gun.

"My brother. Thomas. Thom. He won an Academy Award this week for a screenplay he's written. I can't imagine it. Thom with an Oscar. He's gotten everything he's ever wanted." They surprised her, relaxed her somewhat, these thoughts of Thom. "I get so proud of him."

"I had a brother, too," the man on the floor said. "Billy. He hasn't been around for a long time." He didn't say anything more.

They had exchanged brothers' names, yet not their own.

Here they sat in the golden light from a lamp, he running from the law, she a hostage.

She turned to him awkwardly. "I'll have to get up early in the morning. Before daybreak. I've got all sorts of chores I've got to do."

"No chores tomorrow," he said. "You know I can't let you go out there and start hauling hay and hitching up horses. It's much too risky for me."

She raised her chin, willing herself to meet his gaze head on. "Is that how you think, then? You measure the risks for yourself, yourself only?"

He ignored the question, instead asked one of his own. "The elk are going to have to survive tomorrow without you," he said. "They're wild animals, aren't they?"

"The elk, yes," she insisted. "But you've forgotten the horses."

They stared at each other.

When they spoke, they both spoke together.

"That won't—"

"You can't—"

They both stopped.

They stared at each other again, for a long time, without saying anything.

"You're thinking I don't have any rights to be here," he said suddenly. "Well, I've got a right to a life, don't I? A right to be alive. That's something. Not much, but something. A powerful something."

"Your chances of staying alive were better in the pen."

"Staying alive. And being alive. They're two different things. Think about it. Two different kinds of life."

"I'll think about it," she said. "I'll think about it all night." She left the window, came to sit on the side of the bed, clasping her hands together between her knees. "I won't be able to sleep."

"Wish you'd stop telling me what you can't do, lady. It makes no difference to me. I've already told you that."

Restless, she stood again, went to a drawer to pull it open. She stared at the pile of folded flannel nightgowns and pajamas, stared at them, and reclosed the drawer.

"I'm not changing into a nightgown," she announced. Bedclothes made her feel as if she'd be too vulnerable, too easily overcome.

"That's fine," he said, smirking. "I'm not, either."

"I'm not taking my hair down."

"Fine, lady. Whatever you say."

"And I'm certainly not turning out the lamp."

"Why not?"

"I don't want to be in the dark with you. You might jump on me."

He had to grin at that one, an honest, mad grin. "Yes. Maybe I would jump on you. Or maybe you would jump on me. Let's keep it safe, then, between us."

She sat once more on the edge of the bed, her hands between her knees, her mind woolgathering.

He sighed, leaned his head against the wall, staring at the pine knots that looked like grimaces on the ceiling. Presently he heard her murmuring.

"What?" he asked. "What are you saying?"

She turned her head sideways at him, opened her eyes with reluctance, as if he'd pried his way into something. That's when he realized he'd interrupted her. "I'm praying," she said. *Praying*. While he sat with a Ruger aimed at her head.

"Oh."

"Do you want to know what I'm saying?" she asked in obvious challenge.

No. He didn't want to hear this at all. Not this.

"Doesn't matter to me," he lied.

She settled herself at the edge of the bed again, bowed her head, readjusted her hands. She seemed to think about it a good while before she finally said, "I'm asking God to keep me safe. From you."

Strange how Rebecca's words tugged at desperation within his soul as well. He couldn't turn back. He couldn't change anything.

Keep me safe, too. Keep me safe, too, Ben wanted to cry out to somebody. Only he'd learned a long time ago that nobody, nothing, would listen. But Rebecca kept right on muttering as the lamp stayed burning. Seemed like all night long he stared at the ceiling, finding sneering faces in the pine knots, willing himself not to hear.

5

Thomas Tobias Woodburn stood on the lawn at the house in Pacific Palisades, watching out over the massive expanse of grass and the small clutches of people. They annoyed him, wandering around his house in billowy clothes, following Jillian with their eyes, talking about things that didn't matter.

He'd meant to be writing again by now.

"Thomas." Someone he didn't know clapped him on the back. "Congratulations. *Spirit Dance* deserved that Oscar."

Thomas nodded and poked his hands into his pockets, becoming lost in the movement of sprinklers a full two acres away. Water fanned out over the grass like giant plumed feathers, casting vapors into diamond-sparkle sun and setting up the fresh, fervent scent of moist loam. On the patio, caterers served brunch. He felt an arm slip around his side. Jillian said, "Grayson's let a few press people in. They want to take pictures of you in the office."

He continued to watch the water. "Grayson's your publicist, Jillian, not mine."

She brushed hair the color of sunlight away from her face, a gesture of dissatisfaction. "Yes. And he has my interests in mind."

"That's the reason for the parties, too, I suppose," he said with derision. He'd dreamed of standing in this place, with an Oscar on his mantel, for years. Now, the appropriate parties seemed endless. Tonight they'd have dinner at Cicada. Tomorrow they'd attend an intimate gathering of four hundred at an executive producer's home in Bel-Air. Heaven only knew where they'd be the night after, and the night after that.

She didn't answer him. She slid her arm away.

"This is difficult for me, Jillian. I don't feel like celebrating."

"Thomas. Don't start again. Please."

"I can't think of anything else." She stood close enough, still, for him to reach over and lay an open palm across her stomach.

"Stop," she whispered, wheeling away. "I don't want people to see."

"People will see soon enough. This is my baby, too. You can't pretend this is nothing more than an inconvenience."

She wrapped her arms around her middle as if to protect herself. "Don't do this to me. Not now. Not here."

"You don't want people to see, yet you want to be seen."

"Film actresses wait all their lives to be cast in a leading role on Broadway. It's my first chance, my only chance, maybe, to prove to the critics I can act on stage. If I back out of playing Charmaine now, I don't only lose momentum, I end up farther back than where I began. You've got to try to understand. Everything isn't always as simple as you see it. I cannot play Charmaine pregnant."

"So, to you, playing Charmaine is more important than giving birth to our baby?"

"Many doors are open for me now, Thomas, doors that haven't been open before. I intend to stay free to walk through them."

"That isn't freedom," he said. "It's being a slave to who you think you should be."

"Ah," she said dryly, "and you're the expert on that, are you?"

"The play might not even make it. They may close you down after a month or two." But the chances weren't good of that, not with a headliner like Jillian Dobbs and the huge measure of money already behind the show. The play had just been cast, and it was being billed as the most dazzling special-effects production New York City had seen in the past decade. That in a decade of special-effects productions.

"Even if they shut us down, it won't matter," she said. "By the time they make a decision on that, I'll be way into my second trimester. Nobody'll give me an abortion that late. Suppose I make the show a hit and *then* I have to give it up! No, I have to do this now."

Grayson Hanks stepped up beside them. Thomas wondered if the publicist had heard their exchange. "I have a room full of cameras inside, Thomas. What the dickens out here could be so important?"

"Nothing's important," Jillian was quick to say. "He's just coming."

"Isn't that a part of it, too?" Thomas asked both of them defiantly, obviously feeling boxed. "Aren't we important enough to keep the press waiting?" He followed Grayson inside and settled on his chair, smiling in the uneasy way of someone not among his own kind, as photographers jostled around his desk, taking pictures and asking ridiculous questions.

"Did you get your inspiration for *Spirit Dance* from your wife?"

"Can you work when she's at home and not on the set, or is she too much of a distraction?"

"Does she read your work and give you suggestions?"

"Would the screenplay have been this critically acclaimed if your wife had not played the lead role?"

Until she signed the contract with the studio, Jillian hadn't read a word of his scripts, not even the title page. For the first time in the last three months, he refused to lie. "No," he said. "She doesn't read my work and make suggestions. I wouldn't let her. . . .

"No. Jillian wasn't my inspiration for *Spirit Dance*. This story is based on my sister, Rebecca, in Wyoming. . . .

"Yes. Of course I work when Jillian's home." The past days, his office, these stories, had been his only place of sanctuary.

"You didn't answer my question," said Bev Spaugh of *Entertainment* magazine. "Would the screenplay have been this critically acclaimed if your wife hadn't played the lead role?"

He made certain they knew he'd finished. He waved them away, then stood, sending the chair rolling back against the wall.

"You didn't answer." Spaugh spoke louder, pressing him.

"I'm not planning an answer."

"Hanks promised you'd give me an interview. I'd hardly call this adequate."

In the hearth, a decorously set fire flickered despite seventy-degree weather and the emerald lawn outside. Thom grabbed the coveted Oscar from the mantel. He raised the statuette high above his head and waggled it at them the way a little boy would brandish a baseball bat. "No one tells me what is adequate or not adequate in my own house."

"This isn't your house," Spaugh said matter-of-factly. "It belongs to Jillian Dobbs."

He gave the roomful of journalists a loose, sarcastic smile. "This Oscar is mine." *And the baby she wants to get rid of is mine, too. Put that on your front pages.* Oh, how he longed to say it, but he didn't dare. He saw Grayson Hanks grip the door frame, knew from the way the man turned and peered back casually that Jillian moved behind him in the hallway. Bev Spaugh stepped up in front of him, and he said it directly into her face. "I'm finished answering questions."

Grayson began weaving through the crowd toward him.

"Don't set up any more of these god-awful things, Hanks," he said, aiming Oscar's head at the publicist as if he were aiming a gun. "My office is private. This house is private. My life is private."

"Thomas." Grayson took his arm. "Let's go somewhere to discuss this."

"There's nothing to discuss. If you wanted a trained performance, you should've gotten that Saint Bernard who acts in those big-slobbery-dog movies." Photographers crowded around him and Grayson both, snapping pictures, asking more absurd questions, never stopping, like a frenzy of coyotes on a full-moon night back home. He turned once in the hallway, raised his arms at all of them so they'd stop talking. He smelled Joy, Jillian's perfume. Of course, she'd been nearby watching him.

"I have never seen anybody act like such an idiot with the press as long as I've been in this town," she told him that night as she stalked around the balcony, her filmy nightgown drifting around her ankles the same way clouds drift across the sky. "You've made us the laughingstock of the town. And all on a day that should've been your finest hour."

"Yes," he said. "It was my finest hour."

"That speech you gave on the stage last night. About the mystical elk herd and the way your grandmother wants you to live." She sighed, ever the martyr. "The least you could've done was talk about me."

"Last thing I wanted to talk about was you," he said. "They have no idea who you are. They have no idea what you're asking me to give away."

"And it isn't any of their business now, is it?"

"I don't know anymore, Jillian. Living in this place with you, I've lost all perspective on what's their business and what isn't." He turned away from her, made his way back into the house. To his annoyance, she followed him. She lit a cigarette. He stood watching her, feeling as helpless as he'd ever felt in his life. "Please," he said quietly. "Think about our baby."

She rolled her eyes at him as if he'd mentioned something detestable.

He grabbed her arm, made her face him. "I've never been anyone except who you expected me to be," he said. "I want you to think about that."

"Yes," she said, flicking ashes. "I do think of it. Often."

She walked out the sliding glass door to the balcony and the view, shut the door with a faint murmur, and left him alone. Thomas Tobias Woodburn waited there, not inclined to move, not inclined to make himself free in the opulent room that belonged more to Jillian than it did to him. For a while he sat with his head in his hands, his fingers spurring up through his dark hair.

He heard Jillian go to bed without him. An hour later he made his way to his study, rolled an empty page of paper into the old Royal typewriter he still insisted on using for each first draft, and typed at the top, steadily but not fast: "Fade-in Ext. Mountain shot Elk refuge, Star Valley, Wyoming Day." He returned the carriage to space two lines and firmly set the scene. "Camera sees a herd of elk pawing through snow. Vapor comes from their nostrils in the cold air."

Thom spaced two more lines, centered his character's name, pounded out the first sentence of dialogue.

There. He'd begun.

The paper curled in the night air, tapped with straight-edge precision on the typewriter platen, as if it could be brought alive by magic. Thom looked past it, out into the thin starlight above him in the night sky. After a while, the stars seemed to fill him. He came back to page one, to peck away with shallow satisfaction.

And, as always with Thomas Woodburn, words poured forth, filled his emptiness for a little while. He found writing a relief, as if the function of arranging words on a clean surface purified him of something. Two, three, four in the morning passed, and still, still, he kept at his banging on the keys. Not until dawn, not until the water on the Pacific Ocean began to shimmer with pink like abalone shell, did Thomas finally decide to quit. He rumbled back on his chair, stood, stretched.

He saw the old issue of *People* magazine lying where he'd left it on the shelf. He picked it up, held it a long time in one hand. His own smiling face stared back at him, his arm wrapped squarely around Jillian's shoulders. FAIRY-TALE COUPLE, the yellow headline read. "Exclusive *People* Photos of the Storybook Wedding at Jillian's Bel-Air Hideaway."

Almost against his will, he flipped it open again. Of its own accord, the magazine fell apart at the four-color, double-page spread.

"In a move that surprised Hollywood insiders," the copy began, "actress Jillian Dobbs wed longtime friend and sometime beau Thomas Woodburn in a short ceremony this past weekend. Sources who asked to remain unidentified but who are acquaintances of the couple, say that Dobbs and Woodburn met each other on the set of *Jubilee*, Dobbs's latest smash movie. Woodburn wrote the screenplay.

"Only a select group of family members and business colleagues attended the lavish affair on the lawn of Dobbs's estate on the Pacific Coast. Speculation ran rampant that the ceremony, originally planned to take place at Woodburn's home in Wyoming, was rescheduled to fit into the filming schedule for *Jubilee*. Woodburn's family did not attend.

"'She adores him,' one wedding attendee confided to *People* reporters. 'He's everything Jillian's looked for in a man, and more.'"

Thomas closed the magazine, laid it back upon the shelf. Even though he'd put away the pictures, he still conjured the sight of Jillian as she'd been on their wedding day, wrapped in a gauzy scarf that matched her simple Chanel dress, her toes bare in the sand, her blue eyes the same thrilling color as the sky. She'd seemed like a flash of brilliant light to him ever since she'd first walked onto the set of *Jubilee,* carrying his script in her hand.

Every time he came near her, she seemed to envelop him, like the stroke of sun that comes boldly wherever clouds are sundered in a storm. She was the sort of woman with whom Thomas found himself yearning for experience. She stepped before the cameras the first day of filming, all bright and slender and fiery. He watched from the darkness, entranced, while she spoke his character Tamsen into life.

"How do you *do* that?" he asked her later as she sat on a canvas chair and drank a mineral water, watching the others. "How do you just step out under the lights and *become* someone you aren't?"

"It isn't hard." She set down the water and turned the full, impelling blaze of her eyes upon him. "It's much like being a chameleon and taking on the color of the rock where you're waiting. Becoming something you aren't often helps one to hide."

"And what are you hiding from, Miss Dobbs?"

"From people discovering that I'm not anybody at all."

"Ah, you think that, do you?"

"Doesn't everybody? When they realize how fleeting all this can be?"

He didn't stop to think. He only set out to prove her wrong because he heard the grief in her voice. "I want to show you something. Will you come with me tonight?"

For a long while, she sat silently. He saw the emotions cross her face, her apprehension, her intrigue. Finally she nodded. "I'd like that."

"We'll go from the studio. I'll pick you up."

"Okay."

Late that afternoon, while the sun still flashed in silver coins on the ocean, he drove her all the way to Seal Beach. He parked and held his hand out for her. "Come on."

"I can't walk here," she said.

"Why not?"

"This is a public beach. I can't walk on a public beach. They'll recognize me."

"You're worried about that?"

"Yes." She still hadn't budged from the front seat.

"Well, if that's all it is, I'll take care of that." He climbed back in and started the engine.

"Where are we going now?"

"Wait and see."

He drove them first to a convenience store. He went inside and came out with two things: a Hawaiian-print red hat that said "My mom and dad went to California and all I got was this stupid hat" and a pair of gaudy yellow sunglasses big enough to cover practically her whole face.

"Here." He plopped them into her lap.

"What am I supposed to do with these?"

"What do you think? Put them on."

"But what if somebody—"

"That's the whole idea. Nobody's going to recognize you."

"If they do, I'll lose any chance of being on Blackwell's best-dressed list."

"You care about things like that?"

"Yes."

He took them through the drive-through at Burger King and ordered them both Whoppers with the works and chocolate milkshakes. He drove them back to Seal Beach, parked in public parking, and finally coaxed her out of the car. He carried the bag from Burger King in one hand and intertwined his fingers with hers. Halfway down the beach, she took off her shoes and toted them. They climbed atop a rock to eat their hamburgers while a father and his little girl batted a beach ball back and forth. Boys rode past on bikes, spraying sand and shouting.

"What did you want me to see?" she asked as she wiped mayonnaise off her mouth with the sleeve of the warm sweatshirt he'd lent her.

The sun began to settle beyond the horizon, reminding Thomas of the earth itself, moving in its great circular dance. From behind him he smelled new-cut grass, sweet as mint. "This," he said, indicating the entire scene with one sweep of his hand. "This place. These people. They're all of importance. So why wouldn't you be?"

She didn't speak. She only wrapped her arms around her knees and hugged them against her, watching out as the brazen sun dropped lower, setting off a golden afterglow above the water. Incoming waves plated the sand like fluid silver.

Jillian wasn't as Thomas had imagined her to be at all. She glistened, but he sensed that beneath the shine was something fragile and frightened, something easily broken, like glass. He kept at her. "Not everyone lives at the mercy of public opinion, Miss Dobbs."

"But you do." She smiled at him slyly. "You're a writer, aren't you? Where would you be if no one wanted to make your stories into movies? You ought to be just as nervous as the rest of us."

He stood and grinned down at her, thinking how she'd been obscure at first with her talk of the chameleon and how he took pleasure in answering the same way. She took his hand and let him help her stand. He stepped out of his shoes and they both walked barefoot, the grass cold lace beneath their feet.

They came to a place where the sandy beach gave way to pebbles and rocks worn smooth by time and surf. They stood in silence, listening to the difference. For before, where waves had roared onto sand and backed out in silence, the sea now spilled onto the rocks and did its best to slip back, bringing with it the exquisite clatter of a thousand pebbles gently tumbling together, a happy, hollow echo that didn't end before it began again.

"Ever seen a flock of starlings?" he asked her at last. "At home in Wyoming, the young ones fly across a meadow in bunches, stopping upon every stalk where seeds remain and stripping it bare. When the field is picked clean, they move to another. They are small birds, but they rush forth in one mighty flock, almost like the wind. So it is with my writing. It rushes forth, picks its course through the seeds and the grass, like so many little birds, out of my hands. It's a gift that moves past, something that always surprises me."

She thought about his words a long time before she asked, "So you just wait for stories? Always knowing that they'll come?"

"They always *do* come, in their season. My only task is to accept them, to give them a vessel. I can't help thinking that telling a story is much like living a life."

"But now you see." He could tell she was well pleased to bring it back around to herself again. "What you've told me isn't so different from what I've told you. We're both of us something we aren't. And expecting others to approve of it."

"No," he said. "This is much different. Because you pretend that who you are is something that's within *you*. When I say you become who you are by letting something come in from far, far away."

She still wore the silly hat and the huge glasses. The sun had disappeared by now. Strange, Thomas thought, with the light gone, the sky seemed to flame brighter, the striated colors, pink and orange and gold, resplendent beneath tattered clouds. They walked to the water's edge and began to pitch stones from the beach, competing for distance. Sometimes she came close to bettering him, but not often.

It grew almost too dark for them to make their way back to the car. He reached for her, touched her shoulder. He felt a shudder run through her from head to toe.

"If what you say is true," she said, "then it doesn't matter what anyone thinks at all."

"Yes. That's it exactly."

"Will you remind me of that, often?" she asked, smiling a rare wholehearted smile that he hadn't seen before. "I know myself so well. I know I'll keep forgetting."

"I pledge to remind you." He took her shoulders again, bent his head forward a little.

"Are you ready to go?" she asked carelessly.

"No. I'm not, Miss Jillian Dobbs. There's something I'd like to do with you first."

She rose a little on her toes, stood straight and free. He took off her funny hat. He pulled the sunglasses from her eyes. "There," she said. "It isn't as dark out as I thought it would be."

He lowered his head farther, placed a hand against the spline of her back, pulled her close. In the growing shadows, he found her mouth and kissed her. As he did, she reached behind her own back and took his hands into hers. She pulled away from him just enough to turn his hands up, to survey his palms momentarily. "Just touch me like this once," she whispered. "Please."

With her own hands, she slid his beneath the sweatshirt. He tried to hold them back, thinking she meant to bodily place his hands on her breasts. But, instead, she surprised him and laid his palms together over her heart.

"See now," she said, obviously waiting for his reaction.

He felt her heart's restless thrumming beneath his palms, felt the rise and fall of her uneven breathing. "What is it you're wanting now?"

She smiled somewhat bleakly. "Everyone on the set has told me about you. Your hands have built barns and fences. They've been pinched harnessing horses and blistered digging wells. You have a right to be writing, and to think the things you do. You've touched things that mattered. You've built things that last."

Oh, how the years had ripped past since then. How like a child he'd been, to think he could remind her and remind her, and that she'd grow to understand. He loved her; he depended on her simple, insistent need for him as touchstone, thought it would prove the strength that held them together in a money and image-battered world where nothing held together for long. At her side the day he'd married her, knowing she loved him, he'd felt deluged and intent, full of passionate humility, much like his own character he'd written in a screenplay once who'd won a battle at the cost of many men. He'd known the truth from the beginning, had known she needed him because he brought her something of substance.

As studio notables strolled from table to table and the helicopters flew in low, carrying photographers with cameras and telephoto lenses, as he stood among four hundred people he didn't know and pronounced wedding vows he'd written for Jillian, he felt swept away, as a red-tailed hawk is swept off its flight path by a vicious wind. He wanted her more than he'd wanted anything in his life. And he thought he knew the dangers.

"We could have a ranch in Wyoming of our own, couldn't we?" she asked not long after the wedding.

"With a second house where friends could come to stay." And when she said "friends," he knew she meant people she wanted to woo, directors, producers, investors whose faces no one knew but who could mean the death, the life, of every project. "We could be like everybody else out here. Jane Fonda and Ted Turner had their place up in Montana. Melanie Griffith is down in Aspen. Don Johnson, too, only they aren't together anymore. And I can't even name everybody who's building down in Telluride or up in Jackson Hole. Oh, honey. Let's do it, too."

He shook his head slowly, not liking himself that he was glad of the excuse. "Star Valley isn't like that, Jillian. It isn't a place people go to be seen. And we couldn't raise a house on the land even if we wanted to. It isn't ours any longer. Grandmother gave everything to the government. When the house where Rebecca lives is pulled down, another can never replace it. It'll be left to rot in the snow, every stick and timber."

"Not any of it belongs to you anymore? How could your grandmother give something away that was so valuable? And if she did, why does your sister still live there?"

"There's places people never should've tried to own. Some places can't belong to owners. They only belong to those parts of nature that inhabited them first, the windswept rocks, the animals, the ancient trees."

"Ah," she said quietly, sounding somewhat dissatisfied. "To hear you talk, everyone would know you're a writer. No one else has such idealistic notions as writers do."

When she got into one of her moods, her opinions always jolted him a bit. "You usually like my idealistic notions." He himself took pride in them, as simple and definite as they were. And a baby's life, even talked about, became more than an abstraction.

Jillian needed to feel touched. Thomas could think of no better way for tangibility to pour itself over her than this. On the Woodburn place he'd seen life in its rarest form, free and wild, yet still so entirely designed. He had Howdy and Lucille to thank for it, for all the springtimes he'd spent prowling along the stretch of creek that threaded across the meadow, poking through the budding willows, his hand in Rebecca's as they searched for new-birthed calves. They searched sometimes for days, so well were the calves hidden by their mothers, their tawny bespeckled backs and their small circled bodies as elusive as smoke in the greening underbrush.

And so it would be for them, so much of the miracle, if only Jillian would prepare to receive the heavy, certain life of her own child into her arms.

No matter how bad the night before, Thomas always found hope in the mornings. He found it now, as surely as the sun began again to glisten off the water. He took page two from his typewriter, laid his next screenplay carefully by, and walked into the bedroom to speak with his wife.

"Jillian?" he whispered.

She rolled over and peeked at him out of one eye. "I'm still sleeping."

"No, you aren't. You're awake, looking at me."

She sighed and threw back the covers, lay there waiting for what he would say. When he didn't say anything for a long time, she prompted him. "You never came to bed last night."

"I was writing."

"You've started a new screenplay." He noticed she didn't seem pleased. He knew her well enough. She didn't want him to have any other reason for not coming to bed other than he knew she was angry and didn't want him.

"Yes. This morning I'm satisfied with it. Tomorrow I'll hate it. So I'll just keep going at it and see how I feel when I've worked a month. I'm never certain of what's coming until I've had it on paper long enough to see what's being born."

At the words *being born,* he felt her go tense. "That's always the way with you, isn't it?"

"Jillian. I want to talk more about this."

She stood up and gathered her robe around her. "Oh, haven't we talked enough?"

"No. We haven't. We won't stop talking until you've realized that the two things you're reasoning against don't merit giving one up for the other."

She walked toward the window. When she came to the sill, she turned back to him. As she spoke, tears coursed down her cheeks. "Damn it, Thomas. The things you want go only one way. Can't you see what you're doing?"

"I want my child," he said, "and I want you, too."

"You can't have that. You're like a child yourself, asking and asking and asking."

"It's the only thing I know to do."

"Listen to me." She came back at him, tossing her saffron hair over one shoulder. He saw in her a woman who didn't know her own carrying power, didn't understand half of her own capabilities. Yet she'd seen herself achieve so much. Why didn't she trust it? "You do me dishonor, Thomas Woodburn. You stand there and look at me and think I make this decision lightly. It isn't that way. Do you hear me? I'm hurting over it, too. Don't you know?"

If he did hear her, if he did know, he didn't let on.

"Do you know how lonely I feel?" she asked him now, her voice a shrill treble. "Do you think I don't know what this is costing both of us? Not only you, Thomas, but me?"

"Yes," he said quietly. "That's exactly what I thought. I didn't realize you had already counted the cost."

"Well, I have."

He began to see, at last, how futile his cause with her. She was as she'd always been, shape-shifting, ready to lose herself in the landscape. "We aren't going to decide this amicably, are we, Jillian?"

"Not unless you admit I've made the only decision I can make right now."

"I'll never admit to that."

"That's it, then," she said quietly, yanking her robe tighter around her. "We won't accomplish anything like this."

Outside every window to the west, the sea kept at its constant wind-tossed pounding, the high sun glimmering against each wave, gilding each oncoming swell with magnificent blue. Thomas left the bedroom and went to find one of Jillian's many telephones. He might be naive, but he wasn't crazy. He'd conduct business in this town as well as anybody. He ran his finger down the page until he found their lawyer's phone number. He dialed.

Thomas didn't realize it was Saturday until he got the answering machine. He hung up, searched out John Arlen's home phone number. When John answered, Thomas could tell he'd still been in bed. "What do you need, Mr. Woodburn?" the fellow asked in a coarse voice.

"I need a restraining order or a lawsuit or something served on Jillian. Whatever's appropriate in this situation. I'm the father of the child, and I'm not willing to let her abort it."

"But you don't understand, Mr. Woodburn," he said, sounding somewhat perturbed. "I can't do that. I'm *Jillian's* lawyer. I can't serve papers against her. You'll have to find someone else."

"I thought you represented both of us, Mr. Arlen."

"My retainer is billed each month to the account of Jillian Dobbs."

"I see." So Thomas was reduced to going through the Yellow Pages, seeking someone who specialized in "Family Disputes Kept Confidential." It took him what seemed like forever to decide on someone. Like Jillian, he didn't want to risk hiring any mongers who might sell information to the press. When he finally found a possibility, a man in his office on Saturday morning who sounded decent, the lawyer informed him he couldn't do anything until his secretary arrived to draw up papers on Monday.

"That's the best you can do?"

"Yes."

"But I'm—" He stopped himself, knowing how dangerous it would be to identify himself to the wrong person. After an Oscar for best screenplay and the publicity Grayson had garnered, they'd have reporters swarming the grounds again before lunchtime. "Never mind who I am," he said. "Schedule me in. I'll be there first thing Monday morning."

He hung up the telephone and walked out onto the lawn, watching out over the sea, wondering how long he would stay here. He held his arms straight as he tried to get his bearings. His chest began to heave as though there were not enough air in all Jillian's acreage, in all of Southern California, for all of them, for him and anyone else, even for him alone.

6

Folks in Star Valley, Wyoming, know you can tell a lot about a man by the way he builds his fences. Howdy and Lucille Woodburn started out simple enough, with neat rows of unpeeled buckrail, leaned upon themselves and buttressed along rises in the meadow like the slim vertebrae of some ancient, big animal. But things changed with the coming of the elk.

As the years passed, everybody in town had taken a hand in helping Howdy redesign his fences. Anything to protect his haystacks. Anything to keep the wilderness animals from eating into his profits and starving his cattle.

Taking the buckrail down that first year had been almost as back-breaking as putting it up. But over at the vet's office, Jubal Krebbs had insisted Howdy'd be better off if he could come up with something more difficult to jump. "You oughtta try something like this," Jubal'd started out in 1971. "You'll have to find yourself a posthole digger, though. Don't know where you'll come up with one around here." Nobody around Star Valley had been either desperate enough or stupid enough to dig holes in the rocky soil.

Howdy doffed his Roice's Wyoming Troutfitters cap and scratched his head through what was left of his hair.

"You might find one in Casper," Jubal told him. "That, and you're gonna need spools of barbed wire to string along. You're gonna want at least five strands. Like this." He went back to drawing again.

"You think something like that'll really keep 'em out?" asked Miller Roice. "Doesn't seem like upright posts would make that much difference. Crazy fool animals. They'll jump higher than that if they need to. I saw one come right up over a freeway abutment once. Remember that winter when the whole convention of Ski-Dooers got their maps turned upside down and ran their snowmobiles full throttle across the gully? Spooked the herd so bad, it took weeks for 'em all to find each other again. There were elk everywhere. One of 'em knocked over the Budges' outhouse, with Aretha in it."

"When elk get hungry during a mountain winter, nothing stops them," chimed in Charlie Egan. "You see, Howdy, it's a matter of a fence for you. It's a matter of life or death for them."

"It's a matter of life or death for me, too. I'm making a living up there raising cattle," Howdy said.

"Those elk come in and eat all my graze, my cows won't survive and neither will I."

"Barbed wire'll stop the elk." Jubal laid the pen upon the counter and frowned into his appointment book, obviously taken aback that someone would challenge his professional opinion. "I know it will."

Oh, how this conversation echoed and changed from year to year! As Rebecca and Thomas grew gangly and tall in their adolescence, the fences grew taller, too. First one year: "Best raise the height of those poles two feet, Howdy," Miller Roice said. "You've gotta come up with *something* that's a higher barrier."

Then another year: "Better just get rid of the barbed wire all together," Frank Weatherby surmised. "Never should've put it up in the first place. I say you raise it again and barricade the whole thing with net wire."

And another: "We think you'd be smart to get rid of those wooden posts." This from Jubal and Tuck Krebbs, who'd taken during latter years to working as a team. "You oughtta go with something more durable, something you can pound in deep, like steel."

"But Jubal, you're the one who told him to dig all those postholes," said Lucille, who'd firmly taken to joining these meetings. After the third fence had gone up and three times she'd had to feed everybody who came over to help, she'd decided to attend these gatherings and put in her two cents' worth.

"No one could've guessed what you and your family'd be up against with that high land. There've been times I've thought you should sell off and start the ranch again somewhere else. But if you sold the place to somebody, they'd be expecting to run a ranch up there, too. Then I'd be sitting here discussing this same thing with somebody else who might not have the same presence of mind that you have."

"I've thought about selling off," Howdy said.

Lucille laid a hand against her husband's arm, a hand that had once been soft and perfectly formed, a hand now singular with work and age. "But what about Thomas and Rebecca? They love it so."

"Yes," he said. "I know. That's what has kept me at this for so long."

"I suggest you make the steel posts at least nine feet tall. I'd add another three feet at the top. Use woven wire, at least eleven gauge. And two strands of barbed wire at the top to deter anything that might still be tempted to jump."

"Barbed wire again." Howdy took the latest diagram from Jubal, rolled it up, tapped it on the top of the barrel where Jubal's son, Tuck, had whittled pictures when he'd been a little boy. "This is my last try, Krebbs. My last try. This doesn't work, I don't know what I'm gonna do."

And this fence—Howdy's last-ditch effort—remained standing to no avail a full quarter century later. Lucille had passed on and been buried next to Howdy in the cottonwood grove beside the house, where the limbs rattled like bones upon the roof. Cattle no longer grazed on the Timberline. But Star Valley folks with animal problems—or problems of any sort, for that matter—still gathered at the vet's office on Saturdays and discussed the week's events.

"Did you hear the crazy call that came in over Silas Braxton's radio yesterday?" asked Elmer Crates. "Some fool inmate escaped from the state pen and thought he could cut across the Oregon Trail in a car."

"Now that's a fool idea all right," announced Harvey Perkins. "How long did it take state troopers to catch him?"

"They haven't caught him yet," said Prentiss Smith.

"What?" John Owen bounced his and Lisa Jo's newest boy on his knee. "Can't believe such a thing."

"Heard about it on KSGT from Jackson Hole sometime in the early afternoon. They've got an all-points bulletin out for the guy. Name's Ben Pershall. They say he could be close by, that he's armed and dangerous."

"He got *away* on the Oregon Trail? Must've been driving one hell of a truck."

"Nope. Wasn't driving a truck at all. Did the whole thing in an old Buick Le Sabre."

"That's impossible."

"The guy's either a mastermind or damn lucky." First thing after he'd taken over from his father, Tuck had installed a pegboard on the wall behind the counter. He'd covered it with metal hooks and the broadest selection of collars, leashes, harnesses, and bridles found anywhere in Lincoln County. He passed them now to join his chums at the barrel. They swept along with him, then swung back, their buckles and grommets jangling together. "You know where the

Oregon Trail comes out on the Smoot Highway? The report on Silas's radio said he lost control about a mile east of there. Car plunged all the way down into Caddisfly Creek. Took 'em five hours to get a Highway Department crane up into the backcountry and lift the Buick out of the creek. Andy Rogers got called out just after it happened, about sunup. Angus Riley was down there, too. They said everybody fully expected that car to come up with a body in it."

"And didn't it?"

"No! This man's like Houdini or something. The car was as empty as a church pew on a baseball afternoon. Nobody's quite sure how he accomplished it. The state people up from Cheyenne think he must've planned it, that he scrambled out and got the door shut before the car sank too deep in water. Let that current get ahold of a door, and you might never get the thing back secure again."

"You think he schemed it?"

"I reckon so. Seems he went to great pains, making it look like he'd gotten trapped inside."

"You figure he's running?"

"If I were him, knowing I had a few hours of solace before they'd be after me again, I'd hightail it right out of this place."

"But what if he didn't? Or couldn't?"

"You got a county map, Tuck?" Frank Weatherby asked. "Something topographical? I wonder if those state experts are studying the lay of the land."

"Andy Rogers suggested a theory or two. If this Ben Pershall climbed out of the driver's side, it would've been easier to cross the creek and head downhill along river drainage. Or he might've climbed out on the passenger's side, making it easier to skirt the north bank of Caddisfly and head northwest toward Smoot."

"Where were the officers who chased him?"

"Up on the trail itself. The north side of Caddisfly."

"I say he didn't dare head toward Smoot, even though it would've been easier. If he planned the whole thing, if he was thinking it through, he couldn't've stayed on the north side of the river. Chances were too good those lawmen might've seen him."

"He came down toward Star Valley, then. Yesterday sometime."

"They've set up roadblocks on all three of the highways. If he didn't get out then, he won't be able to get out now."

Tuck Krebbs had rummaged through his file cabinets and had come up with three satisfactory maps. Frank Weatherby unfolded each and spread them clockwise on the floor. He surveyed them for a long moment before offering his opinion. "There's one other way he might've gone." When he spoke, his voice became solid, weighty, deliberate. "There *is* one other way he might've gone."

"What way is that, Frank?"

"Here." He pointed with one broad, knobby finger. "Up and over the top. Coming down through the trees by Rebecca Woodburn's place."

The gentlemen of Star Valley stared at each other for a full twenty seconds before anybody said anything.

"Surely not—"

"There's eighty inches of snow up that high. He couldn't've done it without snowshoes."

"You're saying he climbed clear up over the tundra. I agree. He couldn't've gone that way."

"But he's desperate—"

"Desperate enough to drive his car down that ravine."

"You said it yourself. Don't know whether he's a mastermind or just damn lucky. Maybe his luck ran out. The top of that mountain is as good a place as any for a man to die."

Then Tuck Krebbs started laughing. He laughed until his stomach hurt. "Ain't nobody gonna bother Rebecca Woodburn on that refuge up there, not after that last, best fence Howdy built before he passed on."

"This isn't a time for joking, Tuck. That fence didn't even keep the elk out."

"That convict could've walked in right across the front cattleguard."

Prentiss Smith was the first to take action. He stood up, challenging them all. "Has anyone called up there to check on her?"

"Surely she knows she could be in danger. They broadcast it on the weather channel in Jackson Hole. Right after Tom Dunham did the forecast. And the radio station has been breaking in with developments all day."

"She doesn't get a television signal up there. Doesn't get radio, either."

Frank Weatherby rose, too. "But has anybody called?"

Tuck Krebbs shook his head. "She doesn't have a telephone, remember. She tried to put up that darned antenna a couple years ago and some ridiculous bird made it into a nest. I've long had my doubts about the sanity of a woman being up there alone, as cut off as she is."

"Rebecca Woodburn likes to be cut off."

"My mother visited up there just yesterday morning," John Owen interjected. "She checks on Rebecca ever so often. She said Rebecca Woodburn was out on the sleigh feeding elk like always. Said she seemed to be doing just fine."

"Yesterday morning?"

They all stopped and stared at each other again.

"Yesterday morning was too early." Harvey Perkins poked his cigar out in the ashtray and shrugged into his coat. "Anything could've happened between now and then."

"I'm with you, Harvey," Prentiss said, putting on his coat, too.

"You taking your pickup truck?" Tuck Krebbs asked. "Is there room for me?"

"Yep. If you don't mind sitting in the middle. We sure might need you." Then Harvey hesitated, hanging on to the truck door and poking his head back out at everyone. "Anybody got a gun?"

They glanced around among themselves.

"You think we're likely to need one?"

"I think we'd be stupid if we went up there with no way to protect ourselves or Rebecca Woodburn."

Frank Weatherby, as calm as you please, strode toward his own vehicle, pulled out his hunting rifle and ammunition. "You three young fellows take Old Betsy here. Coral's been jealous at me for fifty years because I never go anywhere without this sweet rifle. Tuck, you know best how to shoot my Betsy. I'm putting you in charge of her. I figure it's time to put the old girl to some good use."

Rebecca roused from her broken sleep. She lay motionless in her own bed Saturday morning, listening for his breath. She knew he waited—as he'd waited all night—with the gun propped on his knees.

Sun beamed in through the windows, setting the room afire with color. She should've been up hours ago, out mucking stalls and graining the horses. She knew Mabel and Coney would be almost frantic. The two muscular horses hadn't missed a day of sleighing since the first heavy snowfall November 18.

Cautiously, without moving another part of her body, Rebecca lifted her head an inch off the pillow and stared along her nose at him. He was there all right, crouched like a cat at the end of her bedstead, the rifle well positioned across his thighs.

His head rested sideways against one shoulder. His mouth hung open; his eyes stayed closed. His breath, which she'd listened for so carefully, came in heavy, even cadence.

She raised herself on one elbow. He was asleep!

With one cagey hand, she raised the heavy bedclothes and folded them toward the foot of the bed. She gathered both legs beneath her, wincing at the rustle of the sheets. She paused a moment, expecting him to stir at the sound, watching with both terror and ecstasy as she realized he wasn't going to respond.

Here was her chance, then. She shifted one leg, one leg only, and lowered one foot toward the floor. She lowered the second foot, placed it delicately on the cold plank floor beside the first. Slowly, oh, so slowly, she placed her weight on her toes. She edged her way off the mattress, began to stand.

Rebecca had no idea where she'd go, what she'd do, when she made it out that door. She took one step. Two. Maybe she'd hide in the barn until help came. Maybe she'd run across the pasture, praying he couldn't shoot a moving mark. Maybe she'd get as far as the road and could flag somebody down. That wasn't likely, though. Not many people passed by on a road that led them nowhere.

Three. On her third step, the floor squeaked.

His hands bolted for the rifle. Two seconds' time and he aimed it at her, his eyes bleary but surprisingly alert. "Where do you think you're going?"

Her hopes plummeted. Her breath stopped, caught in the hard, sharp constriction in her throat. "Where do you *think* I'm going?" she asked. "I'm getting out of bed for the day."

He unfolded his long limbs and stood from the floor, barring her exit. He did his best to adjust the shirt that had fallen open across his shoulder blades. She saw how carefully he plucked at the wrinkled cotton. She'd blistered him with the soup. "You expect me to believe that? After you threw boiling soup at me last night? You're not going anywhere without me, lady. I don't trust you any farther than I could throw you."

"If you please," she said quietly, secretly taking pleasure that he still felt pain and that she could agitate him, "I need to go to the outhouse."

"Again?"

"Yes."

Rebecca preferred to keep this place very much as her grandfather had built it. She thought her way of living respectable enough for one ordinary woman and a whole passel of elk. She hadn't ordered a furnace for the house, and she boasted no running hot water, even in the kitchen.

When she wanted to wash dishes or bathe, she boiled water in an immense aluminum pot on the stove. Of course, she'd never seen the need to install a porcelain commode. In fact, when someone asked her once why she didn't have one, she'd looked up the word in the dictionary and had found it there, right on the same page as "common prayer." Well, she'd say all her common prayers while sitting in the outhouse, thank you very much. She saw no reason to cut holes in a perfectly good floor to add more plumbing.

Rebecca shrugged on her jacket over the same clothes she'd worn yesterday. Thank goodness she hadn't considered changing into a nightgown. Thank goodness she'd found every way to keep herself from becoming vulnerable to him. This man had escaped from prison and now held her hostage. He'd committed a crime punishable by time in prison. He'd been tried and found guilty. He wielded the gun. He wielded the power. She didn't put it past him to violate her bed the way he'd violated her home.

But, he hadn't.

Yet.

He followed her downstairs. Just as she headed for the door, he commanded, "Check on her before we go out." With the rifle barrel, he motioned toward the downstairs bedroom, toward the sleeping girl.

They went in together. Rebecca sat carefully on the edge of the four-poster, her bedraggled braid looped over one shoulder. Gently she reached across the mattress, ran one hand across the girl's forehead. No fever. And the wound seemed to be healing nicely.

"She'll sleep well enough for a while longer," Rebecca whispered.

"Take good care of her today," he whispered back. "I want to get her strength up."

"Of course I'll take good care of her."

"I've gotta get her out of here tonight. We've got a ways to go yet. The longer we stay around this place, the worse off we'll be."

Rebecca stared at him. His talk of leaving filled her with treacherous hope. However, the child's welfare remained at stake. "Don't take her," Rebecca said. "Leave her here with me. She'll be better off."

"No." He shook his head. "You haven't any idea what you're talking about."

"But she won't be—" Rebecca stopped herself. This young lady wouldn't be ready to travel tonight, or tomorrow, or the next day. She reminded herself that she had no say in the matter, that she'd do best to stay uninvolved, to let him fight his own illicit battles. *Okay, then*, she thought. *You're no problem of mine, whoever you are. Please go. Just leave me to my life as it was before.*

As if he'd read her mind, he favored her with a loose, sarcastic smile. "I'm ready to escort you to the outhouse."

7

She proceeded out the door, then down the walk. He followed her as the sun caught the landscape and the snow came alight with color. The cottonwood boughs wove a tapestry of shadow along the trodden path. She went inside the tiny wooden building with the quarter moon carved high on the door. He heard her lock the door from the inside. *Click*.

Ben leaned against the little building. From the barn came the sound of the horses pounding hooves in their stalls. Across the snow-covered meadow the elk showed their high spirits, the sun glistening on their sleek curves as they pawed through the ice or made their way along with clumsy, bovine tossing of heads. From above him a great distance he heard "*Garooo-a. Garooo-a.*" His hands tightened on the gun. He glanced around one side of the building. He glanced around the other. That's when he saw the flock of sandhill cranes floating majestically overhead, following the watercourse and uttering their flight song.

I don't have to do that, he reminded himself. I don't have to have eyes in the back of my head. I'm free. Free.

She said through the door, "You want to stay safe in this place, you'd best let me get at my chores. Anyone could drive in and see there aren't fresh tracks coming from the barn this morning. Anyone comes up here for any reason, they'd be suspicious of a thing like that. All the world will know something's the matter. If you'd just let me grain the horses, maybe harness them and do a little of the feeding—"

He didn't like the way he'd heard the determined locking of the door. If she tried to lock herself in, he'd have to break down the door so he could get to her. He didn't want to chance that. He put his face next to the splintered gray door and ordered, "You come out of there and we'll talk about it."

She didn't answer at first. He stared at the painfully blue sky, at the ground, at his snow-stained prison shoes. Presently he heard her unfasten the latch. The door swung open. "Are you going to make me bargain for everything I need to do on my own land?"

"Yes." With one hand, Ben reached inside the door for the wooden hasp. He wrenched it off, nails and all. "There."

She stared at him as if he were crazy. "The chores," she said. "You told me we'd talk about the chores."

For the animals she needed to do this, and for herself. She longed to perform some act of routine, some daily custom whose very pursuit would sing out to her, Yes! Although you can't see or feel it, the good, small things happen somewhere today, and matter.

She thought he might relent. For an instant she saw him see the need in her eyes. She knew, after everything that had gone between them, he had to consider her request.

"Never learned much about horses," he said. "Do they—"

But he stopped. As he'd spoken, two vans filled with people had turned at the gate. The vehicles rattled in over the front cattleguard and veered toward the house.

He grabbed her, shoved her back against the outhouse so they'd stay out of view. "Who is that?" he asked. "Who's coming?"

The vans proceeded up the drive. They parked.

"It's Saturday," she cried out to him. "I forgot that today's Saturday."

"What happens on Saturday?" he snarled. "Who are all these people?" And here he took her face in his hands, made her meet his eyes. "Answer me, lady. We've got lives at stake here." He glanced ruefully toward the vehicles as the doors began to open and children began to climb out. "A good number of them."

"S-Saturday." She could scarcely utter the words, so distraught was she. Tears filled her eyes. "On S-Saturday, the. . . the schoolk-kids c-come. . . ."

"What do they come for? There isn't any school today."

"They come to s-see the elk. To ride the sleigh w-with me."

"You didn't tell me that," he accused her. "You thought they'd come in and catch me."

That was one of the most ridiculous things he'd said. She frantically took stock of who'd be here, who could overpower this man, who could help her. But she wouldn't risk these children's lives. Or the teachers, either. "Th-they're only third-graders," she babbled now, finding her voice and wanting to make him understand. "They're the ones who've met their reading goal for the week. It's a reward for them. I forgot about it, is all. I've been able to think about nothing but *you*. *You* and that infernal gun you keep waving in my face."

"Well," he said smugly, "you'd best not change your train of thought yet. We have a problem here."

Despite the gun, despite his control over her, she grabbed the tattered sleeve of his prison-issue shirt and tugged at it, pleading with him. "D-don't hurt them. Th-they're not involved in this. It's my fault I didn't warn you. P-please."

The children and their two teachers climbed the steps. One teacher, Mrs. Virginia Anderson, knocked at the door. They all waited for the door to be answered—waited, and, of course, nobody came.

"Rebecca?" Mrs. Joan Byington called out.

Despite the man's preoccupation, he glanced at her somewhat victoriously. "Rebecca. That's your name, isn't it? Rebecca."

She nodded.

It seemed the group of visitors had given up on the house. They'd decided she was already out, working in the barnyard. In a joyous line, the students clambered—or jumped and flew—down the steps. Their belongings flew with them, brightly colored mittens and hats, all manner of thick coats. They made their way toward the stables, where Mabel and Coney shifted restlessly inside their stalls.

"You've gotta get rid of those kids," he ordered her.

"How do you expect me to do that?" she asked angrily. "They know the sleigh goes out every day. They can see it hasn't come out yet this morning."

"Damn it."

"Please," she whispered again. "They'll see the horses haven't even been harnessed yet. I'll tell them I left the hitching job undone so they'd learn to help me."

When the last kid disappeared around the corner of the barn, he grabbed her arm, dragged her after him as he ran full bore toward the house. With one massive arm, he pulled her inside and held her against his length. He surveyed the snow-covered pastureland from the far window. He raised the gun, looked out again through the scope she'd mounted on her Ruger. "This is powerful, isn't it? I can see the whole place. I can train the gun on you, no matter where you go with them. I could shoot from here, you know."

"Yes," she said, praying he'd listen to reason. "I know. But I won't give you reason to." If he saw her start to run or the children begin to panic, he could kill somebody before they made it to the tall, dense wall of timber or the startling buttes. "If we do this, no one will know you're here but me. I won't risk frightening these children or having them hurt."

"You could send one of them back to town with a message," he said, analyzing all of his options. "They'd have the sheriff up here in no time."

"When would I give someone a message?" she asked. "I've already thought of that. They're all together. The minute I start speaking to a teacher, the children will hear. You know I can't risk that, either."

He stepped away from her and leaned against the wall, staring at the ceiling for what seemed an interminable time. At last, she felt his hand go lax around her arm. "Rebecca," he said.

"What?"

When she turned to him, she saw contrition in his expression. But his faded green eyes became less grim and less haunted. He walked over to the window, turned, and came toward her again.

"There are things happening here that I never intended," he said.

On the hearth, Lucille's ancient clock ticked placidly toward the next hour. From the barnyard came the shrill treble of children's voices. One of the students, or maybe even a teacher, gave out a little shriek of appreciation.

"Stop looking at me like that. Go on out there," he told her at last. "I give you fifteen seconds, fifteen seconds only, to get those kids all out of the barn and over here where I can see them. While you harness the horses, the kids and the teachers stay in one big group outside. You get them all on the sleigh, you ride them around in circles or whatever you do, and then you send them home. I stay here in the kitchen with my eye on the scope, my hand on the trigger. If I see you separating yourself from the group, if I see you trying to take a teacher aside, I start shooting. And I don't care who I hit. Do you understand?"

Rebecca nodded.

"And leave the door open. Wide. So I can hear what's going on."

"I will. Thank you," she said, her voice gone thick with relief. "You've done . . . a good thing."

"Now, what I've done depends on you, doesn't it?"

"Yes." She looked back once at his hardened face, just once, before she plopped her plaid hat on her head, tugged on her work gloves, and hurried out the door. She didn't want to give him time to reconsider. In ways, she sensed he was as entrapped in this as she. She suspected his decision today had nothing whatsoever to do with kindness.

"Halloo," she called out, putting on a false smile, hurrying to find the third-graders. "I'm here." She waved her arms.

Children came from every direction, waving too and running.

"Where have you been?"

"We've looked all over!"

"We thought you'd gone off and left us."

"But the horses are still there!"

How do I get them all in one place? How do I make them stay together?

Half of them were already running back to see Mabel and Coney. "Wait, please," she called out, knowing the precious fifteen seconds had long since come and gone.

Please let him see I'm trying, that I'm doing the best I can.

Frantically, she tried to round them up. "You've got to come here and listen to me," she called out, motioning the teachers to help her. Then she knelt in the snow so she'd be eye level with them as she explained it.

"What is it?"

"Why aren't the horses ready?"

"What's wrong?"

"Nothing's wrong," she lied. "I'm behind schedule today, is all. I'm going to bring out Mabel and Coney and teach you to harness them. How would you like that?"

They nodded en masse. Rebecca reached out gloved hands to several of them. "If we do it, though, you have to follow my instructions. These horses are big. And they could be dangerous if you moved too much or got too loud and spooked them."

They watched her, wide-eyed. *Oh, if only you knew of the danger*, she longed to say to them. *If only you understood how important it is for you to obey.*

"Can we help get them out of the stalls?" one little boy asked.

"No." Oh, how she fought to keep her countenance steady. "I'll bring them out." Another bright, eye-contact smile. Then she ran to the stables, her disheveled braid flailing behind her. She carried out collars and reins, all the while willing her hands to cease their trembling. She went back for the two heavy martingales and the tug and girth, the gigantic leather loops that belted and buckled around the Belgians' withers and flanks.

All the while she kept glancing at the house, at the kitchen window, which reflected the fixed, brazen daylight. She caught no glimpse of motion behind the glass. But she knew he stood there, waiting, watching her.

The chore, which never took long, seemed as if it took hours this morning. Rebecca's only thought, as she laid out blankets to sit on, was to finish the ride and get the children home safely. As the third-graders began to step aboard the sleigh and find places to sit, she saw him.

Ben must've readjusted the gun barrel. Sun glanced against stainless steel, sending a shot of light through the pane. The instant the light moved, she saw danger glinting in his eyes, eyes trained perfectly on her face while his two fists grasped the gun.

She turned forward, gave the Belgians a good *thwack* with the reins. "Mabel. Coney. Yah!"

The sleigh lurched forward. The kids squealed. The teachers clapped. And, as all these things happened at once, Rebecca recognized Harvey Perkins's old pickup truck as it turned in off the main road and crossed the cattleguard.

She looked from the window to the road to the children to the window again. She yanked the reins, bringing the horses to a prompt halt. "Confound this." She looked around for someone to hand the reins to, but she realized she couldn't leave the sleigh. If she did, he'd suspect something. She held the reins and held her ground. "Haven't had this many people come to visit all at once since Lucille's funeral."

Harvey parked his truck and climbed out. Tuck Krebbs and Prentiss Smith clambered out right behind them. They gathered, the stubble-bearded three together, without first greeting her.

Tuck carried a rifle, slung low by his thigh. She knew the convict could see them through the window, knew he probably already had found good aim with the Ruger. Which would he shoot? A child? A teacher? Or one of the men she'd known for as long as she remembered, who waited affably in the driveway? Adrenaline shot through her, sending sharp nettles along her limbs.

"Howdy, Rebecca," Prentiss hollered.

"Hello." Rebecca waved back. But she stayed with the sleigh and the kids. This was her only choice. This was her only way to protect them. Oh, if only Harvey and Prentiss and Tuck hadn't come now! If only they'd come when the children were gone home and she'd been able to ask them for help!

The three men sauntered to the sleigh. "Well, what's this?" Harvey asked, grinning. "You taking passengers out today?"

"Sure am." Rebecca pulled the big plaid hat lower over her eyes. "We do this every Saturday."

"Are you kids from John Fremont Elementary?" asked Prentiss.

"Yeah," answered several of them. "We live down in Star Valley."

"Our teachers brought us up."

"You fixed our cat last year," one little boy announced, pointing his red waterproof mitten at Tuck. "Cat ate a rabbit and got a big hairball. You got it out of 'im and saved his life."

"That old gray tomcat of yours?" Tuck asked, obviously pleased to be recognized and proud of his work. "I'm glad to have helped him. How is he doing, anyway?"

"Oh, he's dead now," the little boy said. "Coyotes came onto the place this past fall. Went after 'im and took his head clean off. But you sure fixed him up after that rabbit."

Rebecca stood in the midst of them, in the midst of innocence and peril, every fiber, every sense, keenly focused on the window. Was the motion she saw a reflection of these children in the sun-stark yard? Or did it conceal one man's terrifying, invasive effort to hold her hostage while freeing himself? Even now he kept her captive.

"I'm glad to see you all," she said, grinning at them. "Can I help you with something? Or are you just dropping by for a visit?"

"Don't she look just like Howdy up there on that sleigh?" Prentiss pointed up at her. "There you stand, wearing his hat and everything. You'd sure make him proud, Miss Rebecca. Him and Miz Lucille, too. Still up in the wilderness all winter feedin' animals off the sleigh. Who'd've thought they'd still have family up here, after everything they went through. You Woodburns are made of hearty stock." Only he didn't mention one thing. He didn't mention the animals she fed now were the ones Howdy'd fought so hard to keep out.

The horses pawed the ground. The third-graders got antsy and started to wiggle. Mrs. Virginia Anderson had to remind several of them to remain seated.

"We came to check on you," Harvey announced.

"Wanted to take a look around," Tuck added.

"There's been some talk in town," Prentiss said.

She kept a firm hand on the reins. Mabel and Coney made it obvious to everybody that they wanted to start up without her. "Whoa," she hollered at the Belgians. "What sort of talk?"

"You seen anything strange around the place?" Harvey asked.

"Or noticed anybody strange?" Tuck added immediately, not giving her time to reply to Harvey.

But she didn't answer either of them. She couldn't. Instead she prayed, *Oh, don't ask me this now. Not in front of all these children. Not while the man in the window's got the gun trained on me, or you, or one of the children. Please understand me. Please look at me, really look at me, and realize that something's wrong. Please come back again later.*

Rebecca pictured herself saying, "Yes. There's a strange man in my house right now. Don't act like you've heard anything. Just look around and walk back to your pickup truck, then go back to town and find the sheriff." She pictured the children. "A convict?" they'd all ask. "Where is he?" And they'd start craning their necks toward the house.

"No," she'd say. "You mustn't look at him now. He's pointing a gun right at you." The girls would start to scream. The boys would start to run. The man in the window would start to shoot.

Or she'd say to Harvey, "No. Nothing's the matter. But why don't you three go into the house? Pour yourself a pot of coffee?" And there they'd go, traipsing into the kitchen still talking about how proud Howdy'd be to see her, that rifle Tuck was carrying still unloaded and hanging low, while the man with her Ruger would be waiting for them.

She wouldn't endanger their lives. Not for a convict who, she prayed, would be gone tomorrow.

She swallowed. Hard. "Everything's fine," she said, lying through her teeth.

"Every Saturday morning we gather around down at Tuck's office," Harvey explained. "I don't mean to frighten you, Miss Rebecca, but Elmer Crates came in this morning talking about the funniest thing."

"What funny thing?"

Before he went on, Harvey glanced apologetically at the third-graders from John Fremont Elementary School. Rebecca could tell that he didn't want to frighten them, either. "You need to know these details," he said. "We want you to be on the lookout, up here alone the way you are."

"The lookout for what, Harvey?" If she hadn't already surmised what he was talking about, he'd've driven her mad with his hemming and hawing.

"There's a prison escapee loose, Rebecca. And he could be somewhere close by."

"Really?" she asked, trying to sound as nonchalant as possible, while the children all started to whisper. "A convict? What makes you say that?"

"This crazy, fool fellow escaped from the state pen sometime night before last," Prentiss said. "The guy got clear away and nobody can figure out exactly how he did it. His cell was still locked. And nobody even knew he was gone until they did the bell count at four-fifteen yesterday morning."

"Only thing anybody ever found was one small hole dug and a place cut in the prison fence. He vanished off the face of this earth. Just like that," Tuck added.

She wanted to say, "All three of you sound like you've been watching too many movies." But the problem was, she knew they hadn't. She knew how tall tales and fables grew beside Tuck Krebbs's upturned barrel. But this one wasn't a fable. This one rang true.

"Just wanted to come up and check on things," Prentiss said, and Rebecca thought—as he spoke—of how she'd always loved him. She remembered him from long-ago forever, the same brown face, only not so worn away as it was now, worn away as rocks are worn away by water. He'd always been the one to care enough to check on things. "Frank Weatherby even let Tuck borrow Old Betsy here, in case we found anything suspicious."

Rebecca turned to Tuck. "That isn't your gun? You don't know how to shoot it?"

"Oh, I could figure out how, I guess," Tuck answered, "given the time."

"What makes you think this man's somewhere nearby?" Rebecca asked. And suddenly, despite the gun barrel, despite the man who frightened her so, she felt unforeseen power. The more she knew about him, the more she'd be able to predict his deeds. The more she'd be able to predict his deeds, the more she'd be able to protect herself against him. "Have you found something?"

"I should say so!" Prentiss said.

"Outlaw got plumb away from Rawlins before anybody knew a thing," Harvey said. "He could've gone two hundred fifty miles before anyone discovered him missing. Something like this is unprecedented."

"Everybody in Star Valley's saying this guy's either a fool or a genius, doing the things he did to get away," Tuck added.

"Can we go feed the elk now?" Little Carrie Budge scrooched on her seat. "They're hungry. And so am I."

"I need to go to the bathroom," announced William Beery.

"What did he do?" Rebecca asked.

"He must've been driving along 191, out there where a man can see for half a state and then some. Two deputies from Sublette County had stopped to move a herd of pronghorn antelope that'd congregated on the highway. They were displaying lights and honking the horn, weaving through the animals to make them move along, when the APB came in.

"These fellows thought nothing of it until they drove by the Oregon Trail marker a half mile down and saw fresh tracks in the snow. Somebody'd turned off the highway, taken the old Oregon Trail, and made a beeline straight across the countryside."

"Folks ain't been traveling that trail since 1847," Prentiss put in. "Of course, there's ranchers that recognize the historical value of it and keep their portion cleared out and open. But to think those wagon ruts cut so deep that somebody in a car could make it across Wyoming *now.*"

Harvey said, "Just when these deputies were about to catch up with him, he lost control—"

"He didn't lose control. He planned the whole thing—"

"Nobody'd do something like that on purpose, nobody sane, that is—"

"But maybe somebody desperate—"

"Nobody'd drive a car straight down a gorge into the river."

"I thought he'd *backed* it down into the river."

"They're saying it looks like it flipped from bumper to bumper and ended up going sideways."

"I heard he'd hit a tree. Took the whole thing out, clear down to the roots."

"The car sank in four feet of water. Thing was, everybody thought he was trapped in there. For hours, until they got the car out of the water, people stopped looking."

"Didn't know they had a problem until they got a crane up there, pulled the car out, and didn't find the body." Here Rebecca shuddered. Despite the man's odious doings, she couldn't imagine referring to him as nothing but "the body."

"Have the sheriff or any of the deputies come up to look around this place?"

Rebecca shook her head.

"Don't figure they will. Don't figure the police'll come searching up this draw at all. For all intents and purposes, seems impossible for a fellow to get from there to here. But Frank Weatherby pored over a topographical map in my office this morning and he insisted we'd better come out and check up on you. Frank thinks this man could've climbed up over the divide and wandered across your place. And you know how Andy Rogers always tries to figure everything out on huge charts down at the sheriff's office."

"All the state troopers who're up from Cheyenne think the fellow came down the watershed and through town, that he probably hitched a ride during those first few hours with somebody going north."

"Did they run a search on the car?" she asked, wanting to know everything, anything, that might give her leverage with the man in her kitchen. "Who does it belong to?"

"That's another funny part. Some man in Rawlins named Pete Giddy. Andy Rogers said the guy was housebound because he didn't have a big toe. He'd never even realized his car was missing."

"Everybody's looking for him now," Harvey announced casually. "If that man isn't out of the valley yet, he ain't gonna get out. Those troopers have set up roadblocks on every two-rutter, backcountry road between here and the Idaho State line. They're stopping people on the highway, too. I heard tell there's a mile-long line down on I–80, from them stoppin' and checkin' everybody."

Mabel and Coney chomped at their bits, their huge yellow teeth grinding against the metal in their mouths.

"My butt's sore from sittin' here so long," complained Ellen Sue Tabbert.

"Now, now," admonished Mrs. Joan Byington. "It isn't nice to say the word *butt*."

"I wanted to go watch my big brother play hockey," complained Keegan Sides.

"Yeah," agreed Tara Ankeny. "They're all down at Greybull Pond, with a referee and nets, and everybody's watching from that bench they put up in memory of Charlie Roice's mom. And if we don't get started on this sleigh ride now, I'm gonna miss the game."

"I have to go to the bathroom," said William Beery.

"Do any of you know his name?" Rebecca asked, her voice gone suddenly odd, as if she sought the answer to a difficult riddle. "Do any of you know who he is? Where he's from? What he's done?"

"His name's Ben Pershall," Harvey told her.

"Ben," Rebecca repeated. "Ben Pershall."

"Folks all over are talking about what crimes he's committed," Tuck said. "Nobody knows for sure. Guess we won't find out until the *Star Valley Independent* comes out next Wednesday. Angus Riley Jr. has already started writing his investigative article for the front page. But he won't tell anybody anything he's found out until the papers roll off the press. He's out to double his circulation this week."

"I heard all about it," William Beery said proudly from his place in the sleigh. He'd long since forgotten his need of a bathroom. "Emma Burgess from the Pronghorn Motel told us he'd robbed a bank down in Big Piney."

Tara Ankeny wasn't about to let William have the last word. "Harold Gray down at Star Valley Creamery told us the criminal'd exploded something with dynamite. It sounded gory."

"They don't want anybody to know because they don't want people to panic," said Ellen Sue Tabbert, lowering her head and whispering to her peers melodramatically. "He's a very dangerous man. I got my hair cut yesterday at the barber shop. George Peart says Margaret Cox heard it from Lowell Anderson, who heard it from three customers down at the post office. Ben Pershall killed somebody."

Harvey Perkins gave a loud guffaw. "All this, and I was afraid to talk about it. Imagine that. I didn't want to scare these kids."

Rebecca didn't find the children's revelations quite so funny. "We'd best get going," she said quietly. But inside, she cried out again. *Please look at me, really look at me, Harvey, and realize something's wrong.*

"It's good to see you, Rebecca," he said, disengaging her as Tuck and Prentiss headed toward the truck and the children began to wave. She'd finally released the Belgians to draw the sleigh forward, and they'd gotten under way. "Don't make yourself such a stranger now, you hear?"

8

Ben Pershall sighed with relief as the three men walked away. He lowered the Ruger onto his knee, leaned his forehead against the window, closed his eyes.

"There," he heard Rebecca say as she turned to the children. "Let's stop by the shed and load up the hay."

"Better not have any outlaws comin' around while *we're* here," some child announced. "I'd beat him up with my bare hands."

"I'll just bet you would," Rebecca said, her voice gentle yet affected by pain. Ben watched her again as she let the horses have their head to the corrals. In no time at all, with help from many new hands, they heaped high the allotment of hay bales and Rebecca gave the horses a sharp cut with the reins.

The sleigh headed into open pasture, its runners slicing the snow with an exquisite hiss. As Ben watched, she broke apart bale after bale, instructing each child to pitch great, fragrant clumps overboard.

As they worked, he saw her turn many times from the haying, saw her yank the reins to hold back the horses. He could see that the Belgians were accustomed to roving much farther afield. But she kept the huge pair at a slack pace, all the while placating the third-graders from John Fremont Elementary and giving a good number of elk their breakfast. Despite her fear of him, or perhaps because of it, she kept things well in hand. Either way, she impressed him.

Despite the strength of the sun, fog still rose from the water and lay low over some of the high land. Mist covered each hillock the way a counterpane covers wrinkles in a bed, only torn in places, like fragile, antique cloth reluctantly admitting patches of brilliant sky. A thick stand of pines rimmed the pasture. The evergreens pointed ardently toward the top of the butte above them, arrows aiming at towering rocks where Ben supposed nothing could grow.

As Rebecca and the sleigh and the hay and the children set out to meet them, the herd drifted closer to the house, stepping silently out from among the fir and pine through dissipating tatters of vapor.

The idea struck him suddenly. He stood in this place, seeing things he never thought he—Ben Pershall—would be worthy of seeing. He stood within the presence of something extraordinary. The animals stood like apparitions, their huge dark manes poised, their eyes like those in paintings, at the same time following and remaining still.

The elk weren't afraid of the sleigh or the children. One animal after another joined the gathering in the misted pasture, all bedecked in full winter regalia, coats long enough to curl, white rump fading to tawny foreflank and brown-dark head, as if they'd each stepped headfirst from light into shadow.

The buckles jangled mirthfully from the Belgians' harnesses. Rebecca's voice carried easily across the snowfield. "By this time each year, these elk are desperate, almost starving."

"Why do they get so hungry, with you feeding them?"

"Long ago, the only way the herd could survive was to raid ranchers' haystacks and eat rations planned for cattle. And even those ranchers with extra hay couldn't spare enough. At first all of the ranchers were like my grandfather. They fought to keep the free-ranging elk off their land. But then they started realizing that the elk weren't only being a nuisance. They were *dying*. . . ."

Rebecca'd finally driven them all out of earshot. Ben thought, That isn't so different from me. I came out of desperation to this place. In a way, Rebecca Woodburn's place was a refuge to him, too. At least it would be, if he ever got to stop waving this blasted rifle around at her.

As she reached the far meadow, she swung the horses around and headed back toward the barns.

The elk tarried behind her like worshipers at matins, giving honor to this field, this open expanse of grass and ice. They began to follow the sleigh, slogging their hooves, their long legs, through the snow.

As they came closer, Ben could see they were a winter-worn lot, their fur ragged and already coming loose in splotches, leaving only the bare dark skin beneath. The sleigh approached. Again, he could hear their voices. She'd done it. She'd kept her promise. And it had been ages—a lifetime, it seemed—since anybody'd kept a promise to Ben Pershall.

A lone bull elk began to move from the group to the center of the herd, his great rack of antlers pivoting in perfect symmetry. The animal halted, antlers toward the forest. He raised his head and set forth with a sound not like anything Ben had ever heard, unlikely and challenging, a low, hollow call that rose higher, higher, to whistle across the pasture and echo from ridge to ridge.

Snow fell from a cottonwood bough just beside the house, shimmering like a bridal veil as it veed toward the ground. Another bull separated from the group, moved forth in challenge. Again the bugle came, the third time starting low, rising replete, resonating through the snow-filled gorges and the creek drainage and the deep stand of timber.

Ben stood rooted, not watching his captive any longer, unable to turn from the majesty and the power of the animals. The two bulls took measure of one another, then squared off.

They ran together all at once. *Thwack*. The noise reported across the high meadow. They locked antlers, twisted their heads, sparring.

Each of them went into the fight with their eyes wide and wild, feverish with intention. They twisted in the air, lacing each other with their forefeet. Ben could hear the dull pounding of hooves against body.

After a while, one bull became winded. He backed away often. The other gained ground. Over and over again the winded bull had to be butted and chased. He stood his ground until the very last, until one final blow made him turn tail and vault, disappearing like smoke into the forest, his body elongated with speed.

Ben kept the Ruger lever-action rifle lowered. He watched from his hidden lookout, feeling solitary, indomitable, and alone. The passel of happy children bounded out of the sleigh. Their voices rang with innocence and joy, resonating like music across the snow. "We've missed the hockey game," Tara Ankeny informed everyone, "but this was so much better!"

One by one, they filed into the vans. One voice by one voice, the ancient high spread of land grew quieter and quieter, until, as the vans drove out and the rattle of tires dissipated, nothing was left to break the majestic, familiar silence except the steaming chuffs of the horses, the occasional mewling of an elk, the high, mournful whistle of the wind.

This woman he watched, this keeper of the refuge, guided the sleigh into shelter. She backed the Belgians beneath an overhang and unhitched the crossbar. She rested the wooden implement on an upturned stump she kept there, checking to make certain everything was secure, then led the horses toward the corral.

Ben considered going out, considered brandishing the gun at her yet again, making her hurry back to the house with him. But he thought better of it now, knowing as he watched her that he'd put her through quite an affliction, that she'd be better this afternoon for time spent with the animals.

The Belgians' sides heaved from the exertion of pulling so many, steam rising from their sweat-lathered backs as the cold air touched their warm hides. Ben watched her unthread each tug. He watched her lift off each collar. One. Two.

She hung each of them over a post rather than laying them on the ground.

Rebecca reached for Mabel's throatlatch as if to unfasten it. And, as she did, he knew absolutely, prophetically, what had come to her mind. Her hand closed around the leather. With the other hand, she grabbed Mabel's mane. "Rebecca!" He reached the kitchen door and slammed it open the same moment she made her move. "Don't do this!" he bellowed at her as he ran. He couldn't believe she could swing up on such a massive horse. But swing up she did. She hoisted herself, got one leg over, centered herself victoriously on the Belgian's bare withers.

"Yah!" she shrieked, kicking the horse's flanks for all she was worth, her face rigid with terror. The Belgian, unaccustomed to being mounted and kicked, bolted forward. Coney, left behind, tromped his massive fetlocks in the snow, raised his nose, and whinnied.

He'd never make it to the second horse in time to catch her. For one instant, two instants he remembered the rifle in his hand, remembered the loaded ammunition chamber and the way he'd kept the sights leveled during the past hours. If he wanted, he could calmly raise the gun, take aim, and shoot the horse right out from under her. Or he could shoot Rebecca. Killing seemed easier after the past five years, after hearing so many stories told by cellmates or by others in the can.

Ben flung the Ruger into the snow. With no second thought, he started to run. Rebecca headed the horse toward the front gate, leaning low over the Belgian's neck, pounding the Belgian's rib cage with her feet.

Where the team had driven the sleigh into the yard, the runners and the wide expanse of poundage had packed the snow into a fine surface that could bear weight. But now she headed through open territory, a portion of the field that hadn't been trampled or trudged upon. Mabel's hooves broke through, sank deep, with each lunge of powerful forearms and gaskins.

Ben knew he could intercept her. He sank, too, but deep. She shouted again at the horse, desperate to move the lumbering animal along as she saw him coming. "Damn your furry hide, Mabel!" she hollered from between clenched teeth. "Can't you go any faster?" What was left of her braid streamed out behind her like a pennant.

He had one chance of catching her, one chance of getting her off guard and knocking her off balance. One wrong move on his part and she'd be at the front gate, headed through a long corridor of downed timber. She'd be on plowed road.

Snow, churned by the horse's pasterns, flung into his eyes. He couldn't see. Ben moved by instinct, seeking purchase in the snow. He leapt for her.

"Get back! Leave me *alone!*" she screamed at him, flailing out to knock him away.

He grabbed for her waist. Despite her grip on Mabel's gigantic neck, she began to topple. *Darned huge horse. Too wide to do much good on*. She couldn't clutch anything that big around with her legs.

She fell. All Ben could think of, as he grappled her next to him, was the Belgian's thrashing hooves, the frenzied legs, and the deep snow. They'd be charged, probably trampled.

"Come on, Rebecca!" he bellowed. The huge Belgian snorted and danced about them. Ben tried to pull her out of the way. But she fought for every inch, and when she realized she wasn't going to make it, she whaled into him with her fists.

"Damn it," she cried. "Damn it all to hell."

"You can't do this," he said, trying to protect himself from her blows as they rolled again and snow slid inside his shirt and down his legs. He wanted to shake her. "Listen to me."

She hauled off and kicked him. Right in the shin. "Let me go."

He was amazed at how strong she was. She'd kicked him harder than a mule. But he'd learned how to hide pain a long, long time ago. "You know I can't do that, Rebecca," he said calmly. "There's too much at stake." His life, for instance. And Demi's.

"You kept a gun on those kids the *whole time*. I saw it through the window."

"The gun wasn't on the kids. It was on you. I intended you to see it." Then, softer: "You did a good job out there, you know. Handling the kids and the horses and . . . and everything. I couldn't help but be impressed."

But she was well past the point of caring. "I feel so much better," she said, glaring up at him with hatred, "to have met with your approval."

Mabel, with weight no longer on her back and rider no longer booting her, had wandered away and joined Coney. The two waited in consort beside the corral, billowing their nostrils together in great, breathy snorts.

"If you wanted to get away, why didn't you try it in that old truck?" With his head, he gestured toward the rusty Dodge truck parked beside the barn.

"Truck's harder to start."

Ben and Rebecca stared at each other for a good thirty seconds, while he kept her hands pressed above her head in the snow. She'd gotten covered with ice, too, during the struggle. It had already melted to form droplets across her cheeks. Water ran in tiny rivulets down the side of her nose. "There's no need to be so high-headed about all this."

Boy, did that turn out to be the wrong thing to say. This time when she went after him, she kneed him straight in the groin. "Da—dadblast it," he groaned, clutching himself and losing his hold on her.

She scrambled away. But he crawled after her and got his fist around one Sorel pac boot. He hung on to her leg, momentarily half standing, half stumbling forward, yanking her back, and finally overcoming her. He was breathless, furious. "You don't get it, do you?" he asked. "I could've *shot* you. Do you know that? I could've *shot* you."

"Why didn't you?" And as she spoke, the new snow on her face mingled with surprising tears. "I . . . w-wanted to c-catch up with them. I . . . thought I c-could. . . ."

He hated it when a woman busted into tears. Wyllis used to drive him nuts when she did it. "You're crazy. Stop belting me like that. Stop crying like that."

"I'll c-cry . . . if I . . . want t-toooo. This is m-my house. I can do anything I want to in m-my house!"

"I can't let you go. I can't let you catch up with them. I can't let you tell anybody. You've gotta stay here. It's too important." And now he knew he'd have to keep her longer than he'd intended. He'd heard that man, that Harvey Perkins fellow, telling her about the roadblocks. If he tried to leave tonight as he'd planned, he'd be dead by tomorrow morning.

Oh, so much to think about! He couldn't stay here, and he couldn't leave. With every minute's passing, time became more crucial.

"You're t-tormenting me," she said, accusing him. "Y-you take me to the outhouse a million times. Y-you let me drive around in my sleigh, feeding my elk, tasting my freedom."

"You told me you wanted those things," he said, perplexed. "And you shouldn't say so much about freedom. I'm the one who should be talking about freedom. *You're* the one who locked yourself in the outhouse."

"Y-you're tantalizing me!" She bellowed it back at him with such force that he sat up from the snow and let her loose again. Tears still splayed out from her eyes. She sat up, dusted snow off her britches. "Why don't you j-just tie me up? Why don't you just bind my hands and feet and take away all my h-hope?! Is this some sort of game for you?"

"If you don't quit bawling like a calf, Rebecca, I might consider it." And when he said it, he was only half teasing. "I might also consider gagging you with that bright red bandanna of yours."

"Do it, then," she dared him. "Do it." And he didn't know why, but he was glad to see anger come back to her eyes. "Act like a convict should act. Tie me to a chair. Or a bedpost. Or the fence outside. That's even better."

"You want me to act like a convict should act? Okay, I'll blast you. Right here. And that'll be the end of this nonsense."

But this time she knew he wasn't serious. He couldn't do it. He'd left the rifle lying beside the kitchen stoop. And he kept looking down at her in amazement.

"They don't even keep convicts in the slammer confined like that. Why would you expect me to do such a left-handed thing to you?"

"It would be easier on both of us if you'd stop giving me chances to get away."

"I can't do that."

"Why not?"

"Because I need you to help me—" He stopped short, before he'd said "with my daughter." He didn't think Rebecca'd realized the identity of the girl she'd tended. And for now, he thought it best.

But Demi needed respite, healing, a woman's touch. She needed more than he could give her. He'd known her only as a little girl, a child who'd clung to his legs, who'd loved to play "pinch-bottom bug," who'd raised her arms to him, asking to be lifted and held. Ben found himself on the run with a young lady who confounded him, one with lanky legs, a child's faith, and skin as smooth as a cameo—all wrapped up in one blossoming body. She'd become a teenager on him, one who wouldn't take long in becoming a woman.

"Fine way you have of showing it, Ben Pershall." Rebecca took great delight in calling him by name. After her conversation with the male gathering from Tuck Krebbs's front office, she knew plenty about him. "A fine way of showing you need help. Why didn't you put the gun away and *ask?*"

Outside the barn, Mabel and Coney stamped impatiently, waiting to be rubbed down and put inside their stalls. She stood, finished brushing off snow, and tromped toward the corrals.

To make his own point, he walked to the stoop and reclaimed the Ruger. Then he followed her. "You know the answer to that question, don't you? If I'd put the gun away and *asked*, you'd've taken it back out and wasted me."

She didn't need to respond to that comment. He read her reaction perfectly by her backbone. Unwittingly she revealed herself that way. When she stood on the sleigh and drove horses, her spine curved a little, like the gently bowed pronghorn of an antelope. When she plotted against him—he knew this!—her body went strong and limber, like a willow bough holding its own against the wind. And at her most agitated, when she felt angry or provoked or put upon, she stood as rigid as the handle on a hay rake. She reminded him of just such an implement now, all breathless, snow wet and muddy, as she marched the two nickering Belgians into the barn.

"I could help you in the barn," he suggested as she looped the reins over a peg. The whole place smelled rich, pleasant, like new leather and horse liniment and alfalfa hay and neat's-foot oil. "I could grain the horses or something."

She pulled the aluminum scoop from the burlap feed bag and fed them herself. She poured oats into the long wooden trough while Mabel and Coney crowded in from both sides. "No sense in you helping me. That's not what *I* asked for, is it?"

She was a stubborn one. But then, he figured, a woman would have to be stubborn to make a life for herself out here, harnessing horses and slinging hay on mornings that sometimes reached thirty degrees below zero.

Just below those pegs filled with bridles, halters, and other leathers, he saw her workbench. She had the particle board covered with all sorts of paraphernalia, numbered tags and clips for marking animals and a clipboard of statistics she'd been keeping since Thanksgiving. Ben could see the dates marked meticulously in a vertical row.

To one side sat a metal tackle box and a length of cheesecloth, a wad of heavy twine, and two boot laces. Along the back edge sat a lantern and a row of mason jars, each containing a scat sample. Beside the samples lay a farrier's knife and a large pair of nippers. He could picture her in this place, coming back after going far afield, studying the wapiti food habits, writing notes, repairing gear, putting up and labeling the small specimens.

"All right. I won't help you, then. But it looks like interesting work you do," he commented offhandedly.

"Probably as interesting as what you've been doing," she said right back. "How do they keep prisoners employed at the state penitentiary? Did you make license plates?"

"No," he said. "The woolen mill. I made blankets. Prison issue." Not to mention clothes, shirts and pants, including the ones on his own back. "And I played a helluva lot of jailhouse rummy."

"That doesn't sound so bad," she said.

He couldn't describe life in the can to anyone. He hadn't even tried to make Wyllis understand how horrible it had been, listening to men bellowing, clapping, and cussing or pacing back and forth in their cells.

Most of them, maybe all of them, had been snakepit crazy. Once, during the first month he'd been in the can, some guy in the end cell started hollering that the walls were on fire and that rats and snakes had come oozing out of his walls. And if the noise hadn't been bad enough, the silence had been worse. Every time he'd had a fight and the screws had put him in isolation, the darkness and nothingness had come on heavy, heavy like deep water, smothering him. He'd felt buried alive.

"People don't think it sounds so bad," he said, "but they have no way of knowing."

"Is that why you escaped?" she asked. "Because you couldn't bear it any longer?"

Perhaps because he'd remembered it recently, he felt the silence yet again, the horrible parts of it, hanging between them before he spoke. "That isn't why," he said at last.

She began to load items into a dusty rucksack, a specimen or two, the clipboard, several tablets. "I'm taking these to the house," she said. "I've got research to finish."

"You make it sound totally high-minded."

"It is high-minded. And it's my life. Wyoming Fish and Game expects it. They'll pick up the results at the end of the season, after the elk go back into the trees. That's how things end each year. Then next season, I'll know to do things better."

"This is how you spend your days, then," he said.

"Feeding, documenting, repairing things the same way my grandfather repaired them. These things take all day."

"Except for Saturdays, does anyone come up here much?" He wasn't asking for his own benefit now. He'd begun to wonder at her life, at how quietly she existed, at how happy she seemed to be away from the bustle below her in Star Valley.

"The Boy Scouts come up in the springtime," she said. "After everything melts off, I let them wander around for a day, a whole swarm of them, to gather antlers. Each May they sell them at an auction right outside Jenkins Building Supply. That pays for the feed and keep for next year."

"An antler auction?" he asked, incredulous. He'd never heard of such a thing. "Who'd buy them?"

"Some people buy the pretty ones to lay around in their front yards. Make it look like elk spent the whole winter there and dropped their antlers before they headed up into the high country for the summer. Some make jewelry or buttons. Others build arches and fences, like the arches on the town square down in Jackson Hole. But most of the money comes from people who want to grind them up and take the powder. It's an aphrodisiac, you know. Folks come from everywhere just to take a good batch home. There," she said, stopping herself and hiking the rucksack. "I'm going on again, just like I did about the telephone and the osprey." *You're telling too much*, she had to remind herself. *You mustn't trust him.*

"I'll carry the bag," he said, reaching out.

"Why should you?" she asked. "I've told you I don't need help."

He took the canvas pack anyway, putting his hand over hers on the handle, practically wrenching it from her before she'd let go. "It'll be easier on both of us," he said. "It'll be easier on you, safer for you, if you'd let me try to fit in, to do you some good."

"To do me some good?"

She closed the barn and headed toward the house. Other than latching Mabel and Coney into their stalls, she didn't need to lock anything up. She'd never locked; never before had she worried about anything encroaching. As they walked along, she brushed chaff mercilessly from her gloves and knew she could no longer wait in asking.

They stood beneath the shadow of the wind-tossed cottonwoods beside the house. "What did they put you in for, Ben? Have you killed a man, as people say?"

If she'd've known anything about the state joint, or life in prison, she'd've recognized the expression he purposely put on his face. The other inmates called it "jailface." It started on everyone as a dead look, every feature kept stiff so nothing moved. But maybe stiff wasn't the best way to describe it, either, because stiff meant hard. And it wasn't hard; it was just like death, and *empty*.

This look meant you'd been under everybody's heels for too long. In the can, before much time passed, everyone like Ben learned to use it as protection. You never let on that you might be afraid or weak or hurting. You never let your eyes look straight at anything. You gave yourself jailface every time you got sick or scared or worried.

"Don't ask me that, Rebecca," he answered her, his face gone vacant in a way she couldn't, wouldn't ever, comprehend. "It won't do you any good to know."

9

The girl had awakened. She sat on the edge of the mattress, her bare toes just grazing the rough pine floor, as if she weren't certain whether to lift herself up and walk on them or to stay abed. At Rebecca's entrance she went prone again, bouncing a little. Rebecca tucked those toes beneath the sheets and folded the coverlet over her. "You've had a bad knock to the head," Rebecca said. "You'd best be careful."

"Have I?"

"Yes." Rebecca made her way around, straightening linens.

"I didn't know. I . . . I think I remember it," the girl said, watching Rebecca intently and still obviously disoriented. But then, suddenly, she sat bolt upright in bed again. "Yes." She said it as if she'd just come to full consciousness, as if she'd just remembered a great deal more than a bonk on the forehead. "I do. I remember everything."

"You've been sleeping a long time," Rebecca said. But she stopped short of telling how worried she'd been. She still didn't understand why Ben Pershall hadn't let her contact a doctor.

"I helped him escape, you know. I went to the library and read all these books about Butch Cassidy and the Sundance Kid. Great reading. I was into *Baby-Sitters Club* and I had to turn that one in so I could read about outlaws instead. Learned everything I needed to know about busting people out. Then we pulled it off, easy as anything."

Rebecca couldn't believe it. The girl's words echoed in her head. "*You* helped him escape? Why?" All this time she'd thought the girl a hostage.

"Because he needed me."

"Oh." As if that answered everything.

"Where is he? Where's my father?"

He must've been waiting in the hallway, listening. Ben hurried into the room, the Ruger lowered, and gripped her small hand with his big one. "I'm here, Demi," he said. "I haven't left you."

They knew each other. Not only that, they were in cahoots with each other. Not only that, she was his *daughter*.

The girl named Demi jabbered happily. "I remembered everything all of a sudden, and then I was afraid you'd be gone. I woke up and didn't see you and I thought . . . I thought . . . that you'd left . . . that you'd gone away without me. . . ."

He squeezed her hand, said it again. "No. I wouldn't do that."

His words came back from yesterday, before she'd thrown a boiling pot of soup on him, when she'd accused him of striking and injuring this child. *I didn't hit her. I wouldn't have her hurt for all the world.* Rebecca stared first at the girl, then at the man. "She's your daughter?"

He smile somewhat obliquely. "Yes."

Demi waited with her head against the pillow, her dark eyes huge and expectant and despairing, her face as white as a Sunday tablecloth. "Where are we?"

He spoke with what seemed a heavy irony, so heavy, indeed, that his voice sounded coarse. "We're in a safe place. At least for now."

"Are you sure? Butch Cassidy and Sundance weren't so—"

"Sh-h-hhh." He stopped her. "Quit thinking about old-time bank robbers and such. This is different." All this time, as they'd talked, Rebecca'd watched him lower the gun beside his leg, as if he wished Demi wouldn't see it. "There isn't any reason for you to worry."

Demi reached up from beneath the thick coverlet and fingered the bandage on her forehead. "I hit my head on something in the car."

"Yeah, you did. When we went down into the water. I don't know what happened. It was all too . . ." Rebecca heard him pause, heard him struggle to find the right word. "Fast."

"How far did you come, carrying me?" the child named Demi asked.

"A ways. Over a mountain or two." He winked down at her. *Winked.* As if it didn't matter at all. But he'd achieved a tremendous feat, just rescuing this girl. When Harvey, Prentiss, and Tuck had told her where they'd found his car, she'd started to suspect it. Now Rebecca knew for certain. He'd climbed up over the Continental Divide and tundra, in snow deeper than any living creature should be able to traverse.

"Thank you," Demi, his daughter, whispered.

He clenched her hand even tighter, as if he were eager for something. "You're welcome. I haven't had the chance to do anything like that for you in a long time, have I? But now I can." Rebecca saw it on his face, the hint of pride, the new, precious hope, as if something inside him were coming to life again. For one unsettling moment she felt as if she shouldn't be in the room, shouldn't be observing this different man from another time, this man who revealed joy, delight, as his daughter thanked him.

She turned toward Demi, uncertain, wanting to see more of this different man yet uncertain how to look upon him. "You've slept a long time. I'll fix you something to eat immediately. I gave you some broth last night, although I doubt you remember it." She'd fixed another pan of soup, just something easy and out of a can, and had watched resolutely while he'd eaten some. She'd been disappointed when the girl had eaten only a few spoonsful.

Demi shook her head. "I don't. I don't remember much of anything after Dad brought me in. I just remember being so cold." She plucked at the tiny buttons on the nightgown. "Is this yours?"

Rebecca nodded. "Tell me how you feel, child."

"I feel okay, I think." And her eyes seemed lively enough now, with light in them like light that shone on dark, moving water. "Guess I'd better get healed up fast. We've gotta get going again."

But Ben shook his head. "We aren't going anywhere for a few days, Demi."

Rebecca glanced up at him, surprised. He'd heard about the roadblocks. She supposed he'd decided it wouldn't be safe to take her truck, anyway. Everyone in Star Valley would recognize the rusty Dodge that belonged to the Woodburns. No matter the sheriff's elaborate barricades and careful mapping. Everybody'd be stopping him just to say hello.

When Rebecca left the room, she left so father and daughter would have time alone together. But after a few moments Ben followed her out. He stood in the hallway, watching her, as if he dared her to admit she'd been wrong.

"You didn't tell me. You didn't tell me she was your daughter."

"How much does that matter?"

She looked away, out the back door, where sunlight beat fiercely through the screen. Outside, the sun of midday shone like a holiday gift. Inside, once again, she felt disoriented and lost, as disoriented as if she'd been the one with a blow to the head. "I don't know how much it matters," she told him.

"Perhaps you wouldn't've been so afraid for her, if you'd known she was somebody I cared for."

"Yes," Rebecca said. "Perhaps I wouldn't have been so afraid."

"Perhaps you would've understood why we cannot take her to a doctor."

"Yes," she said. "Perhaps that, too."

"And now you know she isn't someone I've kidnapped and beat over the head. She's come with me of her own free will."

"Yes. I know that now."

He kept his eyes on her, aiming them as precisely as if he continued to aim the barrel of the gun. "Does that make you fear me any less, knowing these things about her, about me?"

This time, she didn't answer. She couldn't. She didn't want to talk to him about fear. She didn't want him to see so much of it within her. "She helped you escape," she said at last. "However could you get a girl like her involved in a thing like this?"

She's been involved in it since she was born, he wanted to say. "I didn't have much—" But he stopped, wouldn't go on. How tired he was of telling himself, of telling everyone, that he'd run out of choices.

But Demi'd come up behind them in the hallway; she'd climbed out of bed without either of them seeing. "I wanted to be involved," she said. "Now where's the bathroom?"

"There isn't any bathroom here," her father said with an odd sort of smile on his face. "There's only the outhouse."

"I'll show her where it is if you'd like," Rebecca offered, looking from one to the other of them, not knowing if he'd trust her to go. But Ben nodded, giving his consent. They looked at each other over Demi's head for a moment, each of them comprehending it. This time, she wouldn't run. She had no place to go, nobody to tell. And because of this, he wouldn't hurt her. "You can't go out in bare feet," she told Demi. "You'll freeze."

"I had boots." But the boots she'd worn had gotten soaked. They were still damp even though they'd spent the night by the woodstove.

"Wear mine," Rebecca said. "They'll only be a little big."

"An outhouse . . ." Demi laughed as she poked her bare feet down into the sheepskin-lined pacs. "Who'd've ever thought?"

They stepped outside into a day so brilliant, snowflakes on the ground flashed colors like so many mirrors. The mountains throbbed with the splendor of light. "It's so beautiful here. How do you ever absorb it all?"

"It's taken me a lifetime," Rebecca answered. "Maybe to see it all, it'll take me a lifetime more."

"I think living all the time in a place like this would keep me from being afraid of things."

"Are you afraid of things?" Rebecca asked her.

The girl lowered her gaze to the ground as if she didn't want to answer. Finally, finally, Rebecca saw her decide it best to be forthright. "Don't tell my father," Demi said. "I don't want him to know. But I am."

10

On Saturday afternoon in Bel-Air, Thomas Woodburn drove his Acura to the television studio where Jillian was filming her latest project. She didn't often go in on Saturdays. But today was the wrap of an exclusive made-for-cable movie, the sort of thing actresses chose with caution. A failure here could make a big-time film actress like Jillian Dobbs look the fool. A success could make her look more versatile, like more of a hot property, especially because it would air while she played Charmaine on Broadway.

Her agent had banked on the latter when he'd suggested her to the casting director. This was a TNT exclusive, a Western based on the newest novel by Elmer Kelton. They'd filmed most of it on location up near Lake Tahoe. This afternoon, they'd shoot two more scenes inside the studio and one last outdoor scene on the sound stage when the light angled correctly over the lot. Three days from now, this movie would be tightly edited, any extra footage lying in snips on the cutting room floor. And Jillian Dobbs would be in New York City, starting grueling rehearsals on Broadway.

Thom steered the car onto the studio lot, light glancing off the polished chrome, and rolled his window down at the security gate. He didn't need to show his identification to the fellow inside the booth. The guard already knew him well.

"Jillian ought not to have to be out here on a Saturday afternoon," he said. "These television people. They'll work the dickens out of her and then expect more."

"It's all in the name of *career*, Joe," he said. "Nothing's more important than getting ahead." He said it to make conversation. But the words themselves sent such pain through him that he felt certain Joe Fathers had seen it.

"That's life in L.A.," Joe said.

"I'm starting to figure this out," Thom said with false animation.

"Is Jillian starring in something else you've written?"

"No." Thom shook his head. "This one isn't mine. If I don't get my schedule cleared off and get back to my office, there won't be another Thomas Woodburn screenplay for a long time. I'd best get at it or I won't even be earning my union dues."

"Being married to Jillian Dobbs, doesn't seem like a man would have to worry about things like that, does it?"

"No. It doesn't," Thom said, his eyes going dark. "It doesn't seem like a man would have to worry at all."

"They're on lot five, Mr. Woodburn," Joe said, pointing the way. "Good to see you today. Oh, yes." He hung out the window, wagged his hat, and hollered the rest because Thom had already started to drive away. "Congratulations on winning the Academy Award the other night. You looked great on stage. Where'd you get a tie like that, anyway? I've never seen anything like it before!"

"Thanks, Joe," he hollered back, waving and ignoring the reference to Howdy's tie. He drove slowly down the side street between the huge metal buildings that served as studios, all of them filled with sound stages and sets, lights, cameras, and costumes, the paraphernalia of make-believe. He found lot five, parked, and climbed out, pitching his keys onto the front seat before he slammed it. Only other place he knew safe to leave a car with keys in it was Wyoming. Back home, everybody figured somebody might need to borrow it or move it out of the way.

A member of the camera crew let him in when he knocked. "Hello, Mr. Woodburn." A gaffer waved down from his roost high in the rafters and then winked boldly. "I don't blame you. If I was married to a woman like her, I wouldn't be able to stay away, either."

"Where is she?" He asked the question to anyone within earshot, knowing they'd all understand whom he looked for.

"In her dressing room," three people answered at once. Then the cameraman added, "They're having some trouble with her dress. Cal Moody wanted them to readjust it before this next scene. We only have another two hours to finish then, before we have to go outside. If we miss this today, we'll all be back next week. And nobody seems to like that idea, least of all the producer."

Thom pushed his way through the hordes of crew members, trying to find Jillian's dressing room without any direction. Ever so often he'd shove up against someone and point. "Are the dressing rooms this way? I'm looking for my wife."

"Yes," everyone answered. "This way." And a few stopped, when they recognized him, to offer congratulations. "Good job on *Spirit Dance*, Mr. Woodburn."

"An Academy Award!"

"Good show, Thomas. When're you gonna write another one that good?"

He found her door at last, marked by her name on a small, engraved plaque. He knocked. "Jillian? It's me." One of the assistants opened the door for him, and there stood his wife, surrounded by costume designers and looking mad enough to destroy something.

"What are you doing here?" she asked.

"I came to check on you. I wanted to make certain—" But there he stopped. He wasn't certain why he'd driven all this way. He hadn't actually come to see Jillian Dobbs. He'd come to make sure she wasn't letting them work her too hard, that she wasn't doing something that might harm the baby. "You were okay."

She saw right through his words. She knew exactly why he'd come. The anger deepened in her eyes even as he finished the sentence. "Really, Thom? Since when did you become so concerned about my needs?"

Oh, how he wanted to say it aloud. *Since I found out you were carrying my baby.* But he wouldn't announce that now, not while five costumers hovered around her, smoothing wrinkles out of a massive taffeta skirt. "This isn't working," one of them said, still plucking at the lavender fabric. "Miss Dobbs, we're going to have to start over again with the corset. Strange that we're having so much trouble. It must be laced tighter for the skirt to fall in a cascading line over the petticoats."

"Damn the petticoats." Jillian's wrath turned toward the women in the room. "The corset's already tight enough. I can't even breathe in this thing."

"You've gained weight, then," one of them pointed out severely. "This skirt had the appropriate fit last time you wore it."

"How dare you! Get out," Jillian shouted to all of them. "Get out of here and leave me alone!"

"We're behind schedule, Miss Dobbs," one of them reminded her on the way out the door. "They're holding us responsible on the set."

"My name is going to *make* this production. You think I care if they're waiting on the set?"

Thomas stood his ground as, one by one, the agitated crew members filed past him. He closed the door behind them and turned back to his wife.

"Why are *you* still here? Didn't you know I was talking to you, too?"

"I knew it. But I'm not going to be thrown out of here like another of the studio grunts. I'm your husband."

She sank onto the chair, the taffeta rustling with the same subdued music as the sound of a rushing stream. "This is too much, Thomas."

"I'm glad you wouldn't let them strap you any tighter into the corsets. It might've done something to—"

She leapt at him. "I knew it! I knew that's why you were here." It seemed to Thom as though she'd gone a little crazy. She reached behind her, fumbled with the hooks on the back of the skirt, trying to get it off.

"Jillian. Stop."

"It's why this god-awful skirt won't fit. My whole body is puffed up like a balloon. You should see my breasts. They're monstrous. The whole stage crew is probably out there talking about it. The director's probably already noticed." Her own mind was taking a brutal toll on her.

Thom felt so many things as he listened to her, confused, hurt, betrayed, furious . . . and afraid. She wasn't rational any longer. It sounded as if she talked about a disease, something horribly wrong growing inside her body instead of his child. "Just get this show finished and come home, Jillian. We're talking about realities here. And the reality of it is, you've got to start taking better care of yourself than this."

She'd fumbled around enough to get the skirt unfastened. It fell around her ankles in shiny folds.

"No. You've got it wrong, Thom." She started to yank at the strings to the corset herself but couldn't get them. She punched a button on an electronic box beside the mirror to summon someone.

"Yes?"

"Get Dixie and the others back in here. I can't get this corset tightened all by myself," she ordered.

"They'll be right in, Miss Dobbs."

"Jillian," he said, practically whispering, "I'll do anything you want. I'll hire a nanny. I work at home. I'll be able to take care of a child. We won't even get in your way, if that's what you're afraid of." Eventually, after all this, Thom knew he'd probably leave her. But he wanted this child. Dear God in heaven, he didn't want her to do anything irrational.

"I'm playing Charmaine on Broadway. This is my only chance. We have plenty of time to have babies later."

"I want to ask you something," he said, his heart breaking. "I want to know why you married me."

"You know the answer to that," she said, but she didn't give him the answer he'd wanted. He began to realize that to a girl who'd grown up in the golden, easy life of California, who'd grown up having her own way, love didn't always have everything to do with it. "I married you because I liked your screenplays. You wrote about real things, in places I wanted to see."

"That's all?" he asked.

"Of course." She smiled blandly, carelessly. "What more could there be?"

"You told me once to remind you," he said. "You told me to remind you that life isn't always about what other people think. It goes much deeper. It can't always be planned. It often comes unexpected."

"Don't give me that speech again, Thomas, please. I can't bear it."

"You believed it once."

"Not for very long," she told him.

A knock came at the door. The costumers had come back. Before he let them in, he turned back to her, his hand on the knob. "I'm not going to let you go through with this, Jillian. I'm going to stop you." He'd be at the lawyer's office before eight Monday morning. When the lawyer served papers, she'd see how serious he'd become. "I don't care what happens to our marriage. But I'm not going to let you diminish what we've had together by whisking our child's life away in a doctor's office."

"You try," she said quietly, new resentment in her voice. "You try and see how far it takes you."

11

Rebecca Woodburn spent Saturday afternoon examining elk skulls she'd found scattered among the trees. She made notes, inspected their teeth, looking for signs of necrotic stomatitis showing in the jawbone, or the thing everybody in Yellowstone worried about now, brucellosis. Demi watched her, peering over her shoulders in fascination while she used twine to measure the circumference of an eye socket.

"How do the bones get so clean?" Demi asked her. "Does the sun bleach them out?"

"No," Rebecca answered. "I boil them in a washbasin."

"Like soup?"

Rebecca shook her head. "No. Not quite the same as soup. It doesn't smell nearly as nice. It's horrible, almost indescribable." She smiled a little. "I suggest you not mention soup around your father, though. It isn't one of his favorite subjects."

"You burned him, didn't you? You threw soup and burned him."

"Yes," she said. "I wanted to get away."

"I figure his skin's hurting," Demi said. "I've been seeing him trying to adjust that old shirt so it doesn't rub up against him."

"It scared me, having a man come into this house and taking over the way he did," Rebecca said, trying her best to evoke gentleness and the seriousness of the matter all at the same time, wanting the girl to know that they shared something, too. "He came here and made me afraid for my life."

"If only Momma hadn't—" The girl stopped and frowned, obviously thinking better of it.

Rebecca looked up from her work. "Hadn't what?"

"Nothing."

And just as Demi said it, Ben Pershall walked into the room. "What is this?" he asked, poking one finger at the massive skulls.

"Research on the elk," Demi announced. "She boils them to clean them off."

"So you examine their heads, too," he said with droll amusement.

"Yes." But the whole time she worked now and Ben watched her, Rebecca thought of the words Demi'd said.

If only Momma hadn't . . . what? Rebecca allowed herself to think of the woman he must've married. What would she be, what would she *feel,* to have the man she'd loved tried for a crime, convicted, locked away? She tried to picture Ben Pershall with a wife, and couldn't.

She covertly studied father and daughter as Demi went on and on about things Rebecca had explained to her, the proper evaluation of eye sockets and inspection of each antler base. Demi favored her mother, Rebecca decided. That explained her blond, wavy hair so different from Ben's, her round dark eyes, her pale, triangular cheeks, the shape of her delicate chin.

Even Demi's full lower lip must have been inherited from her mother, likely so, because Ben's mouth appeared entirely dissimilar, finely drawn and narrow, not given to smiles except when his daughter happened by. And even then, the smiles Rebecca'd seen from him seemed forced and sad ones, never reaching his eyes. From her seat at the desk, she watched him cross to the sink and draw water into one of her pitchers from the metal tap, water just up from the well and so cold that it set droplets condensing on the faucet.

He tilted his head back, raised the pitcher to his lips, and gulped it down in vigorous, flowing gulps, one never separating from another. Perhaps it'd been years since he'd tasted fresh well water. She observed him, guessing he tasted freedom more than he tasted the icy liquid, guessing he satisfied his soul more than he satisfied his thirst.

Ben turned and caught her studying him. Their eyes met as he set the pitcher on the counter, as he lingered, taking his time at backhanding his mouth.

Something peculiar happened in Rebecca's chest. Something caught briefly, a constriction that tightened in her throat. Abruptly she reverted her attention to the skull that smiled broadly on the examination table.

"Can't stand things staring at me," he said.

She glanced up quickly, thinking he admonished her. But instead she found him looking at the skull, too, as the sockets loomed large in the vacuous, gaping head. He began to pace with impatience. "Can't stand things not going the way they oughtta go. We should've been out of here by now. Who'd've thought. Roadblocks in a wool-hat town like this one."

"They'll be gone by Tuesday," Rebecca said with hope. "With any luck, they'll give up and decide you made it upcountry a long time ago. They'll start searching somewhere else." She analyzed the look exchanged between them, her reaction, as methodically as she'd analyze a sample in a mason jar. Fear. It had to be fear. Every time this man came within talking distance, he got her rattled and mixed up.

"Lady, my luck ran out a long time ago."

That was the end of it. That's all he said; he offered no other salutation or good-bye before he blustered out of the kitchen. He strode purposefully down the hall and went outside. Rebecca heard the creaking open of the screen, the slamming shut of the heavy door. She heard the *thump thump thump* of his pacing on the wooden porch.

She glanced across the room at the girl. "Demi?" she asked after a long silence. "I'd like to know about your mother. What's her name?"

"When you look at that elk skull," Demi asked, pointing to it in an obvious act of diversion, "can you figure out how old it is?"

"I'll tell you all that in a minute." Rebecca waited, drumming up courage. She repeated the question quietly, insistently. "What's your mother's name? I'd like to know about her."

"I ought not to have brought her up," Demi said. "We ought not talk about her at all. It isn't my business to discuss."

"Of course it isn't." But Rebecca decided it was best to be honest. "Living up here by myself, sometimes I just know things, is all. I know there's something about her that's hurting you." She gestured toward the door through which Ben Pershall had recently departed. "There's something that's hurting him, too."

Demi sighed. "All right. Her name is Wyllis."

"Wyllis?" A beautiful name. An unusual name.

"I'll tell you about Momma, only I have to stop if Dad comes in again. He hasn't said much, but I know he doesn't like me talking about her in front of him."

"Why not?"

"He just doesn't, is all. You wouldn't, either, if it was you."

"Why? What did she do, Demi?"

"Things've been bad for Mom ever since he's been in jail. They came and arrested him right during the Wild Horse Round-Up parade in Hanna. Everybody saw.

"That was the year they brought in the precision mule pack team from the U.S. Forest Service. The mule team drivers were whistling and shouting 'Yah, mule!' and the mules were doing formations with their hooves clopping in the street. Then Hanna's three sheriff's cars came driving up with their sirens blaring.

"Everybody thought they were part of the parade—that is, everybody but me. I knew something was wrong the minute the mules were doing a figure-eight and the first sheriff's car tried to drive right through the middle of them. Anybody'd who'd known anything about the parade would've known those drivers kept the mules tied together by the tails.

"By the time the deputies got to where we were standing, they'd upset three mules and their fancy canvas packs. Each mule had a raincoat tied to his back. I remember yellow slick raincoats flopping around like flags, and ropes thumping from their sides, and barrels rolling on the ground, making a sound like thunder. Those men ran out of their cars and they had *guns*, real guns, hanging in black woven cases. Everybody kept pressing in and there wasn't a place to move, so I couldn't get out of the way, and one of them shouts, 'There he is. There.' One of them grabbed Dad and said, 'Benjamin Pershall, you are under arrest.' Before anybody could do anything, they'd spun him around and pushed him against the lamppost and put handcuffs on him.

"From that day on, everybody in Hanna looked at her as the wife of a criminal. Nobody talked to her much. Pete was the only one she could tell things to or count on to help her. He was even there that day, hanging on to Momma while she screamed, 'They can't do this! They can't take him away like this!'

"The pumper truck came by, blasting its horn, with one of the volunteer firemen squirting water down on everybody. Everybody started running and screaming and trying not to get wet, and Momma just stood there with the water flopping down on her like a whip. 'Come on, Wyllis,' he said, putting his arm around her and getting wet, too. 'They've done it. But no matter what happens to Ben, I'm here to take care of you. We'll do what we have to do to get you through this.' 'He had the keys to the car in his pocket,' Momma said to both of us. 'We're going to have to walk home.' 'Of course you won't have to walk home,' Pete said. 'I'll drive you.'"

Rebecca took the girl's hand. "It must've been awful."

"I heard you asking my dad questions in the hallway. I heard you wanting to know why he'd gotten me involved in all this the way he did."

"No matter how much he wanted to get out, that wasn't a smart thing for him to do." Rebecca turned back to her work then, doing her best to appear casual. She'd already removed the deceased elk's incisor from the row of gnarled yellow teeth lining the jaw. She picked up a pair of tweezers and turned the tooth beneath her magnifying glass. It was no use. Her hands shook. She couldn't see a thing.

Just as she raised a pencil to jot notes, Demi said, "I did it, you know, not him. He asked Momma to help him, but she wouldn't."

The pencil poised in midair. "What?"

"I wasn't supposed to be in on his rescue. That's the whole story. He'd intended Momma to be there. But she wouldn't do it. I had to go instead. If nobody had been there, he'd've been caught when he reached the fence. And, given who he was, they'd've probably shot him."

"Your mother was supposed to help get him out? But she let *you* go in her place?"

Demi nodded. "He sent her a letter in some strange code. All about Grandma's birthday. And Grandma's been dead almost two years. We haven't even *talked* about Grandma's birthday since I started middle school. So Momma knew exactly what he meant, even though she wouldn't carry it through."

"Why wouldn't she?"

"She just got to needing other people worse than she needed him, I guess. They gave Dad a life sentence. You can't blame her for wanting to get on with things again. She thought it would mess everything up, having him free again, no matter how he got that way, after everything she'd given up and everything she'd gotten over. So, I went instead. I waited there in the dark, digging a hole until he ran from the building. He didn't know it was me until I got him clear through the fence and out. You should've seen his face, all blank with shock. I had a car parked down at Rip Griffin's, the truck stop just off the highway, and I had to tell Dad how Momma didn't come because she's living with Pete Giddy—"

Demi told her all of it, from the heart-stopping run across sagebrush to the plunge down the ravine in the car. As Rebecca heard the story, she thought how he must've felt, this man running for his life, to have someone he'd loved, someone he'd depended on, who hadn't come.

But no matter he ran for his own life. He'd been arrested, found guilty, sentenced. For what? That, she might never know. Something that carried a lifetime penalty. The fear she'd felt took on new magnitude. She felt incapable, incapable of functioning with this new knowledge. Presently she laid aside the skulls without making any notes. For a long while she sat at her desk, considering her own fragility and impotence.

When she went outside at last, she found Ben on the front stoop, his face looking embattled in the afternoon sun, his hair poking up all around his head in uneven, ill-clipped tufts. He seemed his best out of doors, she decided, with his thick hands, his strong countenance illumined in the wind and sun. The Ruger lay at his feet. He squinted up at the high rocks, she supposed waiting for the elk to weave their way out of the trees again. "What do you want?" he asked with gruff nonchalance, as if he didn't much care what she answered.

"I've come looking for you," she said, doing her best to make light of the hammering fear in her heart.

He said nothing. At last he pointed to the rocks above him, high above timberline, the Continental Divide over which he'd come. "What's up there in the summertime?" he asked. "Nothing grows, does it? The trees don't. Is it only barren rock?"

"Why does that matter?"

"Because I came that way. I'd like to know what grows when everything isn't covered with snow."

"Not trees," she told him, forgetting his sins as she spoke, thinking only of the mountaintop, "but a great number of other things. Alpine fescue, the tundra grass. And flowers, mostly old man of the mountain and forget-me-nots, moss pink and heather. And tiny green muskeg that covers the ground like velvet. Seems like it'd be impossible, doesn't it? But it isn't. Sparse and bluster swept, but alive. Everything blossoms in July. After the glacial snow melts and the warmth comes to touch, just to touch, but not to stay."

"It doesn't last long, then?"

"No. Not long. Tundra's very fragile. Almost unbelievably hearty and fragile at the same time. High in the national parks, they don't even let visitors walk off the paths. If too many people walk over it, they destroy it."

"Like life," he said brusquely, still looking up. "If too many people walk over it, they destroy it."

Her trepidation returned. She didn't know exactly how to begin this. She couldn't say, *I know what a blessing your daughter's presence is to you. I know what a heartbreak it is, too.* Instead she asked, "Would a change of clothes suit you? I have some things upstairs in the closet."

His irresolute expression reminded Rebecca that he had cause to mistrust her motives, even as she suspected his. "Different clothes'll help me escape when the time comes," he said. "It'll be much easier for the state screws to get me if I'm still wearing these institution duds. You know that."

"I figure you'll take them yourself when the time comes," she shot right back. "You know you will, as well as I do. I figure I'll just offer them now. There isn't much up there, though. Just some old things of my grandfather's. Work pants and a shirt or two, if you'd like."

When he finally decided to accept her offer, his smile, although somewhat weary, was a smile of sincere gratitude just the same. "Yeah. That'd make a big difference. It'd go a long way toward making me feel like a proper person again."

"I'll show you," she said. *Don't think of what he's done. Don't think of what's been done to him. Don't think of what he's doing. Only be civil, so you'll survive these next days.* "You can pick something out."

Ben left the gun lying on the porch, as if he'd forgotten it. As she led him back inside, back up the steps to the room where he'd kept guard over her sleep, Rebecca's thoughts came, disjointed and fleeting. After so long living in this desolate place and feeling constantly accompanied, she now found herself constantly accompanied and feeling alone. She sat on the bed, her hands clasped about her knees, while Ben thumbed through the tangled rusty hangers in the closet.

"This one," he said quietly as he extracted a brown plaid that Howdy hadn't favored much. It'd been hanging in the closet at least twenty years. He also picked a pair of pants. "These okay?" He held them up to her, much aware that he needed her approval.

"Yes. Yes. Those are fine."

With no further ado, he began to unbutton his shirt. Two buttons. Three. As he went, the fabric veed open from the strain of his shoulders. She saw his body. Tall. Lean. Flat stomached. She saw the red slash across his chest where the scalding began. In several places his skin had raised to blisters.

"I burned you badly," she said, not asking, just stating.

He cast his eyes low, not meeting her gaze. "I've been hurt worse than this," he said. "I've always survived."

The room grew quiet except for the soft popping of wood from the stove below. Again, after a while, they spoke together.

"All the same—"

"It isn't the—"

He had no right to be here. He had no right to bring such vicissitude in her life, to swap her freedom in exchange for his own. But the sight of his reddened, seared skin swam before her.

She couldn't help the twinge of guilt. The story of Wyllis, of his discovery and disappointment at the prison fence, gentled her. *I don't understand what you did. But I understand a part of your bitterness*, she wanted to say.

It felt odd, furtive, to hold these things in her mind while she stood before him, as if she truly *did* hold them, as if he could look at her and see them. She found herself wanting to be decent, wanting to make amends for the bodily injury she'd done him. In two days, two blessed days, this man and his daughter would be gone. In two days, heaven only knew what would befall them. Until then Rebecca could afford propriety. "If someone offered you a bath, you'd probably want that, too, wouldn't you?" she finally asked.

Ben had gotten his shirt halfway unbuttoned. His hands stopped right where they'd been, on the fourth button from the bottom. He tried to mask an expression of total surprise, to no avail. "Yes. I would."

"Well, I'm offering, then." She said it serious and soft, looking at him square.

He started refastening buttons. One. Two. Three. Four. He looked around, waiting. "Only problem is," he said at last with humility, "I can't imagine where a man would take a bath in this place. Maybe I'm crazy. Maybe I'm expecting a washbasin to appear outta nowhere."

"Maybe it will."

"I've already seen my fair share of the other private facilities in this place. You gonna set up a galvanized steel tub in the middle of the kitchen like they did in the olden days? I don't see many other options."

"No. Not a steel tub in the house. Much better than that. We'd take Demi, too, only I don't think it would do her good to be out in the cold."

"Take Demi?"

"I'll get her back in bed for a rest. Put on your shoes. I'll get you a towel to dry yourself off with."

"Put on my *shoes?*" Surely she couldn't mean she expected him to take a bath outside somewhere. At once, he suspected her again. He figured this had to be another of Rebecca Woodburn's cracker-brained schemes to escape him. But, in the same instant, he decided to risk it. A bath just sounded too good, too much like a miracle. "Can't imagine. Just can't imagine."

"Come with me." She beckoned as a little girl would beckon, as if she wanted to impart a secret. "It isn't a long walk."

12

The afternoon sun had dwindled to dusky, early-evening gentleness. Each hue of the mountains, the blues, the greens, the delicate mother-of-pearl pink in the sky, seemed as translucent and carefully applied as a watercolor wash. Ben carried the bundle of clean, dusty clothing tucked securely, miraculously, beneath one arm.

Oh, the idea of donning real clothes again. Oh, the joy of wearing *anything* that wasn't prison issue! For one timeswept, treasured moment, nothing else mattered, not the officers out to capture him or take his life, not Wyllis, not Billy. He lived only for this, the highland place where ancient floes and bare rocks towered over him and where sometimes, briefly, forget-me-nots and moss pink bloomed.

Please, please don't run this time, he begged to this woman who feared him, this woman who led him silently on the path across the meadow. This once, just today, he wanted to pretend he was someone who could be trusted, walking with someone who trusted him. *Please, please don't let this be a deception,* he begged her.

Ben wanted to look at Rebecca. He wanted to tell her that because she hadn't tried to escape after Demi awakened, she'd gifted him with dignity. Maybe dignity didn't seem like so much. But when you'd lived in the state slammer, you learned real fast not to argue for anything less. When you spent sixty months with screws telling you when to get in line, when to bend down, when to say something and who to say it to, taking power for power's sake, you tended to place heavy stock in things that gave you a right to act on your own. You tended to yearn for things like Rebecca Woodburn gave, places in your heart that weren't fenced in by stone, things that made you feel like a human being.

Ben glanced sideways at her. She looked intently toward the western sun, her lips a little parted, her hair in a blaze of setting sunshine. He got the impression that she was terrified again. Terrified and doing this act of kindness as a way of survival. "You go this far from the house every time you take a bath?" he asked, trying to bring her back.

He'd been right about her terror. She didn't answer for the longest time, as if she had physically to pull herself from some far place to be with him. "Not every time," she said. "During winter, we always took sponge baths. Lucille used to say, 'People *keep* a long time here in these mountains.' Folks never do sweat or get to smelling bad when it's this cold out."

They headed toward Caddisfly Creek. In the distance, Ben saw where the creek bent artlessly into a grove of winter-bare willows. From the grove came tendrils of steam.

He pointed. "Is that where we're going?"

"That's it."

They brushed through the willows and came upon a mystery. In contrast with the winterland that cloaked the mountainsides, here stood one place as green as Eden, the rim of the water bright with growing things. In this pond, Ben saw fishes swimming about.

Rebecca whispered, "This is the place to come if you can't wait for springtime. Look." She toed the moss at the edge of the water. "This is saxifrage. Here's watercress. And these are golden alexanders. They stay leafy all year."

With fresh clothes in hand, he bent to check the water's temperature. He cupped his hand into the pond, letting the surprising warmth flow past his fingers. The tiny fishes seemed to dart at him in strict formation from everywhere, to peck at his skin.

"Hey," he said, laughing strangely as he pulled his hand away. "They're nibbling me."

Their eyes met. "They want to know what you are."

"What's going to happen when all of me gets in?"

Vapor rose around her. "They won't have you for dinner, if that's what you're asking." He saw disquiet in her expression. "As soon as springtime really comes, there'll be frogs, too. You can hear them crinking from all the way up at the house."

"You're afraid of me," he said abruptly. "All this, and you're more afraid now than you were before. Why, Rebecca? Tell me."

"The water bubbles up here and mixes with water from the creek. When Thom and I were children, we put rocks around to keep it in, to make a deeper pool. This stays warm when everything else is frozen and cold. I brought you here for a bath, and I—"

"Tell me why you're afraid of me." He dropped his clothes on the snow, grabbed her arm with one firm fist.

"You know why I'm afraid of you. You've broken into my home. You've held a gun on me for two days."

"There's something more, though. I see it."

She tried to yank her arm away but couldn't. "Stop holding me. You wanted a bath. Go ahead and take one."

"Something's changed. Something in you." And as he spoke, he suddenly understood. "You've talked to Demi, haven't you?"

"What does that have to do with anything?" She turned her back to him, picked up the pants, the old shirt, and began draping them over the pliant burgundy branches of one willow. As she hung them, he saw her hands shaking. "These'll get wet if you aren't careful. They'll freeze stiff before you get back to the house."

"What did my daughter tell you?"

She stopped fiddling with the sleeves and collar. She stood with her back to him, not moving, staring into the complex webwork of limbs. She didn't answer.

"What did Demi tell you, Rebecca?"

At last she replied, "About the day you got arrested. How they handcuffed you in the crowd and took you away."

That seemed a lifetime ago for him. He remained silent, waiting for her to go on. When she didn't, he prodded. "I need to know what it is you know."

"Do you? Is it so important?" This time when she spoke, her tone stayed stoic, so different from the pasture this morning when she'd been vulnerable, when she'd started to cry. "Okay. I know how Demi helped you in your escape. I know that your . . . your *wife* was supposed to come help, but she didn't. I know it isn't your fault that your daughter came instead, that she came because you'd been betrayed."

Ben toed the green succulence at water's edge. "Demi told you all those things, did she?"

"I know about the parade and the mules doing figure-eights and Wyllis screaming." She told him the rest of it fast, without pausing, as if it made no difference to her. "I know they sentenced you for a lifetime."

Dear sweet heaven, Ben thought. That's it, then. She knew perhaps the whole of it. Clinically, as if there were nothing left inside him, he repeated the terms for her. "I'm serving a life sentence. And unless the warden recommends to the Wyoming governor that my sentence be commuted to numbers, I won't ever be eligible for parole."

He could see she didn't want to acknowledge it. She didn't want to comprehend it. She didn't want to be alone with a man who'd done something vile enough to be punished in such a way. "You'd best get to your bath," she said. "The sun'll be down soon. And we haven't brought a lantern with us."

He doffed his shirt as she turned away into the willows. He held it for a moment, letting the filthy, threadbare fabric drape. With no further ado, he took the garment in two hands and rent it in half, divided it as mightily as his heart was divided. His own words echoed.

I'm serving a life sentence. I won't ever be eligible for parole.

He pitched the shirt high overhead, watching as it sailed deep into the willow thicket, never to be seen again. The pants came next. He pitched them away, too, taking great joy in their strange, leisure ballet as they skimmed the air.

She handed him the soap she'd brought, and Ben sloshed into the water, sifting around in the pond until he found the place where it ran warmest and deepest. He dove under. The water was hot enough to tingle, to wash over his skin and make him feel encompassed, unable to catch his breath. All about him, the tiny fish flecked the water. He brushed them away from his arms and came back up. "You can turn around," he called out to her after he surfaced and shook his head. "I've gotten in."

He stood, watched her, listening to the water slapping against the ice on the shore and lapping over the rocks in the creek. The sounds reminded him that he hadn't heard music in a long time. Music. As he stood in the warm pond, the melodies of this place encircled him like a symphony. This time he did turn, holding his hands to the sky as the water jostled, danced, made harmony like strings and woodwinds around him. Today, this moment, the world belonged to him. The sounds of the stream bespoke something so basic and primal, it couldn't be shared with words.

Rebecca found a rock that protruded from the snow. She sat upon it in the way he was growing accustomed to seeing her, clutching her knees beneath her chin. Without saying anything, she pointed into the pool beside him.

Two muskrats swam one after another, their rattails slapping haphazard S's in the water. At pond's edge, one blade of wild grass—its head heavy with last fall's seed—dipped low to brush the current. Pushed along by the warm stream, it rose, circled like an oar on a tiny boat, before it dipped yet again. A slim weasel, still bedecked in winter ermine, vaulted past on the bank, leaving behind a queue of perfectly furrowed paw prints in the snow.

With him in the water and away from her, he noticed Rebecca didn't seem quite so fearful. Indeed, as this place had come alive before them, she'd gotten an expression so childlike and guileless, he wondered if she even remembered his presence. Thinking of all it would take to love this land as she loved it, to live on this land as she lived on it, he decided she was like no woman he'd known before. Childlike, and not childish. Not simple, and living a life of powerful simplicity.

"Doesn't it hurt you some?" he said. "Growing up in this place and knowing it might've been yours? That must've been one of the hardest things you've done, giving up ownership like you did."

"It all depends on what you think ownership means. Lucille always said there were some things that ought never be owned by anybody. This place was one of 'em. When she died and we found she'd deeded the land to the elk herd, it didn't surprise me much."

"It should've made you bitter. You could've made a living here, could've run it as a ranch the way your grandfather ran it."

"No sense being bitter about things you can't change. I'm making a living here," she said. "Living works one way or another. But I never could convince Thom—"

Her brother, Thom. Hearing about Thom made his heart ache because of Billy. "Maybe Thom's like me," Ben said. "Maybe he can't change who he's been."

Rebecca jumped from the rock and readjusted towels and shirts on the spindly limbs of the willow. She looked as if she suddenly needed to be somewhere else. "Some folks think that. Some folks think it was easier for him to cut loose and leave Star Valley than it was for him to stay here and make a living after Lucille'd given away our inheritance. Most people didn't waste time in telling us we'd been cheated out of everything that'd been rightfully ours."

"Tell me about him," Ben said. "Does he ever come back to the refuge?"

"No. Not since he's married Jillian."

"Jillian Dobbs?"

"That's her."

"Ought to be something, Rebecca, marrying a woman like that who everybody admires."

"It wasn't like him, really. He wasn't often impressed by famous people when they came here to go fishing or something. They'd always go down to the Roices and ask to be taken out in a boat. And folks at the barber shop would be gossiping about them for weeks. Thom never seemed to pay them much mind. He was always thinking about writing all the time, nothing more. But perhaps that's why he fell in love with Jillian Dobbs. He wasn't impressed, so he had the chance to get to know her."

Ben shook his head, gave a *humphff* that sounded like a laugh, a sad laugh. She saw it, understood it, knew he wanted to talk about his own brother, too. "So, tell me about Billy."

He stared down into the water for the longest time, letting the pond quiet until he could see the reflection of his face, studying it as if he saw another face, not his own. "There isn't much to tell."

"But you haven't said anything. Not anything about him at all."

Still, he looked down at the water. "I loved him. I loved him, is all."

"Is Billy older than you? Or younger?"

"Older by two years."

"Billy and Ben," she said. "Billy and Ben."

Her words, the very coupling of the two boys' names, seemed to open a gate for him. He smiled, a bit of the sadness gone. "Folks in Hanna used to see us riding by on bikes and say, 'There goes those Pershall boys. Up to no good again.' They said it loud, thinking either that we couldn't hear it or that we ought to. My mother worked at the Western Family grocery store, and while she was behind the cash register or stacking cans on shelves, we took care of each other."

"What about your dad?" Rebecca asked.

"He did what every man in Hanna did. He worked in the Hanna coal mines. He got to be foreman right near the end, then died where men in Hanna die, too. The mine caved in on him when I was fifteen. Billy was supposed to start college at UW that fall, but we couldn't afford it. He never got to go."

"That must've been bad," she said, "for you and Billy, too."

"He started hating Dad, started hating him for leaving, couldn't argue with him because he'd already gone. And all the while Mom and I depended on Billy. We let him step in and take a father's place for us, let him start his own job in the mines. Without warning, we started desperately *needing* him."

"That must've been bad," she said again.

"No worse than what happened to you." He didn't want to speak of it anymore. She could tell by the sudden desperation she saw in his eyes, a desperation she didn't understand. "No more horrible than having land you've grown up on taken from beneath you the way a trickster yanks a tablecloth from under dishes."

She looked down at the place she stood, at her pac boots sunk deep into snow, at the fine traceries made by the weasel as it had darted past. "The land is still beneath me," she said. "No one's yanked it away."

"No," he said. "It's because nobody's been able to yank *you* away."

Rebecca looked at him long, her eyes brimming with honesty, even humility. "Isn't that almost the same thing?"

"I hadn't thought so," he said. "Maybe I've been wrong."

"We made talk on people's porches every night well into that September, Ben. As if they thought they'd make it better, at least a dozen of them—Jubal Krebbs included—wrote the government with ideas how to better preserve the elk herd than to keep it here. If it'd been up to the other ranchers in this town, they'd be taking turns stuffing the elk with alfalfa hay and then blasting 'em off out of their front yards, one by one, during hunting season."

He had to smile at that. It was exactly what he'd been thinking of earlier, exactly the gift that she'd unknowingly given him. "Dignity," he said. "All this to give honor to wild animals."

"And in giving honor," she said, "we give honor to ourselves. Cyrus Cotten told me once about his dad shooting an elk out the bedroom window. Got him right between the eyes while Cyrus's poor mother lay there naked except for her nightcap pulled down over her eyes. They'd been in the middle of things when Mr. Cotten said he just got the urge, right during the heat of it, to strike a high position and have a look at what might be out the window. There stood a ten-point bull, ready to blast and dress out and fill up the Cotten family freezer. He could've taken four more if he'd had a mind to disobey Wyoming Fish and Game rules and Mrs. Cotten hadn't been hollering at him to come back to bed and finish what he'd started."

Ben began to laugh.

"Howdy and Lucille taught us a long time ago what a toll it would take if the herd got too tame and started coming all the way to town to forage. They understood the depletion it would bring to the dropseed and wheatgrass and thistle. To overuse the elk's natural browse would've made a serious struggle for the moose population and the deer, too. Folks didn't understand conservation much when the Woodburns started talking it. Back then, a lot of people took my grandparents for fools. Now, everything proven, a few of them still think it for old-times' sake."

She'd made such a speech, he'd finished with his bath. He'd soaped, soaked, and rinsed every part of his body in the warm, fresh water. It felt like a miracle. "I'm climbing out," he announced as he began to step up toward the moss-covered bank. When she turned away this time, she amused him. Not three minutes ago, she'd been speaking with great candor about Mr. and Mrs. Cotten and their sexual experiences. Now she'd demurely presented her back so he'd have privacy.

For an instant, he let himself remember. He let himself remember what it felt like to have a woman watching him, a woman wanting to touch him. It had been five years. Five long, empty years.

He sloshed out and toweled off, all the while balancing first on one bare foot, then the other. Ice smushed up between his toes. "Could you hand me those pants?" he asked.

Rebecca reached to the willow and retrieved them for him. Without looking, she handed them back. He hopped into them, one leg at a time, dispersing ice chunks up and down inside them as he went.

He liked the dusty smell of these pants. He'd never before thought of dust as an honorable, homey smell. But nothing in the slammer had ever gotten dusty. Prisoners on cleaning detail doused every square inch of cement and steel with disinfectant or polish or scrub soap. He'd forgotten real-world scents, had grown accustomed to the acrid, antiseptic smell of prison until—like a clock's ticking that fades because of its constant familiarity—he'd lost all sense of the ornate, alluring power of smell.

Only now, as his body quickened to the freedom around him, did he realize all he'd missed. The fresh, searing bite of mountain air. The fervently green earth where new grass rooted, thriving in the mist from this spring. The woody perfume of the woman who stood before him, hugging her elbows tight around her middle. Seemed like she always had to be occupied, either fiddling with something or holding her arms against her.

Ben zipped, snapped, adjusted the old, dusty relics over his hips. These ancient pants would wear fine, thank you, just fine. He poked sockless feet into hated shoes that, during his journey, had begun a befitting curl over the toes. "You can give me that shirt any time," he said. "I'm ready for it."

She pivoted, the shirt in her hands. She didn't hand it right over. She twisted the collar. He saw her looking him over, examining his size and shape, watching the rise and fall of his chest. "I've got a tube of salve back at the house," she said. "I oughtta put something on you for that burn."

"You got any horse clippers?" he asked. "Last time I went to the commissary for a haircut, they'd brought in some old barber from Tie Siding. Between you and me, the fellow had one eye that wouldn't focus right. He told me all about it the whole time he was snipping around my ears. If I could use those horse clippers, maybe I could buzz it, smooth it out around my head some."

She handed him the shirt at last. "I've got clippers. I bet it'd make you look better all right."

Above them, from a promontory of open woodland, one lone coyote raised its voice, an early, baying tribute to the moon that would soon glimmer beyond the horizon. From nearby, a second coyote began to rail, mirthfully merging its voice into a duet. From the high open ridge across the creek, a third started yapping. Down below, from the forested hills across the meadow, a fourth, a fifth, joined into the chorus. The sound echoed, multiplied, surrounded them. The animals sent up such a racket, Ben said, "Well, I'll be dogged. Sounds like every coyote that's ever lived is alive and howling now."

"They're denning," she said, "coming back to old grounds, looking for a place to birth their pups."

The two of them grappled their way out the way they'd come, through the willows. The house stood beneath the outline of the mountain, its scalloped log corners etched with feeble light. Ben poked his hands in his pocket, realizing that—without the gun—he needed something to keep his hands busy, too.

A silent canine silhouette moved from the shadows, its ragged fur the same sandy gray as the sky when the dust kicked up. The animal waited directly in their path. "Stop," Ben whispered, taking her elbow. "Rebecca. Look there."

"It's a coyote. Down here this close. Crazy varmint's come alone out of the trees. Ought not to be doing such a thing with us walking up on him like this. He isn't afraid, and he should be. The way the wind's going, he caught our scent a long time ago. Back before we came out through the willows."

"Left the gun back at the house. I didn't—"

"Figure you'd need it?" Oh yes, she'd noticed he'd left the Ruger lying on the porch, that he hadn't lugged it with him to the pond. Oh yes, she'd noticed. "You won't need the Ruger. Not with a coyote. They'll only kill an occasional sickly calf or a sheep if they're starving. Mostly they dig for rodents the same as dogs do. It's strange, though, having one come down in the field like this. Howdy used to say that was a sure sign of a spring storm, having a coyote confront you in the open like this. As if they know they have to hunt urgently. I was a little girl the last time I saw a coyote do something like it. Thom and I had just arrived."

"Was your grandfather right? Did a storm come?"

"I don't remember. I remember lots of storms right after we got here. But many of them happened in my own heart. I was a little girl keeping my little brother loved, all the while I grieved for my parents. After my parents died and we were brought here, it took me a long time to be happy. But not too long. I was young and willing to forgive. This place has its own way of bringing about healing."

"That, I can see," he said.

The coyote stood as a sentry would stand, its ocher eyes trained upon nothing but distance. The animal stood its ground. Man and beast stared each other down, dumbfounded. Ben could see every detail of the wild face in pencil-sketch precision, the leathery nose, the dark whiskers splaying from the pointed muzzle, the girth of gray-tipped fur surrounding a focused, feral expression.

"Funny thing about the animals, though," Rebecca said. "Things do seem to be a little off. Same thing happened this morning when the children were on the sleigh. You saw the way those elk bugled and sparred."

"Yeah, I saw it."

"Never should've happened like that this time of year. What you saw from them is an autumn mating ritual. Winter's only two-thirds over. They oughtta be saving body fat for survival instead of sparring for a harem. Those cows' bellies are already sagging. They'll be calving in another two months." She shook her head. "Plenty of time for stealing females from one another later. They should've saved their energy. They'd better hope no more big snowstorms blow in this season or they'll be done for."

They'd finally gotten close enough to the coyote to spook it. It stared at them one moment longer. Then it loped off, under no particular duress, and disappeared into deep woodland.

13

Rebecca cooked them venison steaks for supper. She opened the woodstove, set up stones and a grate to make a fireplace of it, an encouraging, gentle scene as the meat sizzled and dripped onto the flaming pine logs below. They ate enormously in front of the fire, their legs sprawled in every direction on the old pine floor, their plates propped on their knees. Demi sat against the couch, her head—which seemed so much better—lolled back against the cushions. "Heard the coyotes out there," she said. "They were yowling something awful. They made me want to sing right along with them." Then she launched into a rousing rendition of an old cowboy song herself. "Good-bye, Old Paint, I'm leaving Cheyenne. Good-bye, Old Paint, I'm leaving Cheyenne." Then, "You remember that song, Dad? You used to sing it to me all the time."

"I remember." He hadn't thought of it in the longest time. When she sang it, an entire life came back to him, happiness, an old friend. He began to sing it, too, his singing voice gruff and uncertain from being unused. "Good-bye, Old Paint . . ." How long had it been? How long? Something seemed to break free within him, to soar. "I'm leaving Cheyenne," he bellowed with his head flung back.

"I used to think that song was sad," Demi said. "I thought when all the cowboys'd left Frontier Days and had come through Hanna, they'd all had to tell their horses good-bye. Just like I had to tell my horse good-bye at the end of summer camp."

"Speaking of horses," Rebecca said, putting aside her plate. "I've got those horse clippers you needed for your hair, Ben. They're on the desk, if you want them."

"I do. Only I. . . "

"What?"

"I reckon I'll need help with this project. I always got Wyllis—"

"I'll help you." Demi volunteered almost too quickly, as if she tried to make up for everything her mother wasn't there to do. "Let me try."

"You ever used clippers before, girl?"

"No. But there's gotta be a first time for everything. I need to learn anyway."

"The intent here is to smooth out my hair shape, not add more nicks to it," Ben reminded her.

And Rebecca'd sensed something in the girl, the same need she must've given credence to when she'd rescued her father. "I think it'd be okay. I'll teach you."

"Really?"

"Yes." She retrieved them from the desk and flipped them on so they made their merry buzz. "Look," she said. "It's simple. You use the width of the blade as a guide, then run it straight around the ears like this. And around the top like this."

"Sit still, Dad," Demi said, applying everything Rebecca taught her. "You mustn't move."

All in all, the haircut went well. But when Demi got to the back of his neck, she accidentally gouged into his skin. "Ouch!" Ben jumped out of reflex, the same way he'd jump at an insect that bit him. "Be careful, would you?"

"Oh, Dad. I'm sorry." Tears came to Demi's eyes. "It was going to look really good before I screwed it up."

"You've done fine," he said. He reached up and took her hand. "Finish up with it, and I know it'll be okay."

"But it's bleeding." She put the clippers back to his neck and tried to complete the task. Her hands kept shaking, though, and Rebecca could see the teenager was afraid to try again.

Ben insisted. "You're doing fine, Demi girl."

"I don't think so." Demi handed over the clippers, and as Rebecca took them, she realized the girl spoke of much more than just her father's barbering. "I don't think I'm doing fine on any of this, Dad. If I'd've been careful and hadn't hit my head . . . Oh, I don't know. We could've kept going if I hadn't gotten hurt."

"Don't you be thinking about that now. You couldn't help what happened. Maybe I should've kept going straight instead of trying that god-awful backslide down the gully. Right or wrong, there's nothing we can change now."

"You *did* plan it, then," Rebecca gasped. Harvey's, Prentiss's, and Tuck's words echoed in her head.

He didn't lose control. He planned the whole thing—

Nobody'd do something like that on purpose, nobody sane, that is—

But maybe somebody desperate—

"Are you afraid, Demi?" he asked.

"Maybe. Maybe I'm afraid. And maybe I'm mad at myself for feeling that way. But I keep thinking I shouldn't be here. I should be at home in my room doing physical science homework and watching *Sisters* on television." And it seemed crazy to realize that after all this she'd missed only one day of school. None of her teachers even suspected she'd been gone. "I've been thinking about things today. All those books," she said. "All that stuff about Butch Cassidy and the Sundance Kid hiding out, how no matter how many horses they stole or how many banks they robbed, they didn't get caught. It made me feel so brave, like I knew what I was doing. But I don't really know what we're doing. Nothing of what I read was *real*. All that stuff was just pages out of a *storybook*."

"Demi, don't."

"I'm a teenager," she said. "Isn't that what they say about teenagers? We don't understand reality. We don't understand our own mortality. Life is a story, like *Nancy Drew* and *Baby-Sitters Club*. The one I read about Butch Cassidy and the Sundance Kid said that they hid out for a long time and doctored horses brands. They ran away as long as they could. They even lived *here* in Star Valley for a while because they knew a posse of lawmen couldn't get in until after May first because of the snow. But, still, they got killed in the end, when the sheriff found them."

"Yes, they did. They got killed all right. And they deserved it."

"What're we gonna do? What're we gonna do if we get caught? I'm starting to think about it a lot."

"They got killed because they deserved it."

"What about us?" she asked. "Do we deserve to get killed, too?"

He looked at his daughter a long time before he answered. Then he shook his head. "You don't." He closed his eyes and scrubbed his forehead. "Dear sweet heaven, Demi, what have I done, getting you involved in this?"

"You didn't get me involved in this. Mom did, remember?"

He took a deep breath, and Rebecca sensed he did everything he could to hang on to his composure. The desperation lay like dark jade in his eyes. He said what he did in a halting, broken whisper. "There isn't one moment that I forget that."

Demi gave the buzzing clippers to Rebecca. "Here. You do Dad's neck."

Rebecca set out to finish the cropping of the silent man's nape, gingerly running the droning blades up his head. The hair fell away in slight, pale wisps. It covered her fist as she worked. She smoothed out the mar where Demi had slipped and cut him. She evened the part on top, made uniform the two cowlicks that sat balanced on either side of his crown. It reminded her of Thom's hair, when Lucille hadn't had time and had asked her to comb it. Thom's hair never would lie down flat on his head the way she'd wanted it to. When Ben Pershall had been a little boy, she bet his hair stuck straight out on both sides, too.

What could he have done, what crime had he committed—this man who had been a boy once, a boy with cowlicks on either side of his hair—that the state of Wyoming found punishable by a life sentence? Perhaps she'd know Wednesday when Angus Riley Jr. finally got out this week's issue of the *Star Valley Independent*. But the good Lord willing, Demi and Ben Pershall would be long gone by the time the newspaper hit the stands.

The thought reminded her: If man and daughter were to travel soon, Demi needed another good night's rest. "You'll be wanting to borrow my nightgown again, won't you?" She'd changed into her own clothes this morning after Rebecca'd laid them beside the woodstove to dry.

"Yes. If you don't mind."

After Demi left them, the movement of warm fire-light filled the room like flowing liquid. The silence was pleasant, as embracing as the radiance from the hearth. "This is a fine evening," Ben said at last, leaning back against the edge of the couch. "If a man had to pick an evening, one that'd be in his memory for a long time or one that'd be his last, he'd pick one like this. Best I've had for"—he made a show of counting back the time—"five years, ten weeks, four days, and—"

"And twenty-seven minutes," she finished up for him with an awkwardness. "But you mustn't talk about it being your last. I won't hear any of that." She stopped suddenly, realizing she spoke the truth. When had it changed? When had she stopped wanting him to be captured and brought back to the state pen? Perhaps Demi's plaintive questioning had done it. Perhaps she, too, wanted to see a man achieve victory in the eyes of his fourteen-year-old daughter. After everything he'd suffered, it didn't seem so much to ask.

He ran a hand over his newly shorn hair. "Best haircut I've had, too. Since—"

"Please," she said, holding up a hand. "Don't count back the time again. I heard you the first time. And you mustn't give me credit for the haircut. Demi gave you a lovely barbering."

"Yes, she did. In more ways than one." His expression sobered. "Thank you for helping her while she helped me, Rebecca. That's the way she is, always jumping in at the beginning without thinking, then backing away afraid afterward. Maybe I should've turned her away when she came, should've crawled back in through the razor ribbon and the hole where she'd dug it. But I keep reasoning that away. I keep telling myself that by the time it would've taken me to crawl back inside the fence and convince Demi to leave, we'd've both been caught. Never intended to be on the run with a schoolgirl. Never intended her to even know about it until I came home. I thought I could trust—" He stopped, not wanting to belabor the story. "I could've saved Demi from this. I could've turned back."

"Sometimes it gets too late to turn back," Rebecca said. "Like the truth when it's spoken. You can't take back the truth once it's said."

They sat in silence again, while the glow from the remaining coals ebbed and flowed beneath the grate, heightening and fading as with breath. Rebecca looked long at it, indulgently and listlessly, in a way that gave Ben full realization of her loneliness. He watched her as she watched the fire, thinking how like two people she seemed, like an old woman and like a young child, at times hardened, at times eager. Even as she'd fortified herself in this high land, she'd left her life intertwined with vulnerabilities. Even as he'd guarded her in her own house, he'd become acutely aware of her.

She seemed to want to say something, only she didn't. Ben shrugged. He would wait, then. "I keep wondering," she blurted out some time later, "about Wyllis." When he said nothing, the rest of her question tumbled out. "I keep wondering how a woman could've sent a child to do such a thing."

He shook his head, at a loss. "Wyllis has always been a deliberate woman. It was the reason I could write her such a letter and know she'd understand. I think of her sitting beside the clock that night, knowing Demi'd come to the prison fence and was digging. I make myself sane thinking she did it for safety instead of selfishness. I suppose she decided we wouldn't be taken seriously if anyone saw a fourteen-year-old girl digging. It just seemed too absurd."

"She's worrying now, isn't she?"

"Of course she's worrying. I'm certain the authorities have been through the house several times, searching. She'll have told them Demi has gone to visit a friend and that she has no idea what's happened to me."

"She's your wife," Rebecca said. "You expected she would come that night, didn't you?"

"Yes, I expected she would come."

It seemed enough to say. They both fell into an intent examination of the grate and the pale blue flame that rose occasionally from the embers, as if each wanted to read there the outcome of his time at Timberline. She stood to carry the plates to the kitchen. "Oh!" After everything else, she'd thought of the salve. He watched her as she rummaged through the oak medicine cabinet, looking for it. She pulled out ancient tube after ancient bottle of medications, ointments, and remedies. "Lucille's kept these right here on the third shelf since I was a little girl," she said, holding up a small bottle. Thantis lozenges. "They work on sore throats. I used to get them all the time."

"It's your house now. Perhaps you should clean out the medicine cabinet and begin with modern things."

"No sense getting new things when old things aren't used up." She selected an old bent-up tube of Dr. B. Denton's Burn Ointment and closed the cabinet. He saw her catch a glimpse of herself in the beveled mirror, saw her stop to examine the reflection of her face in the old, mottled silvering. She hadn't done up her hair since he'd been in the house. The braid, which yesterday had been tidy as a new store-bought rope, dangled in several loose sections around her neck. Wisps of her dark hair poked out every which way from her ears like the quills on a hedgehog. While he watched, she pushed several tendrils back into their intended formation and touched her face.

"You're pretty, Rebecca," he said. "You know that, don't you?"

Her fingers halted where they lay upon her own skin, her short fingernails opalescent against her cheek. Again came that look she'd given him when he'd complimented her supper, the beguiling one of pleasure and awkwardness. She looked down at the floor. "I've never thought much about it," she said.

"Haven't you?"

"No." And then, quieter: "Guess I haven't had a reason to think about it for a long time."

When she glanced back up at him momentarily, a soft light glowed in her eyes. She glanced back down, as if she couldn't bear to meet his gaze.

"I've got you some ointment," she said, her voice gentle. "Dr. B. Denton's."

"I'm not certain I've heard of it before."

"I'm not certain they've manufactured it any time during the past twenty years."

"Oh no," he said, backing up. "You're not putting that stuff on me."

"It's all I've got."

He realized she'd looked up at him again, that she was biting her bottom lip while her eyes sparkled with amusement. She must've gotten an inkling, as they discussed Dr. B. Denton's, how singular her life seemed to him. "If you'd like, you can drive down to Hayden's General Store and buy something different."

That convinced him. "Maybe not." Together they sat back on the floor where the firelight played over the walls. She held the balm in her hand for the longest time, not offering it. Ben reached up, almost touched her face as she'd touched her face in the mirror, but thought better of it. He returned his hand to his knee. The eloquent sadness in her eyes haunted him. He wanted to tell her that, yearned to tell her that.

Finally he pursued it. "Can I ask you something, Rebecca?"

"What?"

"Why do you separate yourself from people? You get lonesome being so far from everyone, don't you?"

"No. I've had everything I've needed here. This house. The elk herd. The high mountains." And the other part of herself that was so much a secret, the part of herself that was more like a wonderful spirit, the part that answered her in silence when she spoke silently to it. Where it came from or what might bring it, she didn't know. She only knew that she could search for it all day and never find it, or she could raise her eyes from the pages of her notes or step out to the barn, and there it would be, something more than herself and part of herself, a warm certainty that made everything, everything she thought of or touched, more beautiful and significant.

"You're lonely," he coaxed her. "I can see it."

"Yes," she said. "I'm lonely now."

"Why?" he asked. "Why now?"

She admitted it to herself even as she admitted it to him. "Because you've come," she said.

Outside the window, the moon had come at last into fruition, its fullness poised admirably above the ice-clad slopes. A great horned owl hooted its lyrical alto from the eave of the barn. *Who-oo-ooo. Who-oo-ooo. Who-oo-ooo. . . .* The snow-crusted fields shone iridescent with starlight, as if the flush came from within instead of high in the heavens. From a bare cottonwood, one nightjar sang its three-syllable song of eventide.

"Guess that Dr. B. Denton's stuff will make me stop hurting, won't it? When I get it on, that is," Ben said, reminding her.

"Oh." She opened her fist, found the tube still there. "We'd best get this done."

He began to unfasten the buttons on Howdy's old shirt, one by one. She unscrewed the lid.

"It soaked through by my shoulder blades. By the way it feels, there's blisters back there, too."

"You'd better let me see."

He pulled one arm out of the shirt, then the other. He turned for her to inspect his back. He felt her fingers alight there momentarily, as weightless on his skin as a wafting feather. Her touch, soft as it was, went through the man, every foot and inch of him. His broad shoulders lifted in a deep breath.

"You're right," she said. "I hadn't realized I'd gotten you all the way around."

"You pitched a helluva lot of soup in my direction."

She bit her lower lip again and said nothing more.

He reached for her, removed the antiquated tube from her unresisting fingers. Rebecca's gaze slowly followed the course of his hand. Taking her fingers inside his own, he held her there while he squeezed a good amount of the clear, cold gel into her palm. Immediately she felt it begin to go warm as it absorbed the temperature of her own skin. "Now," he said, never moving his eyes from hers, "you can rub it in."

She laid her gel-laden hand in the midst of his breastbone as lightly as she'd laid it before. He flinched. She jerked her fingers back.

"No," he said. He reached for her hand again, held it gently there in midair while he spoke. "I didn't mean to—"

"I won't—"

Their words intermingled, faded to a different sort of silence, a soundlessness that held explosive possibility. He placed his index finger under her chin and raised her face to meet his. "You've got to understand something, Rebecca. Something important. All those days, all those months, all those years I've counted back. It's been that long, too, since a woman has touched me in gentleness. My body's going to react to this, Rebecca. I'm a man."

She rose on both knees, as if his words brought invitation instead of deterrent. "I've hurt you," she said. "I did it to protect myself. But I wouldn't've injured you in such a way. After everything else that's happened to hurt you, I'm sorry for that much."

"It's a far cry from any mercy I've been shown before," he said. Just the voicing of it proved enough for Ben. Just now, it was everything he needed. "Thank you."

One by one, she uncurled her fingers and laid her fingertips against him. He knew she felt his breath catch, knew she felt the pounding measure of his heart. "If it stings, that means it's working," she said. Last time this tube had been used, it'd been Lucille telling her the same thing. He shrugged completely out of the shirt, left it lying in a heap behind him, forgetting it.

Her hand crept up his chest, spreading Dr. B. Denton's Burn Ointment across his seared skin. She daubed the oily salve along the length of his sternum, taking care not to put pressure on his tender wounds. After that she moved around to his spine, making ribbony, lavish strokes until the substance turned hot, soaked in. She didn't stop or speak again until she'd finished, until the dancing light of the fire played over his sheening torso. She rocked back on her heels, let out one long breath of her own. "There," she said faintly. "There."

∘ ∘ ∘

Ben kept guard over Rebecca on this, the second night, without the Ruger. "If you don't have to sit propped up with that gun all night," she said, "you might as well find yourself a chair and sleep."

"I might drop off some," he confessed, "after you've gone."

"The horsehair chair in the corner used to be my grandfather's. You could try that one."

"Everything around this place used to be your grandfather's. I'll stay on the floor. I'm getting accustomed to it."

"Ben, I want you to take my truck when the time comes to leave," she said abruptly. "It's the only way I know to get Demi clean away."

"Anybody sees me, they'll know the truck is yours," he reminded her.

"Yes. But I can't figure any way around that. If Thom was here, perhaps he could come up with something better. Thom could create possibilities out of nothing. He always seemed able to come up with the best ideas, even though he was the youngest one. A writer's mind, I guess, even from the beginning."

After she adjusted the lantern to her satisfaction, she prayed. He'd known she would, as sure as he'd known she'd leave what was left of her braid ruthlessly intact. When she'd finished he said, "Tell me about your brother, Rebecca. You make it sound as if he's much different from you."

She turned out the lamp. Darkness enveloped them. This, this was perhaps the first message she'd given him that, yes, tonight, she trusted his presence.

"Thom's different," she said, "and similar, too." The bed springs rasped and Ben knew Rebecca'd flipped to a more comfortable position in the bed. The blankets swished and he knew she'd readjusted them to her liking. He heard the gentle change in her voice, a change he was beginning to know.

"We were an awful lot alike when we were kids. He used to put on snowshoes and follow after Howdy on the sleigh. You should've seen him then, so little, in one of Gramp's biggest ragg-wool hats. He used to hold my hand and all I could see of him was his runny, pink nose and cheeks chapped as red as ripe crab apples. I remember saying to him, 'Grams needs to learn better how to warm-wrap you. There's gotta be some way of keeping your face from freezing without smothering you like this.' He always looked like a great horned owl himself, neckless, starting at the top and getting rounder and rounder. 'She's wrapped me up like this because she don't want me catchin' cold. Poor Grams. I don't guess she knows what to do with us yet.'"

"You didn't always live here with Howdy and Lucille?" Ben asked.

"No. Our parents were killed when I was ten and Thom was six. Strange, though, I've always had to hold on to things to keep remembering. It was easier for Thom to remember, even if he let things go. He asked me once, after we'd been here a while, if I could still see their faces. You know what? I couldn't see, not their faces all together in one piece like I was looking at them. Thom said he still could, and I laid awake all night in the room where Demi's sleeping now, crying because of it."

"It must've been awful, especially with you being the older."

"It was. I tried and tried but couldn't picture them. All I could do was think of how they'd felt to me."

"How they'd felt to you?"

"If you think about it, you know what I mean. When I'd sit on Dad's lap, he'd squeeze his arms around me. He smelled dusty and worn like his truck seats. His chin made me scratch. Momma was always in the kitchen, busy and singing Christmas carols even in June, and she'd get me all slimy with dishwater when she bent down for a hug.

"'You aren't the only one. I can see 'em and feel them, too,' Thom said, always boasting. 'I can feel them all happy and full and strong, like as long as they are watching me, nothing could bother me or make me afraid.'

"Thom always knew how to say things right. 'When you grow up,' I said, 'I bet you'll write something important. I've never known anybody always thinking about things and saying things the way you do.' 'You know, Becca,' he said, 'I feel that way when I'm here.' 'Which way?' I asked. 'Like you'll write something big someday?' 'No,' he answered. 'Like Dad is squeezing me. All circled up and full, where nothing can get at me. I'm never gonna leave this place, Becca. Ever.'"

"And look." Ben gave a low, sympathetic chuckle. "You're here and he's gone to Los Angeles, marrying movie stars."

"Yes, it's funny, isn't it?"

Some time passed before he got up the bravery to ask her the next question. "Do you ever think of leaving Timberline, Rebecca?"

"Yes. Once, I did."

"When?"

"Before Lucille died, I was engaged to be married. But he didn't want to stay up this high in the mountains. He wanted a house down close to Star Valley, where it wouldn't be so difficult to make telephone calls and grow vegetables and raise a half dozen children. I kept thinking I could do both, maybe live down there and drive up here and keep everything in order at the ranch for the Woodburns. But I realized I couldn't. We still ran a few cows up here then. I realized I couldn't live two lives at the same time."

"You gave up a marriage for the land. Then the land wasn't yours anymore?"

Rebecca knew what he truly asked her, even though he didn't voice the words. *Do you have regrets? Are you sorry you did things the way you did them? Would you make a different choice today, given another chance?*

"Cyrus Cotten wasn't so much to give up," she said. "Not when you look at other things I might've lost."

"He's the one, isn't he? He's the one whose father shot an elk out of the bedroom window."

She didn't answer. But Ben knew he was right.

"A refuge and a prison can sometimes be much the same thing, Rebecca. Maybe our lives haven't been so different from one another's."

She sat up in the bed. He heard the rustle, saw her profile against the window. "Tomorrow is Sunday," she said. "Oh, but I've said it wrong. *Today* is Sunday." She laughed a little. "We're only waiting for the sun to light the sky, aren't we? Everyone will be going to Morning Star Baptist today. You should see the churchyard. They landscaped it last year, took a special collection during revival so they could line the driveway with Lombardy poplars. No sooner did they get them all planted than a beaver came around and took them down again, one by one. They paid a pretty penny, the deacons did, to get a driveway lined with stumps."

He readjusted his knees, leaned over to knead his own ankles, which were going to sleep much faster than he was, propped at their odd angle. "I don't know that I can see Wyllis's face anymore," he announced to Rebecca abruptly. "Strange, isn't it? It's only been a month since she's been in at the pen to visit. For the past five years, that's all I could see of her, was a face behind a glass."

"You've loved her a long time, haven't you?"

"I thought so. Or maybe I've just loved who she used to be. No matter what, though, I understand her. She sees it that I forsook her," he said. "She never said it aloud, not from the beginning. But I made choices, too. Choices that separated us."

"The sun's coming up soon," Rebecca said. "It doesn't seem like this night lasted very long at all."

They watched it together, the foreglow that appeared to the east of the butte above them and gently anointed the sky. When he finally fell asleep, she crept from the bed and covered his slumping body with her grandmother's worn wool blanket. For a long while she knelt above him, scrutinizing his face. She wanted to remember it after he'd gone, wanted to remember it the way she couldn't remember her parents' faces, the way he couldn't remember Wyllis's.

At last, satisfied, she dressed easily, not worried that she would wake him. When she went out to feed and harness the horses, the sun had risen full above the old house. And the morning church bell had begun to ring from below in the valley.

14

The Sunday service at Morning Star Baptist Church began promptly at eleven with the tolling of the huge bell in the steeple belfry. Each Sunday Pastor W. D. Owen selected one strapping boy of elementary-school age to swing up and down on the cord in the foyer and give the bell rope five or six strong yanks. Immediately after the last hollow chime reverberated and faded, members of the flock stood and opened their well-worn Baptist hymnals to page 324, and Pastor Owen signaled the organist, Becky Farrell, to launch into her most rousing rendition of "Higher Ground."

On this particular Sunday, a suited visitor entered the door, shook hands heartily with Deacon Silas Braxton, and made his way undirected to very nearly the front of the sanctuary. "Who's that man on the third row, the one who just sat beside the Weatherbys?" Jane Lumin asked Beulah Hardaway. "I've never seen him in a service here before."

"You ought to be thrilled," Beulah answered. "An honest-to-goodness visitor. We don't get many of those in Star Valley, do we?"

He had a weatherbeaten, cruel look about him, the seeming hardness of a man who'd been in the midst of difficult things and had survived them. His hair color was indistinguishable, a rather seedy mixture of gray and the shade of dusty grain. His suit seemed incongruous with the rest of him somehow. It looked new, as if it had just come off the ready-to-wear rack at Sears & Roebuck. The shoulders spread too wide, the sleeves hung too short. It did not fit him well.

The man did not carry a Bible. And, as they watched him, they saw that he did not put anything in the collection plate, either. "He looks restless up there by Coral, jostling around in his seat," Jane surmised. "He shouldn't've sat so close to the front."

"Some people like to sit close to the front because they don't like to be distracted from God's word," declared Vern Chappell, leaning forward from the pew behind them. "I ought to move up there myself with all the noise you women make."

The visitor did not introduce himself to anyone. After welcoming the nameless man from the pulpit, Pastor W. D. Owen opened his massive Bible and instructed the residents of Star Valley to begin reading from Proverbs, Chapter 30. "There are three things that are too amazing for me," he began—very loudly—to recite, "four that I do not understand: the way of an eagle in the sky, the way of a snake on a rock, the way of a ship on the high seas, and the way of a man with a maiden."

"Good heavens," whispered LaDean Hayes. "Why doesn't he stick to the basics? He knows we're not very good at this."

From across the aisle, Beulah agreed. "I never can understand it when W. D. decides to teach us something difficult."

"You instructed him in senior English, Beulah," Ardith Haux commented from down the row. "You ought to be able to understand him."

W. D. did not seem to notice the flurry of conversation. He delved into his message with great vigor. He explained how a sparrow must flap and fight to catch the wind, while an eagle stands high atop a butte, raises its wings, and waits for the wind to lift him. He explained to his flock that they should live their lives in such a way, not flapping, fluttering, or worrying but waiting with raised wings to be lifted.

"During the past two days," he continued, "Wyoming authorities have combed Star Valley in search of a man escaped from prison. They have one clue, one clue alone. A bashed-in Buick pulled from the headwaters of Caddisfly Creek. No one knows if this man has survived. No one knows whether he took part and succeeded in a plan that required both lunacy and genius. But we all *do* know that valley residents have banded together to protect one another from something that might've brought catastrophe."

Here, W. D. searched out Tuck Krebbs in the audience. Tuck sank low on the green-cushioned pew. The pastor gestured expansively. "Yesterday, Harvey Perkins, Prentiss Smith, and Tuck Krebbs followed their gut instincts. They drove up the mountain and checked on the Woodburns' place, even though authorities have determined this convict could've traveled that path. These men wanted to make certain nothing had happened to harm Rebecca Woodburn. Despite the odds, despite determinations by people who'd know, these men let their intuition guide them. They went up to check on one of our own."

"Did they find anything?" Ben Mitchum asked from the third pew on the right.

"No. They didn't find a thing," W. D. answered, not taken aback at all because someone had asked an honest question in the middle of his sermon. "But what I'm saying is this. No matter the outcome, these men displayed kindness. In the end those acts of kindness will be the remembrances that matter. It is the small things, the times when we let God carry us, when we respond to who He's made us to be, that will add up to become big. The big things, or the things we think and play up big at the time, wither away as the days pass.

"Tuck had to close up the vet clinic and lose business. Harvey and Prentiss had to leave the care and feeding of their own animals. And after this trouble, they found Rebecca safe, surrounded by schoolchildren who might also have been in danger.

"We don't always understand God's ways. But we must understand how He draws people together in His love. We must learn to trust the movement of life the way we trust the movement of the wind, to know that—like an eagle—we will be lifted and carried only when we admit we are afraid and incapable of performing a task. We always get into trouble when we're like the sparrow, frantically beating air with our own wings.

"Let us pray."

They bowed their heads as he offered the benediction. When he'd finished, they all filed into the foyer and spilled out into a spring noon reminiscent of so many others. One by one, they lined up to give the pastor their views on what he'd said.

"Good sermon, W. D.," Tuck told him on the lawn. "Don't like it much when you talk about me, though. Always makes me feel like everybody's watching."

"Guess that's why I do it, Tuck. I believe it's good for a man to feel like somebody's watching him."

"I always enjoy it when you discuss current events," LaDean informed him while she shook his hand. "That's one thing that always keeps me awake the entire service."

He returned her handshake heartily. "Thank you, LaDean. Thank you."

"Your sermon today made me remember your days in my class, William," said Beulah Hardaway, who'd been calling him William ever since he'd been listed as such on the high school attendance records. "You wrote your term paper for my class on *Jonathan*

Livingston Seagull, paying special attention to the symbolism of the bird's flight."

"I did?"

"Come now. You must remember."

W. D. Owen had raised three children, had made his way nicely through several dissimilar yet parallel discourses in theology, and had counseled the folks of Star Valley on everything from the particulars of the marriage bed to the dairies where their holstein milk sales could bring in remarkable prices to the spiritual hazards of driving to Jackpot, Nevada, for a weekend of wagering. But no matter the length and authority to which he'd taken dominion over this flock of the Lord, his old high school English teacher still had enough gumption to make him shake in his shoes.

"It must've been a good paper," he said, doing his best to divert her, "if *you* remember it."

"Such a shame. To think, after all that work you did on it, those precise footnotes, and *you* being the one not to remember. I drew on it myself today during your message. It's always hard for me to understand when you preach from Proverbs."

"I'll keep that in mind, Mrs. Hardaway. The next time the Lord prompts me to do a sermon from Proverbs, I'll remind Him that you always have a difficult time with that."

"I did like the part when you talked about the criminal, William. Do you think they'll catch him around here?"

"I doubt it," W. D. told her honestly, relieved to discuss anything except his term paper that—even now, after her prodding—he couldn't call to mind. "Star Valley's such a small town. If that convict is hiding out anywhere around here, I think the state people or Andy Rogers down at the sheriff's office would've found him by now. They're very scientific about the way they do things."

The visitor, whom neither had seen approaching, stepped up to join the conversation. "Oh, I wouldn't be so certain of that. I know the man they're searching for. From everything I've seen of him, he's a dangerous man who defies scientifics. Perhaps the authorities should readjust their theories somewhat. They might have more luck that way."

"Welcome to Star Valley, Mr. . . ." Once again, Pastor W. D. Owen extended his hand in greeting. This time he was doing his best to keep the expression of consternation off his face. In this town, they were not accustomed to strangers coming in and telling them they ought to be readjusting anything.

"Are you a part of the investigation?" Beulah asked, and as she did, a large group of townfolks gathered around them. Everyone seemed interested in his answers.

"No. As a matter of fact, I'm not. I came to this place to see what sort of information you people might be able to give *me.*"

"But you said you knew him," Silas Braxton prodded.

"Yes, but my involvement is more"—he searched for the correct word—"personal."

They glanced about among themselves, none of them certain how they should proceed.

"I'd like to see the river where the criminal's car went down," the suited man announced. "Is there anyone who might be willing to take me on a tour of that area for a fee? I'd like to do some poking around of my own."

"What sort of poking do you need to do?" Jane Lumin rolled and unrolled her church bulletin at least three times, finally making a miniature club out of it and whacking her own thigh with it out of nervousness.

"Don't know exactly. I figure I can find some clues of my own, once I get pointed in the right direction."

Ordinarily five or six good people, including a couple of the women, would've jumped at the chance to make this extra money on the side. But this man put them off a bit; something about him seemed calculating and out of place. He waited for any response. When he didn't get one, he shrugged as if it didn't matter.

"Guess I'll have to go elsewhere. Thought I could find the help I needed at a church."

"Stop on over at the barber shop tomorrow," Tuck Krebbs suggested. "You get them telling you what they know, you'll end up with a whole passel of 'em fighting over who's gonna take you up the mountain. At the barber shop, they compete to see who can sound like an expert."

"Are you Tuck Krebbs?" the man asked. "Are you the fellow referred to in the sermon this morning?"

Tuck's face went as red as the bog wintergreens that bloomed in the woody lowlands each summer. "Yes. That's me."

"This woman you went to check on, the one the reverend spoke so eloquently about this morning? Woodcock? Woodhaven?"

"Rebecca Woodburn."

"You say you saw no sign of the convict when you visited her?"

"No. But we didn't search much. Rebecca said everything was fine. She's a straightforward lady. If something'd been wrong, she'd've figured out some way to tell us."

"This place where she lives. Is it difficult to get to?"

"Not if you don't mind hairpin turns and one-lane roads," Tuck said. "Not if you don't mind ascending mountains. Is that car a four-wheel drive? You'll be driving on gravel and ice when you're climbing up high, you know." They could see he drove a rental, with a license plate that indicated he'd picked it up at the airport in Jackson Hole. "I certainly wouldn't go up that far alone," Tuck added. "Rebecca Woodburn doesn't like to be bothered."

"You men bothered her yesterday, didn't you?" he asked politely.

"Guess we did at that," Tuck said.

"I don't suppose any of you would be willing to accompany me to her place this afternoon, would you?"

"Why would you wanna go up there? We already told you we didn't find anything."

"Yes," he said cautiously. "You told me that. But I know my—" He stopped, cutting himself off abruptly, as if he'd been about to utter something he didn't want them to hear. He shook his head, seemed to change his mind quickly. "Good-bye," he said instead. "Thank you for such a lovely service." He nodded his head once more at W. D., then strolled with extreme nonchalance toward his car.

It wasn't until the man climbed into his vehicle and roared away that they realized no one had found out where the visitor had come from. "Well, I've never seen such a thing," Silas Braxton commented. "That fellow was one of the most unfriendly men ever to lay foot in this churchyard. Sitting at the front like that, waiting until after the sermon, and asking us questions like we owed him answers. All that, and he never once offered us his name."

When the Rural Electric Association set up its first power lines into the wilderness above Star Valley, no one had been more excited than Howdy and Lucille Woodburn. They'd operated for years with a light plant, hidden away in an old ramshackle outbuilding, an ancient generator with a gasoline motor that kicked off under extreme protest if it kicked off at all. They'd long planned their days around the rising and the setting of the sun, knowing that—after darkness came—they'd be using precious fuel to supply meager, flickering light for their evening desk work or reading.

Seemed a miracle when the lights could come on at the flip of a switch and stay on for hours if need be, until dawn if it behooved the residents. As years passed, they'd kept the light plant in working order, shut up in the dilapidated shack and laced with cobwebs and all manner of dirt, filled with enough gas to keep it running in case of emergency.

Rebecca showed Demi how to check it this afternoon, shoving open the door, blowing off the dust, and jamming her finger on the generator button to see if the thing would crank to life. It did, after a good number of tries. The needle on the volt meter inched upward. Rebecca poked the button and turned it off. Best to save the gas for when she'd need it. Up here, you never knew when that might be.

The Sunday morning feeding had gone as usual, except, after a while, Demi had come out to help her. "See this," she'd told the girl as she'd taught her how to manage huge clumps of alfalfa hay with the pitchfork. "Break the bale open, then string it along behind the runners." Elk followed the sleigh's tracks across snow-crusted pastures, the animals nudging the snow and using green teeth to rip at the fragrant hay the girl had pitched over. One contrary old bull slung his head, belligerently horning all the others out of the way, despite there being a long line of hay, plenty for all.

She stepped out of the generator shed now, thinking that if she'd still been running Howdy's herefords, she could've come up with something to straighten out that ornery old animal. She brushed off her hands and glanced over to see Andy Rogers's sheriff's car, followed by the vehicles of two Wyoming State Troopers, barreling up the long two-rut drive.

Alarm hit Rebecca like an electric shock. "Demi!" she said quickly to the girl at her side. "Get in the house fast and wake up your father. They're gonna want to search the place. No!" She grabbed Demi's arm as the girl started out in one direction. "Go the other way. Behind the house so they won't see you."

Demi slipped behind the shadow of the house, past the skeleton poplars that were just beginning to give off the faint allusion of green.

Dear sweet heaven, Rebecca thought. All this, and I want to protect him.

The cars crunched to a stop, heedlessly smashing the winter-brittle sage that rose through the snow. "Hello, Andy." Rebecca brushed off her hands again, needing something to occupy them, anything to keep them busy. She'd made her decision without thinking the moment she'd told Demi to run. She'd set events into motion that couldn't be revoked. "What're you doing up here on a Sunday afternoon?"

"Have you heard about the criminal that's escaped?"

"I have."

"We're tracking him," Andy said. "Mind if we look around?"

She didn't answer him directly. "You fellows've been beat up here. Harvey, Prentiss, and Tuck came up yesterday morning to make sure everything was okay. They didn't find anything." Then she added her own lie to it, knowing she had no other choice, hoping against hope that Demi had gotten to Ben, that they'd hidden away somewhere in the house where they wouldn't be found. These past few days she'd watched a man scrapping for his freedom. She'd watched his face as he told of being betrayed. She knew a part of him that hadn't been seen. She couldn't watch that die now, not here, not this way. "Nothing's been out of the ordinary."

The other officers parked their cars, climbed out, and doffed their hats momentarily. "Hello, ma'am."

"Hello."

One of them explained, "Haven't had much luck following our sketches and topographical maps. Thought we might try something else for a change. Thought we might check where everybody said it *couldn't* happen. No reason to launch into an investigation and leave any possibility unaccounted for. Though we *have* viewed this part of Lincoln County as a last resort."

Rebecca gave them a thin smile. "Many people who've lived here all their lives see it the same way."

"You mind if we take a look around the barns? Andy tells us there's lots of old outbuildings up here, places a man could hide if he wanted to."

"I suppose there are." She glanced around her own property as if she were seeing it for the first time. "Take your pick. I've been working in this shed, restarting the generator. Besides that, there's the barns and the storage buildings. You won't want to miss those."

Just don't search the house. Whatever you do, you mustn't look through the house.

It occurred to her, with bone-chilling exactness, that the moment she'd told Demi to run and find Ben

Pershall, the moment she'd told the officers "nothing's been out of the ordinary," she'd become an accomplice to his crime. For one moment she faltered; for one moment of turbulent longing, she tried to get away. "I'll just—" She pointed toward the house, wanting to make an excuse to run inside and see that Ben was safe. But she realized she couldn't.

"We do want you to come with us," Andy said. "You'll know best where the hidden areas are, where anyone could linger or be concealed. Will you show us?"

She only nodded. She didn't talk. Words brought fear. Everything she might say would be a falsehood. She turned her back to the house, followed them to the barn.

I could tell Andy, she thought. I could take him inside, show him Ben and Demi. He'd be fair and tell me what to do. I could run forward right now and say, "Andy?"

So she did it. She stepped forth. "Andy?"

But Andy Rogers didn't hear her. He'd begun discussing the case with the uniformed officer at his side.

Before Friday, Rebecca'd laboriously kept control of the land, the elk herd, this life. Since Ben Pershall had come, things had happened too fast; they'd zoomed out of control at the slightest cause. Anything she might tell Andy now would be duplicity to Ben, in some ways as costly a betrayal as the wife who wouldn't come to the wall.

The second state trooper opened the massive barn door and stepped inside.

Rebecca pointed to the Belgians across the way, speaking with a lightness that cost her. "There's Mabel and Coney over in the stalls. They've worked today and had a rubdown, so they shouldn't bother you any. Be careful they don't kick you if you get close."

"Are you in this barn every day?"

"Every day," she said, "even into summer." After she turned the horses out to pasture, she still came in to tinker with samples or to jot notes, to examine the formation of antlers or the abundance of natural graze or the internal parasites she kept secure in a glass vial. Occasionally, when the ice had melted off the meadow, she kept species of other sorts here, too, field mice kept in makeshift cages, an ailing chiseler, a horned lark that rested in a box until it was able to fly. This barn, odorous and dark, had long been one of Rebecca's happiest places.

They pulled flashlights out of their belts and shined bright dust-ridden beams up over their heads into the haymow. "Is there a way to climb up there, ma'am?"

"The ladder."

She led the officers to it, showed them how to ascend. One went ahead and searched every corner, stirring the hay up into knots as he jabbed around in it. "There's nothing up here," he hollered down. "Hasn't been anything for a long time."

"Are there other places we should investigate?" Andy asked her.

"Yes," she answered, and she took them to the storage area where she kept the leathers and to the shed where she kept so much hay. It went like this for a long while, as Rebecca let the men search buildings that hadn't been looked inside for years. They moved, one by one, down an entire row of dilapidated store-houses and sheds.

Suddenly one of the state men halted. He stooped low, jerked his head in the direction of the woodland. "Wait. Get down!" he shouted. "Something moved back there."

Rebecca's heart stopped. What had he seen? The officers yanked guns from holsters. Together, in one synchronized line, they crept toward the trees. Had Ben and Demi come from the house? Were they trying to get away? "Freeze!" Andy Rogers yelled.

The two dark shapes kept moving, the shadowy forms of animals sloughing through deep snow.

Andy threw down his arms in disgust. "Of all things." He shoved his weapon back into his holster as if he were embarrassed to be involved. "It's only a cow moose and her calf. You state people have a lot to learn about patrolling Lincoln County."

Rebecca's legs almost buckled with the relief. "Please tell me it's over, Andy." She said this with the intense quietness that signified deep feeling. "Please tell me you've finished your investigation up here."

"I suppose so," Andy said. "Only thing left is the house."

"The house?"

"You don't mind if we go through the house, do you, ma'am?" one of the state troopers asked. "Just to make certain, you understand. In case someone's been inside without your knowledge."

Rebecca's face went pale in the gathering afternoon clouds, and they took it for a different sort of fear than it was. "Living up here alone the way you do, anything could happen. You must think about things like this for your own protection," Andy said. "You can't be too careful."

"I don't think it's—" She stopped, knowing if she persisted and they found him, she'd be suspect.

"Necessary?" Andy asked. "Of course it's necessary. I've heard what your life is like up here alone, with only the animals to care for. Everybody wonders about it."

"How can you have heard what it's like? If there's nobody up here but me to see it?" The officers had started for the house as they talked, not tarrying for her answer. She tagged along beside them, halfway running to keep up.

"Will you show us where a man could hide here?" Andy asked.

They state troopers had gotten to the door ahead of her. They waited for her to press open the screen. "Inside?" she asked loudly. "I've never thought of such a thing. Imagine somebody hiding in here without me knowing it. Please," she said, doing her best to sound gracious. "Don't just stand there on the stoop. Have a look around."

This log house, built so long ago, didn't have closets. She thought of several crannies where Ben and Demi could be, each of those places dangerous and somewhat exposed. Inside the armoire. Beneath beds. In corners. Behind doors. In shadows beneath the stairwell.

The three lawmen haphazardly searched these places while Rebecca kept vigil beside a cold stove, and thought, These men will find them. They aren't expecting a thing, but they'll find them.

One tramped upstairs and rifled through the armoire. Another went through the kitchen, bending low to peer under the table. Andy Rogers perused the nook beneath the stairwell. Rebecca glanced around the room, taking quick stock, wondering what Demi'd left around that would give them away.

The officers found nothing. They shook their heads, replaced their hats. Confidently they bade her good-bye.

"The coast is clear, ma'am," one of them said. "We were correct about this place. A search was unwarranted. But you learn after a while, it never hurts to check things out."

"No, it never does." She gripped the huge pine door, waiting to close it, holding herself up by sheer will. "I suppose you're right about that."

They set off down the path toward the driveway. She followed them out, waving. "I hope you find that criminal," she called.

"Me too," Andy called back. "And soon. It's been two nights since I've had a hot supper and a bath at home, not to mention sitting by the fire and playing dominoes with Leslie."

In the lee of the building, protected somewhat from the wind that had begun to whirl loose snow around their feet, the men paused at the outhouse. "What's this?" one of the troopers asked. "We didn't look through here." He reached out to take the handle, and Rebecca had a premonition.

"That's an outhouse, Jarvis. Haven't you seen one of those before?" Andy asked, laughing.

"Not in about a thousand years."

The man named Jarvis tried the door. It didn't open. "That's funny." He spread his feet to get better leverage on it and yanked.

Rebecca hurried out and stopped him. "What are you doing?" She laughed, wanting to make the fellow laugh at himself, too. "What do you want to see inside an old outhouse? There's nothing except a seat and a deep hole."

"I don't know, really," he answered. "Just thought I'd try the door. Guess it's force of habit. I've been opening doors all day."

"That one won't open."

"Oh?"

Ben had taken the lock off yesterday morning after Rebecca'd locked herself in. She knew that today it should have opened easily from the outside. The hardware to keep it shut lay somewhere cast aside in the barn, where he'd thrown it. "I keep that old place nailed up now," she lied. "I was always worrying somebody would come along and fall in." She watched their faces, hoped against hope they'd give up interest in the old, weather-bleached privy.

For one long moment, she forgot to breathe. Andy Rogers toed the ground where, mercifully, the wind had swept the snow and left nothing but an icy glaze. A thousand men might've trampled there, or no one.

Jarvis leaned up against the splintered door and chose that moment to pick his teeth with a thumbnail and look around. "Good God, but this is a desolate place."

The other state trooper poked his nose right at one rusty hinge and said, "My grandfather used to sell hinges down at the hardware store in Lyman when I was a kid. Haven't seen an old one like this since I was about five years old."

Rebecca waited . . . prayed . . . desperately uncertain whether her heart pummeled because she feared they would find him, or because she'd chosen to hide him in the first place. The wind picked up, fretting limbs high atop the cottonwoods. A cloud skittered across the sun.

Please, she prayed. *Please*. She forced herself to take one simple breath. Then another.

"Well." Andy clapped his hands. "Guess we've covered the place, then. We'd best get on down the mountain."

Jarvis straightened up and readjusted his belt. "Guess so."

They never gave the closed outhouse another glance. They sauntered to their vehicles, and she waved each of them off. Rebecca barely waited for them to disappear down the road before she ran back to the privy. "Ben! Demi! They're gone. It's safe."

She tried the door herself and it swung open. Demi came first, tottering out into the afternoon wind. Rebecca grabbed her elbows to stabilize her.

Ben came next, his head bent so she couldn't see his face. He said nothing.

"I thought they would *never* leave," Demi said blithely. "They were here forever, weren't they?"

"Yes, they were."

"I knew where you were," Rebecca said. "I knew it the minute he tried that door and it wouldn't open. Crazy thing is, I wouldn't've figured it out if you hadn't taken that lock off yesterday."

"Demi," Ben said quietly, "go inside. Now."

"But—"

"Go inside."

Demi walked into the house as the two looked after her, Rebecca suddenly wondering what it was he had to say. He looked so serious, and she didn't understand.

He took her shoulders, held her where she had to look up at him. "What did you protect us for? That was your chance to have them arrest me. That was your chance to finally get away."

"But Demi—"

"Did you do it for Demi, then? Did you do it because you thought they'd hurt her if they found her?"

"No. I wasn't just protecting Demi."

"You sent her in to warn me. Why?" His eyes were dark jade and serious, as if her reply meant everything to him.

She answered as honestly as she could. "Because I didn't want you to be led away in handcuffs from my house." Or maybe they would've shot him, but she tried not to think of that, as he studied her face. "I couldn't make myself . . . I didn't want . . . If something had . . ."

She tried those different ways to say it but couldn't. He kept staring down at her, hanging on to her, like a man who'd almost drowned, then had been rescued safely from the sea. Her eyes were damp when she looked up at him. Suddenly, incredibly, he wanted to wrap his arms around her.

"I was scared," she whispered. "I didn't know where they'd look for you."

"You lied to them." He said it again, as if he needed to say it aloud to believe it. "You lied to protect me."

"It was the only thing I knew to do," she said. Despite the strain his presence had put on her, she'd managed for the past twenty-four hours to keep her composure. She kept it even now as she said, "I didn't want to do to you what Wyllis had already done. Somehow it didn't matter what you'd been convicted of or what you were running from. I wanted to keep you from harm."

Something about his face had gone gentle. He looked handsome and lost, like a little boy who'd been afraid and had found reassurance. "Thank you," he said. "You don't know what you've saved."

She had to smile. "Your life, perhaps."

"No," he told her. "More than that. Much more than that." Ben wanted to say, *Maybe someday I'll be able to tell you*. But he didn't dare voice it. He'd be leaving tomorrow. And by the time he'd gotten Demi back to safety and finished what he'd escaped to do, he might well be dead. She'd never have any idea, any idea at all, what a treasure she'd given him.

He released her shoulders. And before she could draw away he took her face in his hands, holding her where he could search her eyes. Without asking anything in return, she'd given him parts of himself he hadn't even known to ask for. Dignity. Sanctuary. Reprieve. As the hours passed between them, he'd become intensely aware of her as a woman. Last night, when she'd rubbed him with salve—touching him more compassionately than he could remember Wyllis ever touching him—the effect to his body had been devastating. Today, when she'd trusted him enough to let him hide away, she'd gifted his soul the same way her fingers had soothed his body.

Like drifting water, he moved his hands down her temples, across her jawbones, feeling the curves and lines of her face, knowing her intimately in this caress, as if he might be blind. "It's been years," he told her. "Years."

She reached up and gripped his wrists with her own hands, hanging on to him as he touched her. "I know that. You said it last night."

"Are you afraid?"

"I'm always afraid. That's one reason I'm still feeding elk and living on this place. It's safe. The safest place I've ever known."

He did the one thing he'd been yearning to do. He released her face then and gathered her into his arms, pulling her tight against him, tighter than he'd ever held anybody. He wanted never to let her go. "Rebecca." He whispered her name with reverence, voicing it as he'd claim riches. Suddenly it was everything he could do to keep himself away from her.

A rock jutted from the snow beside them. As if sensing this was her last chance of escape, she loosened his arms and stepped back from him, climbed up on the rock so she was looking down. "I don't know what I should do anymore, Ben," she whispered. A great sadness came to her face, sadness born of land and history long disavowed, of the dark nights she'd spent alone. "Things that are right seem wrong. Things that are wrong seem right. You're making me think too much of what I want."

"Rebecca," he said again, and pressed his face to her chest, as if the only place he'd ever find safety was with her. She wrapped her arms around his head, turned delicately, and touched her cheek to his new-shorn hair. With the grace of native grasses that danced at water's edge, she sighed, a sigh that seemed to lift her and settle her against him all with one breath.

She raised her eyes to the sky and two ravens flew past low, wings beating the air with a rhythmic, airy *whoosh*. When she met her gaze with his, she knew what would happen; she knew he would kiss her. She waited, looking up, her heart reaching as high as she could see into the clouds, clouds as gray as the mourning doves that chortled around the haystacks, clouds heralding a storm, dangerous, lovely.

She gave herself over to him, slipping down off the rock and into his arms, their shapes fitting perfectly, their eyes meeting, giving credence to the joy of this, and to the peril. As she'd known he would, he pressed his mouth down upon hers. She welcomed him, rose on her toes, parted her lips for him. Their tongues danced together, moving with great freedom.

15

Angus Riley Sr., publisher, editor, and sole proprietor of the *Star Valley Independent* for forty years, brought out only one special edition of his weekly paper during his lifetime. That had been twenty-three years ago, the summer an entire family camping beside Caddisfly Creek had to be rescued after they'd climbed trees to get away from a black bear cub and then couldn't climb back down.

The Rileys had been newspaper people from the beginning, born and bred. Angus Sr. covered the event with impetus and skill, racing behind the Lincoln County Volunteer Fire Department trucks to reach the scene, jotting notes on his stenographer's pad, detailing the exact size, location, and wardrobe of each treed human, clicking shot after shot on black-and-white film with his dented Nikon camera.

On the front page of the *Independent* that infamous week, he'd run a photograph that he'd taken lying down, lens pointed directly up the trunk of the tree through the limbs and the pine needles, focusing on the soles of the little boy's PF Flyers, his dangling shoestrings and—above the shoes—his tearstained, terrified face.

When the boy remembered his father, seemed like it was always a memory of that week, of standing on tiptoe at three A.M. to see the desk while Angus Sr. banged out editorial comment on the old Royal typewriter and his mother jostled banner headlines on the page. He remembered the burned smell of the light tables, the nostril-flaring stench of developer, the warm, encompassing odor of the photos after they ran through the waxer and were ready to be stuck down.

Angus Sr. talked about it right up until his dying day. "You get a story big enough to do a special edition, by God, you'd better do one," the old man bellowed from his bed at St. John's, gripping his son's arm. "Move the pub day up, schedule an early run at the printer's, work twenty-five hours a day if need be. Work everybody else twenty-five hours a day, too." Except the only employees he had then, and the only employees Angus Jr. had now, were his wife, who came in every night to do page layouts and write headlines after supper, one high school boy who covered Star Valley basketball, and a revolving list of volunteers from the Lincoln County Extension Service who sent constant recipes outlining how to prepare everything from Star Valley cheese soup to tongue sliced thin and marinated in huckleberries.

First thing Friday morning, when he'd heard the announcement on Jackson's KSGT about an escaped convict abandoning his car in Star Valley, Angus Jr. knew he had a story to make his father proud. All weekend he'd sequestered himself on the phone, digging for information, making call after call. "Who is this man?" "What was he convicted of?" "When did the escape occur?" "Where do you think he's headed, and why?"

Each week, the *Independent* rolled off the presses in Afton by eight A.M. Wednesday, early enough for Postmaster Lowell Anderson to sort through the huge canvas bulk bags and get each issue on the mail delivery route by Wednesday noon. But during the wee hours of Monday as a storm began and the snow floated down in an ever-changing tapestry outside, Angus picked up the phone and dialed the printer.

"H-hello?" came the garbled, sleepy voice on the other end.

"Clear some press time for me, Herb," Angus announced merrily. "I'm bringing the newspaper in."

"What? You're bringing it in now?"

"I'm on my way. I'll be there in twenty minutes."

"Damn it, Angus. It's the middle of the night. I know what you've said about the special edition and all. But I didn't have the *Independent* scheduled to run until after three this afternoon."

"I've been putting these stories together for thirty-six hours straight. *Straight*. I haven't slept since Thursday night." He bent over the light table, the phone receiver still to his ear, and scrutinized the best front page he'd ever constructed. Damn, but his dad would've been proud if he could've seen this one.

"I'm a newspaperman, Herb," Angus beseeched him. "You work me in now and I come out in the mail a full two days earlier than I would've otherwise."

"Yeah, but if you come in when I've already scheduled you, you'll still go out on the newsstands this afternoon."

When Angus had gone to J school at University of Wyoming, his professor had said, "You know as well as I do that the best journalism comes out of weekly newspapers. You're the only ones I know who've got time for investigative reporting, time to get something thorough on paper and try your hand at good writing all in the same issue."

Angus had believed the words then as he believed them this instant, just as he knew this issue, this one early edition, would be the one to prove those words true. Even now, with the work on it practically finished, he felt rushed from behind, pushed by some part of himself that had been born when he'd first understood urgency. As they talked, he picked up the black opaqueing pen and went to work on a white dot he'd spied near the top right-hand corner of page four.

"This is the stuff everybody in Star Valley wants to read about," he told his printer confidently. "You know how many complaint calls I'll get if they have to spend a quarter to buy this thing off the newsstand tonight rather than wait for their paid subscription tomorrow?"

He'd started investigating as soon as the sun had

risen and Gladys Crates, dispatcher at the sheriff's office, sent the call out over the scanner Friday morning. With his father's old Nikon swinging from his neck, he'd backed down the ledge. Twice he'd slipped, sending rocks and dirt bouncing into the water.

The roof of the car protruded from the current, dividing the water as it frothed over the metal. Angus pointed the camera, focused it, began shooting different angles of the wreckage. "Anybody alive in there?" he'd asked the uniformed men on the bank.

"Nobody's been able to get out there to see."

"Not likely."

"We ain't positive."

"Sure doesn't look possible."

"If he was alive at first, he probably isn't now."

One of them said, "You want to get good shots, you might as well wait until the crane gets here. They're bringing one in from the Highway Department. We're gonna hoist the whole thing up out of the water. And if there's a body hanging out of the front window . . . well, that oughtta give you a picture."

Angus nodded, feeling somewhat queasy. "Will you show me where the car came down?"

The morning sun had climbed higher, leaving sparse shadows on the rocks. A state trooper named Jarvis led him across an array of boulders and pointed upward. He could see the great gash in the earth and the trail of uprooted sage. He kept taking pictures. In the end, after Angus got back to the office and developed them, the best one happened to be a close-up shot of a state trooper, his face savage with disappointment as the crane brought up the car that didn't contain a body. He tagged each photo with idents and started punching numbers into the telephone again.

At first no one from the prison would give him anything. The state office had sent terse press releases to Channel Two in Casper and the Cheyenne daily paper. That's all anyone intended to tell. But when he finally reached the office of Wyoming head warden Duane Shillinger, he got lucky. Shillinger answered his questions, even faxed him a detailed map of the state pen with a line drawn to highlight the man's escape route.

"Who is this man?" Angus asked everyone. "Is he hiding in Star Valley? What did he do? And why did he escape now?"

Angus began to piece together on paper the life of Ben Pershall. He'd been born in Hanna, had grown up in Hanna, had worked in Hanna. He was married, but his wife, a lady named Wyllis, had neither seen nor heard from him since his last letter. And, interestingly enough, the man's daughter—a girl named Demi—had been reported absent at school Friday. Wyllis told him in an even voice that the girl was home with the flu. He didn't know if that had significance or not. He wrote a story about it anyway. He wrote stories about everything Shillinger and Wyllis had told him. All of it. The Hanna mine. The explosion. His brother.

Tonight, as the snow gathered first in the needles of the evergreens and then began to coat the streets, the fences, the power lines, Angus knew he'd do anything to make the printer accept his press run this morning. "I'll pay extra if need be, Herb," he said, "but I think you ought to remember I've been a dedicated customer for a long time."

"I remember that." From his end of the line, Angus heard the man's bed groan as he sat on the edge of the mattress and tried to pull himself together. "Okay. Okay. You've won, Angus. Give me fifteen minutes to get dressed. I'll go over to the print shop and have the presses ready by the time you get there."

"Thank you, Herb. Thank you." Angus Riley Jr. kissed the receiver squarely before he slammed it down. "We did it!" he bellowed to no one, striking the air in victory with one clenched fist. He held each page to the light table, the banner headlines, the photos, the map of the state pen showing white against the black negative background. When he was finally satisfied, he loaded them into a big flat box and tucked them under his arm.

He didn't wait fifteen minutes. He'd be standing by the side of the print shop, tapping his foot in front of the door, before Herb ever got there.

Angus scraped a peephole in the ice on his windshield, climbed into his car, started off. The entire time he drove, he leaned over the steering wheel with his nose almost to the glass, doing his best to see the snow-covered road in the darkness. The entire time he drove, he grinned. By early afternoon everybody in Star Valley would know everything there was to know about the man who'd driven his car off the Oregon Trail, who might be armed and dangerous and hiding out nearby.

* * *

Ever since she'd been a little girl and had first moved to Timberline, Rebecca kept having the same dream. It had never frightened her, not even at the beginning when she'd been a child. Even then she'd awakened with a sense of anticipation, as if she'd failed to notice something in her own life she should've known about but had missed.

She dreamed she explored her grandmother's house, and every time, she discovered rooms she hadn't known were there. She found another kitchen, a huge loft with a set table ready for a meal, a beautiful arrangement of princess rooms with streaming curtains and a tiny sitting corner that opened off at the top of the stairs.

"Why didn't I notice this door before?" she always asked herself in the end. "Why didn't I realize this was mine?"

In the wee hours of Monday morning, she dreamed the dream again and woke up with her blood racing, the feeling strong on her heart that whatever she'd found anew and treasured was missing, that she'd searched all night through new rooms to find something and couldn't. She heard a dog bark in the distance. She heard coyotes begin baying their moonsong closer by. She lay without moving, drawn to the relentless darkness.

There were no stars tonight. The clouds she'd noticed at dusk had moved in to swallow the tops of the mountains, moving among the trees in wet billows, heavy, sinking smoke that obscured everything. She remembered Thom talking about a night like this when he'd first been writing, how he'd say

"Somebody's stolen the backdrop" every time the clouds moved in and the towering rocks disappeared.

She wouldn't sleep again for hours. She stood and walked to the window, poked her nose against the glass. Outside, it was too dark to see, but she could almost feel it in the heaviness and the silence. It was snowing. Hard.

Rebecca laid her head against the cold glass, letting it numb her skin. Snow wasn't a good sign for the animals, not this late after such a severe season. Despite Rebecca's constant haying, most of the elk had spent their strength and winter fat just surviving the bitter cold.

For the third night, she wasn't alone in her room. She heard Ben rise from his place on the floor, heard him cross toward her. "You ought to have slept on the sofa," she said, "or in a bed."

"I like it where I've been," he said. "I like staying close to you."

She held her breath until he touched her. She'd waited for it, longed for it, ever since he'd kissed her outside. He rested his hands lightly, possessively, on both of her shoulders. She leaned her head back, touched his hands with her hair, closed her eyes. "What's out the window?" he asked.

"I can't see anything," she said. "I'm just thinking."

"About what?"

"About you, Ben. You'll have to leave soon, won't you?"

"Yes. I'll go tomorrow," he told her. "I've waited as long as I possibly can."

"They've still got roadblocks out. It'll be dangerous."

"I know that."

"Because of this storm, you might be safer. It keeps going like this and you'll be able to pass right by them on foot and they'll never see you."

"You think this is as big a snow as all that?"

"I do," she said quietly. "I saw into the clouds this afternoon. Living up here alone, I've always been able to know. Seems like the only thing that ever happens around this place is weather."

"You're like nothing I've ever seen, Rebecca."

"No," she said quietly. "It isn't me. It's something more than me. Something that's taught me—" She turned to him then, each of her elbows clasped in the opposite palm, and waited for him to give her some gesture, some signal, that would invite her into his arms. He did, reaching for her, pulling her close. She burrowed her face upon his chest the way a pine marten would burrow. Neither of them spoke for the longest time; they had nothing to say. They'd both been alone and lost. Now, for a day, a night, this moment, they had each other.

"Want me to go down and turn on the porch light for the rest of the night?" she asked. "Then you'll be able to see the snow."

"Yes," he answered. "I'd like to be able to see everything you do."

She padded barefoot down the stairs, careful not to awaken Demi, and flicked on the old black switch beside the door. Muted yellow light made a pool along the side of the house, the snow-ridden cottonwood branches casting a woven mesh of shadow onto the ground. Huge snowflakes fell through the air, seemed to hang like a wayward trout hatch around the lamp. She joined him at the window.

"It *is* snowing," he whispered. "Look at that." Even this close to the house it was something, coming heavy, sheltering them behind it like a veil. In the meadow, where the elk huddled in restless circles, driving currents would encompass them, ice encrusting their backs.

"Stay here," Rebecca said. "I'll hide you forever in this house if need be. Don't go."

"Don't have any choice. There's somebody I've gotta find in Hanna," he told her. "No sense escaping if I don't do what I got out to do." And from what the scandalmongers had told him in the joint, he didn't have much time left. With every passing minute, a bad situation became more urgent.

"You've got to find somebody besides Wyllis?" Wyllis, who'd assuaged her own guilt by sending a child to do a woman's job. "Who else could there be?"

He didn't answer her. He couldn't.

"Ben, it's too dangerous for you to go back there. Hanna's only thirty-five miles from the state pen."

"They looked for me there three days ago. Maybe they won't be looking for me now."

"How can you be sure?"

"Being sure has nothing to do with it, Rebecca."

"But you could go to Canada. Or Mexico."

He gazed down at her for a long while, saying nothing. He wanted to ask, *Would you go with me, then?*

If I ran off to a different country, would you run off with me, too? Five years ago he'd gone inside a dark mine in Hanna and had set providence into motion, beginning an order of events that imprisoned him tighter than the bars he'd been locked behind. He and Rebecca had their own roads to traverse, their own destinies to heed. Oh, how Ben longed to disappear with her to some exotic place, to make these exquisite days last, to see her strolling unfettered along paths he'd known and could quietly share.

Ben saw her watching him, deciphering the play of emotion on his face, interested. He smiled, covering it lightly. "You and Demi. Always talking about Canada or Mexico."

"You don't—"

He kept her from speaking by putting his finger beneath her chin, lifting it, kissing her, as the yellow porch light shone upward through the snow and the cottonwood limbs. When he'd finished kissing her once, he pulled away and said quietly, "I've been locked away for so long. And when I'm with you, I know who I am."

Rebecca reached up, touched his face, willing this man's features, this one dark hour, to memory. "Is that enough for you, then?" she asked. "Just knowing who you are?"

For sleeping, she'd changed into a white flannel gown for the first time since he'd arrived, and she stood before the light in the window like an apparition or a cloud. The braid she'd worn still hung down her back, bedraggled, with half of her hair gone unfettered. Ben took hold of it, began to unweave it the way a man would unweave the forehard of a rope. "Yes," he said. "It is enough."

His words brought tears to her eyes. He stood before her, his very presence a promise, like the dream rooms she knew were there but had never entered. She waited while he set her hair free. He combed through it with his fingers, splaying it out and draping sections over her shoulders in much the same shape as the petals draped on a mountain fairybell. She whispered, "It is enough for me, too."

"Your hair's pretty this way," he said. "Beautiful."

"I don't take it down. It bothers me while I'm doing the feeding."

"All the same," Ben reminded her, "you don't live your life on the sleigh."

"It doesn't matter, though, about looking pretty," she said. "There's never been anyone to see."

The tears she'd begun earlier still came and—because he knew her, because he felt he'd always known her—he understood they were tears not of sadness or remoteness, but of joy. "I see," he said, "and I'll always remember."

When she'd dressed for bed, she'd fastened every one of the pearl buttons on the gown, clear up to the ruffled collar that enclosed the hollow of her throat. She took the collar now with both hands, moving the first button with two fingers, the way a lover would toy with a nipple. "And will you look at the rest of me, Ben?" she asked him, her voice soft, suddenly hoarse. "Will you look at the rest of me and tell me that's beautiful, too?"

She saw him swallow, saw his Adam's apple bob once up and then down. "Rebecca," he whispered, scarcely able to believe, after everything, she'd make herself this vulnerable to him. "Dear sweet heaven. If I look at you . . . if I touch you . . . I haven't been with a woman in half a decade."

And no other woman had given him as much as she had given him. No other woman had been able to salvage his soul.

"I've thought of that." She reached for the shirt he still wore, the shirt that had hung in Howdy's closet, dusty and unused for all these many years. She released the buttons, ran her hands from Ben's shoulders to his chest, savoring the life, the pummeling heart, the rise and fall of breath she felt beneath the aged textile. "I've thought of a great many things. Mostly, Ben, I've thought of this being the only chance for us, and perhaps the only chance for me." She stepped closer, offering up the little row of buttons to him.

"You'd trust me that much?"

She nodded, her loose hair moving with one motion, a great rippling wave. "I would. I do."

He laid his fist against the throbbing at her throat and began to follow her bidding, undoing the buttons. A tremor, as fast and delicate as the beat of a wing, passed over her. It came and went so quickly, it might have been only a shadow from the churning snow outside, reflected across her face and then gone. He gathered her in his arms, toted her across the room, laid her lightly, ever so carefully, upon her own bed. "Rebecca. I want to be gentle with you. So, so gentle."

"Life hasn't been gentle with me."

He sat on the edge of the bed beside her, brushed her hair away from her face the way he'd done when Demi'd been first in school. "There's all the more reason for me to be, isn't it?"

She reached up her own arms, held on to his neck. Confound these buttons! he thought as he started carefully at them again, fumbling with each tiny circlet as if he'd never undone one before. She lay, watching him with a smile, her limbs akimbo over the quilt where only two nights before he'd held a gun on her and she'd knelt and prayed.

The room smelled like her, woody and fresh like saxifrage, rich like horse sweat and leather, elusive like pine smoke. He could feel the heat of skin where his leg pressed against her own.

Ben had her halfway unfastened now, the ruffled flannel open to her navel, her bosoms still hidden within the bodice of the garment. Even so, the fullness of what he could not see cast a tantalizing shadow across her breastbone. He glanced up at her face and could see how her expression changed. She looked almost wanton with her hair so free, her face flushed and warm—relaxed and round as a child's face just awakened from sleep—brought to new life.

"You're beautiful, Rebecca. . . . Beautiful. . . . Beautiful," he told her over and over again while he undressed her. "Beautiful." "Beautiful." And because he said it, because he meant it, she felt the word, became what he said, felt embraced by her own hunger and the perfect desire in this man's eyes.

The muted light from the porch shone on her. She felt pure bright, golden, treasured. She beamed, saying nothing, accepting his words and the honor they gave her each time he offered them up, as praise and invocation were offered up in church. He kissed her beautiful soft face, her ears, her nose, the crooks of her arms, her breasts. He undressed, too, let her casually, carefully, run her fingers over his chest and count the number of mending blisters.

When it came time to make love to her, she clung to him. And their words, their very breaths, mingled like the currents of water that sang at creek's edge.

"I don't want to hurt you—"

"You won't."

"I'll stop. . . ."

"I'll never want you to stop."

"I love watching your face."

"Hold me. Just hold me, Ben. Please."

He entered her and she cried out with a short, breathless shout.

"Rebecca," he whispered. "My beautiful Rebecca." For he hadn't known she'd be a virgin, hadn't fathomed as they lay naked together upon the bed and the snow swirled ferociously outside the window, the full measure of the changes he'd seen in her face. She might have been engaged once, but no man had loved her bodily; no man had been here, within her, except for him.

"I'm the first, aren't I?"

She nodded up at him, beaming, her hair strewn out across the pillow. "You are."

Ben reveled in it, was astounded by it, felt washed clean by her innocence after all the guilt he'd seen. After everything she'd given him, even this, he knew he'd been able to give her something in return. He'd bestowed blessing, had been blessed. And when they finished it, while he lay against her with his chin on her shoulder as if someone had carved their bodies to lie this way, as if someone had fitted their elbows so they could cradle one another in safety, he couldn't keep himself from crying.

"What's this?" she asked, feeling his warm tears running onto her arms. "What's this?"

He hadn't cried since his father'd died, not since he'd been sitting on the stoop by the spittoon filled with dirt and lipstick-red geraniums and the Hanna policemen had parked halfway in the grass because there was no curb. Together, they'd walked toward him, their black-belted hips at his eye level. "Son," they'd said, "is your mother here? There's been an accident down at the mine."

"She's at Western Family. She works there."

"You'd better call and get her home. We need to talk to her."

In the bed, beneath the quilts, he pulled Rebecca against him, held her tighter just as she'd asked. "Ben? What is it?" Rebecca asked, wiping his tears away with her hand. When she'd finished, all that remained was a flat, salty sheen to dry.

He bundled her into his arms. "You make me see the goodness in things, Rebecca. It's you who makes me cry. To think I'd run across all this, to think I'd find you in a place so hidden." The room smelled different now, after the intermingling of his body with hers, like musk and heat and magic. "If I came back to get you someday, would you come with me?" he asked. "If I survived everything and then ran off to a different country, would you leave this place and run off with me, too?"

She raised herself above him with her elbows. She put her lips to the top of his head, held them there against the stubble of his hair for the longest time, her eyes closed. "This place," she told him, "is everything I am."

He searched her face, knowing already he'd make love to her all night long. Their time together now had to last a lifetime. "Did you stop to think that everything you are, Rebecca, might be more than you give credence to? That you could go and come from it? That you might not have to stay at Timberline because Timberline stays with you?"

She studied his eyes, his mouth, his proud chin. Being with Ben like this for the first time, feeling beautiful, needed, and touched, she could almost think it, could almost imagine such a thing might be possible. In this man's arms, beneath his body, she'd discovered another portion of herself. How many parts can a person have? she wondered. How deep could someone go, how wide, how far?

As if to show her, as if she never needed to ask such a question because he already knew, Ben pulled her down, kissed her, ran his hands elegantly again over her skin, and reassured her.

16

The first thing Monday morning, Thomas Tobias Woodburn walked into the law offices of Schuster Reid and Cornell and settled himself upon the worn couch to wait. He must've crossed, uncrossed, his feet at least a dozen times as the minutes passed. Each time he did, the receptionist, who was doing her work upon a sound wooden desk shoved up against one wall, glanced over at him and smiled weakly.

"He's always a few minutes late on Monday mornings," she told him finally. "I never make appointments for him first thing. He only does this to himself. You must've called him on Saturday."

"I did," Thom told her. "I had a matter that couldn't wait. I would've been here Saturday if you'd been here to prepare the papers."

"Another matter that can't wait." She smiled again, not belittling him, just letting him know she understood. "We have practically a hundred of them every week."

A full ten minutes later, the door shoved open and in walked a rather disarrayed lawyer, his suit coat flying open, his tie pointing to one side, his Styrofoam cup of coffee jostling almost to the edge every time he tried to reposition his papers. The receptionist stood, obviously glad to see him. "Timothy!" she said. "Your client's been—"

"Oh, good morning." He waved them both back onto their seats. "I'll be with you as soon as I get settled, Mr. . . . Mr. . . ." He frowned. "I didn't get your name over the phone, did I?"

"No, you didn't. I wouldn't give it until I'd met you. I have to make certain this meeting is confidential."

Timothy Schuster's curiosity got the best of him. "Come on back with me, then." He jiggled his coffee cup yet again. "We shouldn't make him wait any longer, Constance, should we?" He grinned at her as if she'd been in on it all along. "We'd best get started right away." Once he'd shut the door behind them, the young lawyer became all business, pulling out a legal pad and pen. "Why don't we begin immediately?"

Thom leaned forward onto the cluttered desk, doing his best to read the man's eyes for earnestness, dependability. Timothy Schuster had his own set of photographs lining his shelves, his own family, a very pretty blond wife and two tousle-haired children that looked close enough in age and appearance to be twins. "Promise me first," he instructed the lawyer. "Promise me none of this goes anywhere beyond this room. Not to the press. Not to the buddies you play golf with on Sundays. Not to your wife's relatives who might discuss it with their friends over tea."

"This sounds serious."

"It is. More serious than you'd think. I'd've gone to a better-known celebrity lawyer, except—" He stopped himself on that one. *Except ours is on retainer and all the bills are charged and paid under Jillian's name. He wouldn't represent me against her.*

"You'd better let me in on this," he said. "You have my solemn vow. Constance will be the only one who sees it outside my office. She'll have to draw everything up."

"I want Constance to promise, too."

"I can vouch for her, Mr. . . ."

Here, Thom decided he'd gone long enough making the man wait at loose ends. He'd decided to go forward with this. He liked the looks of this man's family, of this man's children. He would sympathize. "Woodburn. My name is Thom Woodburn."

The fellow examined his face through narrowed eyes. "You look familiar. Your name sounds familiar."

"My wife is Jillian Dobbs."

Of course, as with everyone else, it was Jillian who jogged his memory. "Of course. Of course! I remember you from the cover of *People* magazine with her. Everyone said it was a marriage that would—" He stopped. He'd been about to say "a marriage built on a solid foundation, one that would last." He thought better of bringing that up right now. "Just why is it you've come, Mr. Dobbs?"

"Mr. Woodburn."

"Ah, yes. Mr. Woodburn." He made the first note on his pad.

"I want to file a lawsuit against my wife."

Thom's pronouncement didn't seem to faze him much. "Very well. A lawsuit for divorce?"

"No," Thom replied. "A lawsuit for the life of our child."

"I don't believe I understand."

"She is pregnant, Mr. Schuster. She doesn't want to be pregnant because it will cost her a role on Broadway. And I'm not willing to give up our child because she believes only in the importance of the performance. I'm sure you'll see that is why time is of the utmost importance. I've got to file this thing, have it drawn up legally and served on her before she has a chance to do anything drastic."

Timothy Schuster studied him long and hard. "Have you spoken with anyone else about this? Has anyone anywhere given you the idea that something like this might work?"

"No. But I'm the father of the baby. And I have my own legal rights." Suddenly, at the man's expression, Thom's blood ran cold. "Don't I?"

"No father has ever won litigation of this sort, Mr. . . ." He glanced at the pad on his desk. "Mr. Woodburn. Indeed, California is the only state in the Union where it's ever even been questioned. Your best chance is to hit her with litigation that will tie things up in court until she's well into her second trimester. But that's not a guarantee. They'll rule in her favor. You will have spent plenty of money, made a media spectacle of yourself, and she could still go somewhere and do away with the fetus, even at that late date. It might buy you some time to make her change her mind, but it's a grueling option."

Thom stared into the eyes of the man across the desk, trying to read what lay behind those poker-player eyes. He'd long wondered whether inscrutability was born within lawyers or whether it was a widespread, learned trait. "It's the only choice I have, isn't it?" He'd do anything, everything, to save the baby. His marriage wasn't at issue anymore. For now he knew where Jillian's priorities lay. "Given all these things, do you feel capable of taking me on, Mr. Schuster?"

"Of course I do. I'd be crazy not to. I'll make a fortune off of you and your wife, and I'll make a name for myself, besides."

"I want you to put everything together today." He amended that. "This morning." He amended again. "Now."

"That can certainly be arranged." Timothy Schuster spoke without the merest trace of a smile upon his face. "But I'm an L.A. lawyer. You'll have to secure me with a nice retainer."

"Ah, yes. That isn't a problem. How much?" He drew the checkbook from his pocket and made ready. Schuster named his figure, a steep one, perhaps steeper because he knew his client to be a man of means.

"You do your job, it'll be worth every penny of this," Thom said as he scribbled his signature and extracted the check from its book with a great rending. The lawyer punched a button on his telephone console and summoned Constance. She came in immediately.

"Is there anything you're working on that can't wait until tomorrow?"

"Yeah." She gave an abrupt, amused laugh. "All of it."

"Tell me something. If you started on a document this moment, could you have it ready to go by noon?"

"That depends. I can have it done in fifteen minutes if we've got a master filed on the computer."

"We don't have a master on this one. We've never done anything—" He stopped, obviously not wanting to explain it to her while Thom sat twiddling his thumbs on the chair, observing. "We have a new project, one that must be done"—and here he quoted his client, his half-closed eyes still revealing nothing—"today. This morning. Now." The lawyer handed her his notes and marked one page in a huge bound book that contained a monstrous array of legal briefs. "Get started as best as you can. I'll be out to guide you further as soon as Mr. Woodburn has gone. Put the phone machine on. You can't spare time for interruptions."

"Yes, sir."

The lawyer turned back to his client once the massive book and the directed secretary were out of the way. "Noon, then. We'll be ready to serve Jillian Dobbs the papers by noon. You want me to courier them over?"

"I want you to deliver them yourself. You've got to make certain she gets them."

"Of course."

For the next three hours, Thom drove in a pointless circuit around Bel-Air, willing the clock to speed up or slow down, anything, anything that would take an edge off the passage of these punishing hours of morning. A man had to do what he had to do. If that didn't work, he had to try something else. Try, and try again. Endure, and keep trying.

To the west, thunderheads boiled up over the ocean. He knew they'd move inland soon, full of fury and pounding rain.

He didn't know where he would sleep tonight. For this moment, because he'd done what he had to do, that much didn't seem to matter. He felt ensconced inside his own bravery. Behind the tinted glass of the Acura, Thom skirted the town on side roads, trying to lose himself by looking into lawns and driveways and lace-curtained windows of other families, the vestiges of their encouraging, gentle lives giving him simple hope for his own.

But was anything the way it looked to be on the outside anymore? Thom didn't think so.

A quarter past noon, he parked in front of a convenience store not a mile from the house. Timothy Schuster pulled up three minutes later. "I've got the papers right here," he said, handing Thomas a thick, folded bundle. "You'll need to look them over and sign them."

They climbed onto the front seat of Schuster's sedan, and as Thom read everything carefully, each man kept his own solemn silence, each recognizing the other's presence, each wrapped in his own dark uneasiness. Presently Thom lay the document in his lap. "This looks to be in good order to me."

"Here's a pen. You'll need to sign all those places."

The lawyer pointed to several pages that he'd marked with a slapdash *X*. Thom took it in hand and scribbled his signature, once, twice, three times. Thomas Tobias Woodburn. His shoulders slumped more each time he completed his name, as if each time he signed, he bore more weight.

"You'll need to date those, too." Schuster pointed to yet another blank that needed filling.

Thomas refolded the papers gravely, handed them across the front seat of the car. Timothy Schuster shoved them inside an official embossed envelope and sealed the flap. "Schuster Reid and Cornell, Attorneys-at-Law," the envelope read. "You want to go with me to deliver these?" Schuster asked.

"I'd planned on it." He wanted to be there to soften the blow to Jillian. He knew what this would do to her. These papers, this lawyer he'd hired, would cost her Charmaine. "We'd best go on to the house and get this over with."

Each man drove his own car. Schuster followed Thom. They steered onto the impressive circular driveway and parked, one behind another, beside

Jillian's BMW. Thom sat a moment, his hands idle on the wheel, before he cut the ignition. He joined Timothy Schuster and they walked up the front stone steps together, like two friends.

Schuster rang the bell. And rang it again. For the longest time, no one answered.

They looked at each other. "Hello?" Thom called out, suddenly realizing how absurd it seemed to be waiting at the front door of his own house. He pulled a key out of his pocket and unlocked the front door. "Come on in, Schuster." He stepped inside. "Jillian?"

Nobody answered. The back sliding door stood open to the immense lawn and then, a ways off, the ocean. The curtains drifted inward, flapping recklessly on the brink of the incoming thunder shower. Outside, the sea's rhythmic murmur had become a roar.

"Jillian?" he called again, over the sound of the water.

No answer.

It began to sink in that something must be wrong, with Jillian's car parked out front and the house standing wide open. Thom went to the doorway, with Schuster behind him, hoping he'd see his wife's silhouette against the seething clouds and the water to the west. Perhaps she'd gone to walk along their section of private beach, to enjoy the pounding water as it came on with a tumult, then retreated, plating the sand with silver. She loved the power of an incoming storm. She'd told him once that she'd bought the house after viewing it on a day such as this.

"She's probably out walking. I'll need time to find her."

The lawyer stood aside, slapping the fat envelope against his hand. Thomas shut the sliding door with a mighty *thwack* and silence overtook the house. From far off, down the hall past Thom's study, they heard footsteps.

"There you are. You've come back. But Jillian isn't here." Grayson Hanks poked his hands into his pockets and jiggled things, as if he were much at home here, as if it were Thom who was the guest. "She tried to find you this morning, but you'd gone out early and hadn't told her where. She called me instead."

"Called you for *what?*"

"To drive her to the airport."

"The airport?" He cast a quick, suspicious glance at his wife's publicist.

"Yes." Grayson smiled in answer to the suspicion, a cruel smile that hinted of wiliness. "She's made a trip."

"What kind of trip?"

"A short getaway. To Mexico."

"Mexico?"

"She's at a clinic in Acapulco. It's always best for a woman as well-known as Jillian to leave the country for this procedure. We wouldn't want any adverse publicity, you know, with the way both of you are in the spotlight."

Thomas's very breath left his body. He felt as if someone had belted him in the lungs. He squeezed his hands together until a sharp pain lanced through one of them. It was everything he could do just to get out the next question. "A clinic?"

"Yes," Grayson said with satisfaction. "She's scheduled for an abortion this afternoon."

Behind Thom, the neighborhood, the winding streets and sun-dappled sidewalks, sprawled in hideous perfection. A lawn mower droned. The sky swam. For long moments he couldn't get his bearings.

When words came, they came hard and foul. "You bastard." He wanted to fly with his fists. He wanted to belt Grayson Hanks with all the force he could muster. But even that, even a fierce blow, wouldn't assuage the helplessness that overwhelmed him. "You let her do it. You *encouraged* her to do it."

"Yes, I did, Thom. And you didn't."

"You have no right to meddle in our lives. You have no right to encourage Jillian to do anything with my baby."

"Jillian pays me for my meddling."

"You bastard," he said again.

Timothy Schuster switched his weight from one foot to the other. "Woodburn. If you'll calm down—"

"Good God, man. She's killing my baby. She could be doing it now, while we're standing here . . . in Mexico, where no one can stop her."

"That's the key, isn't it? No one can stop her, Thom." Grayson smiled just enough to darken the shallow lines on each side of his mouth. "I don't know why you're so upset about an abortion, after all. Women do it all the time. How do you know it's your baby, anyway?"

"She's my wife," Thom stated logically, zealously. "Who else's baby could it be?"

At the expression of pleasure on Grayson Hanks's face, even Timothy Schuster realized Thom had made a grave mistake in leading to this. Grayson said, "How do you know the baby isn't mine? It could be, you know."

Dead silence. Dead hatred. Neighbors' children playing, their voices lilting, a musical promise in the breeze.

"Get out of my house, Grayson." If the lawyer hadn't been standing there, a bundle of legal papers in his hand, Thom might've throttled Grayson Hanks. He might've wrapped his hands around the man's neck and tightened, tightened, squeezed out all the hate and helplessness that held his own heart in a deadly vise. "I don't want to see you again. Ever."

"You can't fire me, you know," Grayson said evilly. "I'm Jillian's employee. Not yours."

As the man walked away triumphantly, the truth of his words hammered into Thom. Everything here was Jillian's. Jillian's house. Jillian's publicist. Jillian's career. Dear, sweet heaven, maybe the Oscar he'd brought home had come to him because he was Jillian's, too.

Timothy Schuster stood behind him, waiting, the thick envelope poking up out of his suit pocket, a document that taunted him now, papers with no jurisdiction in Mexico, a summons too late served. The lawyer cleared his throat as if to remind Thomas Woodburn he was present, concerned.

Thom turned in the hallway of the huge, empty house. He stared at the man as if he'd never seen him before.

"Will you fly to Mexico?" the lawyer asked. "Are you going after her?"

It was the most ridiculous question anyone had ever asked him. "Why would I want to go after her?" *Why would I want to see her empty body?*

Schuster handed him the papers. "You've paid for these. Might as well take them and file them away."

"A father has no rights, does he? No rights at all."

"Not where a woman's choice is concerned. And certainly not in Mexico, where chances are you'll be locked up for a decade for starting a street brawl, which it looks to me like you're in the mood to do."

As is common in a man suffering from shock, Thom's mind traveled in a hundred different directions, none of them a direction that he wanted to go. "She didn't come with me to Wyoming when I wanted her to. I wanted to marry her up at Timberline, Schuster. I wanted her to make friends with Rebecca. I wanted her to love that place the way I do."

"What place? What are you talking about?"

"Oh, she had plans for it at first. She wanted to wear an antique dress and stand barefoot on the old porch with the elk in the background. She wanted to give the press people from *Women's Wear Daily* and *People* and the *National Enquirer* all a ride on the sleigh. But once she found out we couldn't build a second home on it and have people from Hollywood fly in for dinner, she never wanted to go."

Schuster shrugged. "It's your own fault. You wanted her . . . this." He included the entire house in one sweeping gesture. "Sounds like she's been leading you every step of the way."

"I don't like to be led."

"I wouldn't, either."

"She let herself get pregnant in the first place. Why did she do that?"

"Maybe to prove a point. Maybe it was an accident. Maybe she just likes the way you write and she wanted to make certain she stayed on your good side so she could star in your next screenplay. Who knows? Who cares? Get on with your life, buddy. That's the only thing I can think of in all this that will matter."

This man called him "buddy." This man he'd paid a retainer to just this morning now treated him like an old friend. Well, he didn't want any friends in this place. He didn't want to have any. Certainly not some two-bit lawyer whose name he'd picked out in desperation from the phone book.

"I'm here to help," Schuster said. "I'll start Constance on the divorce papers this afternoon if that's what you want. After all this, I could give you a ten percent discount on the fee. Of course, we can't serve papers until she gets home—"

The sentence echoed in his head. *Until she gets home*. This was Jillian's home, her landscape. It would never belong to him. What's more, he didn't want it.

"You may leave now," he told the lawyer. "Drive out of this driveway without looking back. Forget that you ever knew my name."

"But—"

"I have other plans. I won't be needing your services any longer."

He needed a place to heal. He needed a place to hide inside himself a while, to grieve the child who had not been born. Thom knew, as an osprey knows when it soars to the same aerie summer after summer, where his soul needed to travel to mend. He waited in silence, staring at the ceiling, until he heard Schuster's car pull out of the driveway. He picked up the phone and dialed the airline. He knew the number by heart.

"I want to book a flight for LAX to Jackson Hole, Wyoming," he said. "Date of travel?" He stopped to think, couldn't remember, had absolutely no idea what date was today. "How about now?" He laughed at himself for having to stop and think about it. "Today. On the next flight out."

Thom answered all the reservationist's questions easily now, becoming more and more certain as the conversation moved on. "No. Not round trip. Only one way. First-class, coach, whatever you have. Just get me a seat on the plane."

"There's a storm system over the mountains, sir," the woman warned him. "It started snowing across the northern Rockies about midnight. All flights through Salt Lake City are being delayed. I can't guarantee what's happening in Wyoming. That airport's usually one of the first to close down when there's a lack of visibility."

As she'd been talking, he'd opened his briefcase and had begun piling things in. The first five pages to his new screenplay. A picture of Howdy he'd kept on his desk, Howdy giving him a piggyback ride the first day he and Rebecca had arrived at Timberline.

"I don't care about the visibility. I've been flying in and out of Jackson Hole since I was a little kid."

"It's only fair to warn you. I can get you on the flight, sir. But there's no guarantee that you won't be rerouted."

After he got off the phone, he'd pack a few clothes in a suitcase. But now Thom reached for the golden statuette waiting on the mantel beside his desk. He wrapped it in the only thing he could find, discarded manuscript pages he'd dug from the trash. He situated the Academy Award carefully so it wouldn't slide around when he carried it. He closed the briefcase lid, turned it sideways, felt its pleasing heaviness. "I'll chance it. I've been rerouted long enough," he said, totally serious. "The devil take the weather. A little snow never hurt anybody. I'm going to fly home."

George Peart's barber shop was always busy on Mondays. Folks stopped by to get the week started out right, to get their mustaches trimmed or "their ears lowered," George always said, before the routine of the next five working days settled in. Of course most of the ranchers and dairymen in this valley didn't work five days a week. They worked a full seven.

Although the men waiting on red plastic chairs numbered as many as usual, the snowstorm outside left the ranchers and dairymen conspicuously absent.

A storm of this magnitude, this wet, this heavy, this late, wreaked havoc with Star Valley livestock. For those with cows who'd already dropped their calves, the situation became perilous to both life and profit at the bank. A newly born calf would freeze to death where it lay if someone didn't come along and carry it to safety. And unless a fellow knew the lay of the land where he searched for calves, chances were he'd get disoriented and frozen to death, too.

Winter in Star Valley wasn't something to be reckoned with. Worst thing a man could do would be to underestimate the power or the treachery of the season, to predict its late arrival or its early demise. This high in the mountains, cold wasn't gone until it was gone. And it always came back again before anybody was ready.

"After a while, these state agencies get like a dog chasing after its own tail," Lester Burgess commented from where he sat in the row, rattling the pages of last week's *Independent*. "This article came out last Wednesday, I've read it three times already, and every time I have to sit around and wait somewhere and read it again, it still makes me mad."

"I'm the same way." Judd Stanford spoke even though George Peart was spinning him around on the barber's chair. He bent his chin halfway down so the barber could burnish his neck with his round, fluffy brush and send loose hairs flying. "I always thumb through it again about this time each week, thinking I'll find something new. Never do, though. Always end up reading the same stories three or four times."

"This issue oughtta be a good one to read when it hits the streets on Wednesday." George gestured with his comb for the next patron in line. He noticed when Ben Mitchum rose to take his turn that Judd Stanford got his chair and sat down again. The more chairs he bought and lined along the front window, the more people stayed. "There'll be stories about that fugitive they tracked all the way to Star Valley."

"Haven't you heard? Angus Riley is coming out with a special edition this weekend. He's been at his office or out getting pictures almost nonstop since they found the car. Paper oughtta be delivered any minute. Carol Mortimer said she heard Angus starting up his car and driving to the printer early, before the sun was even up."

"In this weather?"

Outside, the snow came so hard that it was impossible to see where the street ended and the sky began. The door swung open and everyone glanced up in anticipation, wanting to see who'd be next to come in and make some angry comment about the weather. They all grew quiet at the same time, the very moment they saw his face. For this was not a man they recognized, not one with whom they could call out haughty greetings or make casual jokes. Most of them turned, hiding their discomfiture, pressing their backs flat against the plastic chairs.

He wore the same ill-fitting suit he'd worn yesterday. He stood in the doorway, wet snow pelting in from behind him, eyeing them all one by one and looking at ease. That, in turn, made them all the more uncomfortable, made them feel like the strangers in this place instead of him.

Finally Vern Chappell spoke up, letting them all in on what he knew. "Aren't you the fellow who visited at the Baptist church yesterday?"

He didn't answer Vern. Instead he crossed the room and strolled along the line of chairs the way a car cruises a full parking lot, as if—magically—one might appear open for him.

Judd Stanford jumped up. "Here." Even Judd, the only lawyer in Lincoln County, wasn't wearing a suit in weather like this. He gestured toward the plastic seat that still held the molded impression of his rear. "You take my place. I've already gotten my hair cut. I ought to get back to work."

He kept walking, as if he hadn't seen Judd jump, hadn't heard him speak. He walked all the way down the line once, surveying them. Then he walked back. Even George Peart watched the show, clippers poised above Ben Mitchum's nape. He made a cut when he was shook up like this and he could very well end up with somebody's skin. He'd certainly done it before.

"Who are you?" George asked finally. "What do you want with us?"

As if the barber himself had at last come up with a question this man liked, he poked one wide hand into his pocket. "At church yesterday, they let me know that I could come here this morning and find myself an entire gathering of experts." He pulled a leather wallet out of his back pocket, extracted a good number of crisp twenty-dollar bills, fanned them out to make certain everybody with the notion could count them. "Anybody in this place willing to give up his place in line to show me around this godforsaken valley?"

Silence. They were all too busy counting twenty-dollar bills.

"I need to be shown several places," he explained, knowing he had commanded their full attention and perhaps a bit of their respect at last. Respect could be easily bought, he'd learned. "I'd like a tour of the headwaters of Caddisfly Creek so I can examine the area where the man drove his car off the trail. I'd also like someone with knowledge of backcountry roads and an acceptable car to drive me to Rebecca Woodburn's place."

He smiled sweetly, doing his best to make himself more palatable to them. He'd found out yesterday afternoon that he did, indeed, need one of them for guidance. He'd stopped by Shervin's Conoco and had asked for directions, thinking he'd be able to find the place on his own. The fellow who'd sold him his gas had been cordial enough, and not until the attendant began to draw a detailed map of the area did he realize how truly complicated this was going to be.

The instructions he'd been given were like the instructions everyone in this county seemed inclined to give. "Take the second dirt road after the lone tree." This in the midst of a national forest, where no tree stood alone. "After you pass the osprey nest and the brown barn on the left, cross the second cattleguard and go right when the road veers up the hill."

This when the road seemed to spread out in four different courses, all of them heading uphill. "Take the one-lane bridge next to the pond that's shaped like a bear claw." He'd never before, to be totally honest, considered the shape of a bear claw. Or, his favorite: "You'll see a herd of mule deer on your left. Turn right."

Not three miles out of town, he'd already become hopelessly lost. The snow in the rutted roads grew deeper as he climbed higher. He could see how a car could get stuck up here and its driver not discovered until days later. He could see how a man could stay lost forever in this wilderness, which made him all the more certain, even as he'd decided to turn around, that he had to come back, that his intuition was right, that even though he was lost, he was headed in the right direction.

"And just when"—Lester Burgess folded the old issue of the newspaper and laid it beside him carefully—"did you intend for this grand tour of Lincoln County to take place?"

"Right now."

They met his answer with stunned silence.

"Today," he said, as if to clarify.

"You've gotta be nuts," Vern Chappell said. "Have you looked outside lately? It's snowing so hard you can't see your hand in front of your face."

"It's important that I look around up there as soon as possible."

"No matter how much money you pay, you won't find anybody stupid enough to take you up there today, mister." In an obvious move of dismissal, Charlie Egan reached over and helped himself to the Tootsie Rolls George kept in a basket by the door. He unwrapped three, tossed the wrappers into an ashtray, and poked them all into his mouth at once. "You have no idea how treacherous it is that high when it's blizzarding like this. You could die up there and nobody'd find your body until the June thaw."

"This is the worst storm we've had since the spring of forty-one," Frank Weatherby began again. "That's the year Francis Beery's bull knocked down the gate over at Happersett's."

Margaret Cox, her huge leather mail satchel soaked with snow, shoved in through the door. The bell tinkled merrily, an odd counterpoint to the raging outside. "Hallooo," she called to all of them. "I've been wondering where everybody was this morning. I should've figured it out a full hour ago. Everybody's here getting their hair cut and gossiping about the storm."

"Come on in, Margaret, and sit a spell," George said, thankful beyond measure to have someone else enter, someone who'd take the attention from this idiotic stranger who thought human life on a day like today was worth nothing more than a few twenties waggled under someone's nose. "Judd Stanford's left you a seat. I'll have a fresh pot of coffee in just a minute. You look like you could use some warming up."

"I could use it, George, but I can't stay," she said. "I've got newspapers to deliver. Angus worked all weekend straight and got his special edition of the *Independent* out this morning, just like he's always wanted."

"He did?"

"Let's see."

"Angus is some newspaperman, to get an issue out so fast."

Frank Weatherby said, "There hasn't been a special edition of the paper since Angus Sr. came out with one the summer that all those Texans got treed by a bear cub."

Ben Mitchum said, "Take one out and give us a look at it, Margaret."

"I've got George's copy right here." She tromped the snow off her boots and started digging in her wet satchel, thumbing through the assortment of catalogs and letters so she could show them all. "Here it is."

She opened the special edition of the *Star Valley Independent*, shook it open proudly for all to see. They gathered around her, anxious to inspect the front page, anxious to find answers to the questions they'd been asking each other for days. There the facts stood for them to see, the escape route, the devious plotting, the photos, the headlines.

What they saw made them gasp, fall silent.

"Let me see that," the stranger said, yanking it out of their hands. He read swiftly, his eyes darting back and forth across the page. He scanned it all, every story, as if he looked for something, anything, he didn't already know. The others in George Peart's barber shop waited, not speaking, too stunned to care.

"I'm on my way to take a copy up to Rebecca Woodburn," Margaret told them. "Anybody want to send anything up with me when I go?"

"You shouldn't go up there today," George said quietly, his zest gone, the warning only a vague echo of what it had been minutes before. He'd had no idea, no idea until he'd read it in the paper, that the escaped convict running loose in Lincoln County had done something so awful. "That road's too bad, Margaret. Nobody but you would be crazy enough to try it."

"I know what I'm doing, don't I?" she insisted. "Angus wants her to have her issue of the paper. I'm the mail lady, remember? Neither sleet nor snow nor threat of whatever can stop the U.S. mail from getting through."

"That's a bureaucrat from Washington talking, not somebody who has to take his life in his hands and climb mountains to get to mailboxes."

"My tires have chains. Another hour or two and the road'll be drifted too deep for anybody to get in. *Somebody's* got to get up there and check on that poor girl every once in a while. I don't try to do this now, George, it might be another week before I *can.*"

"I'm going with you," the stranger informed her, handing the paper over to George with no further ado. He'd found his chance at last. After all the cajoling, this mail lady had waltzed in off the snow-frosted streets and offered him the opportunity he'd been waiting for. "We'll be better off up there if we're together, won't we?"

Margaret didn't answer his question. Instead she turned to everybody in the barber shop and posed one of her own. "Say, who is this guy? Isn't he the fellow who was asking all the questions yesterday at church?"

But nobody answered her. They were too busy reading the front page of the *Independent*, too busy absorbing the dire tale and thinking proudly how close they all had come to this one, perilous crime.

FUGITIVE PASSES THROUGH STAR VALLEY, Angus's massive headline read. "Convict Serving Life for Murdering His Own Brother."

17

By early afternoon, huge amounts of wind and a coating of wet snow had brought down the power lines that ran north from Afton. Most people in Star Valley took the outage in stride, adding more firewood to their stoves, readying candles in case the lights didn't come back on before supper.

At Timberline, when the lights flickered and went out, Rebecca smiled as if she'd expected this all along. "I knew there was some reason we checked that light plant yesterday, Demi. The generator's ready to go. We'll get out there and start it up before the sun goes down."

Ben said quietly, "We aren't going to be here when the sun goes down."

"Dad—"

He took his daughter's hand. "We don't have any time left, Demi," he said, hating the tears he saw filling her eyes and spilling onto her cheeks, hating himself for being hard on the outside when he wanted to weep, too. "We help Rebecca get hay out for the elk today and we leave this afternoon."

"Once the feeding's done, we'll go out with a shovel and try to dig out the truck," Rebecca said. "I want you to take the truck, Ben. I don't want you to try it on foot in weather like this."

"You said yourself that this weather would help us." She'd given him a bowl of assorted nuts, and he ate them, finding solace in the simple act of cracking their shells open with his strong fingers, laying the hulls by. "You said we could walk right past somebody and they wouldn't see us."

"Ben. You could freeze to death out there. Both of you. It's too dangerous."

"No. I won't risk taking the truck. I won't risk anyone catching us in it and tying us to you. That's dangerous, too."

"When I think of all the times I begged you to go—" She choked on the words, couldn't say them, couldn't fathom that two days ago she'd been afraid for her very life. She reached her arms out to Demi and they held on to each other, scared again for different reasons.

"There's elk in the middle of a bad snowstorm out there," he said quietly. "We should get started."

"Of course we should," she said somberly, feeling a horrible sense of inevitability about the elk herd, about Ben. "But I'm afraid of what we're going to find. We'll be able to save more of the young ones because you're here."

Ben bent to tie his shoes, the same institution pair he'd worn since he'd arrived, the black toes curled and cracked, white water lines on the leather from snow. She watched his able hands yank the strings tight across his instep and work to form a bow. She laid her fingers against his arm. "Stop. Don't wear those, Ben. You'll need something better. For the storm. For your travel."

"Dad," Demi said again, "we don't have to go, do we? We could stay here. We'd be safe."

"We can't, Demi. There's something that must be done, if only I get to Hanna in time. I've got—" He stopped, panicking suddenly when he realized he'd lost track of the day. "I've been out since Thursday night. What is today? Monday?"

Rebecca nodded, studying his face. "What is it you have to do?" And as she asked it, the realization took full form in her mind. She suddenly knew the significance of what he'd been telling her. "That's why you escaped from jail, isn't it? To stop this . . . this . . . *whatever* in Hanna."

He combed one hand through his windlestraw hair and stared straight up at the pine knots on the ceiling, his silence affirmation enough. She waited, already certain of his answer. But when he turned his eyes back to her and told her, "Yes—that's it exactly," those eyes were full of light and fire. It struck her that they had grown brighter, more alive and resilient, with each passing day of his freedom.

Perhaps that, she thought, perhaps that is what I've given him.

"I'll get you Howdy's warmest things. I've still got his boots. You learn early on in this part of the country never to get rid of a good pair of boots." She turned to Demi. "You can have a coat and hat and mittens of mine."

Rebecca left and came back minutes later toting an armful of things, a wool hat and ragg mittens for Demi and Howdy's old pac boots for Ben. "These'll be big, I think. But they'll keep you warm through the deep snow. I should've thought of them yesterday . . . the day before . . . "

Ben took them from her. He took off the institution shoes, made a ceremony of aligning them side by side near the door. "Today is soon enough, Rebecca. These will serve me well." And then, because he couldn't resist, he took both her hands and pulled her toward him. "As will this," he whispered before he kissed her sadly.

She leaned against him, drawing breath from him, drawing life. And minutes later, when the three of them stepped out toward the barn, the snow and wind hit them full bore, knocking the air from her lungs. This is what I'll feel like when he's gone, she thought. Like something's cut the breath away from me. When three days ago . . . three days ago . . . I didn't know.

The beaten path she'd followed to the barn each day was drifted over. They couldn't find it. They sloshed through the snow, their heads bent low, leaning against the wind, and for the longest time it seemed they weren't making progress at all. Driving currents of snow whirled into their faces. Just when Rebecca thought they'd gone too far, that they'd gotten lost and gone the wrong way, the silhouette of the barn loomed, an apparition behind the thick, swirling veil of snowflakes. Ben got ahead of them and struggled with the heavy door, kicking ice away with his feet so the hinges could swing free.

They didn't speak when at first they got inside. Just getting from the house to the barn had sapped their energy. Demi proudly set to work with the leathers the way Rebecca had taught her the day before. Ben led Mabel and Coney from their stalls, the coat he wore still powdered with snowflakes.

When Rebecca carried in the huge scoop to grain the horses, Ben stopped her, laughing while he wiped away the snow that clung to her lashes and brows. "Even when I close my eyes, I see snow coming at me," he joked. But this could be no laughing matter. Their lives would be at stake while they were out on the sleigh.

The horses ate greedily while Rebecca and Demi harnessed them. "That's right, you two," Demi crooned, stroking their noses as she positioned their head stalls, looking pointedly into four dark eyes that shone vividly clear. "Eat all you want. You're gonna need it when you get out there, believe me."

The horses stood ready almost too quickly. Rebecca gave last-minute instructions inside the shelter, knowing that once they got outside again, they'd have to shout to one another to be heard. "I'll break the bales open, and Ben, you pitch them over. Demi, keep a tight rein on the horses. They may spook some if they can't get a bearing on where they're going. Don't feed until we're right up on the elk. With how fast this snow's coming down, the hay'll get buried right away if there isn't an animal standing over it, eating it."

When Ben opened wide the entrance to the barn, Mabel and Coney both shied as the onslaught hit them. "Easy," Rebecca said, gripping Coney's throat-latch with both hands. "Easy."

"Easy. Easy," Demi crooned, too.

It took all three of them to get the team backed up and situated so the huge Belgians could be hitched to the sleigh. Ben heaped hay bales while Demi gasped for breath against the wind and began, ridiculously, hilariously, to bellow: "Good-bye, Old Paint. I'm leaving Cheyenne. Good-bye, Old Paint. I'm leaving Cheyenne."

Rebecca threw back her head and bellowed, too. "You're supposed to calm the horses down, not rile them up."

"This *is* calming them down. I can tell." Demi grinned, seeming more like a typical fourteen-year-old than she had since Rebecca had known her. She launched into the song all over again.

Ben took the reins first. The Belgians snorted and flung their manes as blowing snow filled their nostrils. "Where are the elk? I can't see a thing," Ben yelled over his shoulder.

"Neither can I," Rebecca yelled back. "Let the horses have their head. Maybe they'll know. They do seem to, sometimes."

The gusts came whistling down off the high mountain gorges, bitter and icy. The blustering snow melded sky and horizon so a person couldn't tell where one ended, another began. Yet after a while, in the white nothingness and stinging cold, Mabel and Coney seemed to accomplish a respectable rhythm with their plodding. "See," Demi said. "It worked. They liked my singing."

Rebecca blinked against the bite of the snow. "It's never been like this, Ben, never since I've seen it." But she had to laugh, tossing her new, smooth braid back over one shoulder. "Of course, Frank Weatherby would know when Star Valley last had a storm like this. He's probably sitting in the barber shop, giving out the date and details of it as we speak."

"Count yourself lucky," Ben bellowed back, "that it hasn't been in your lifetime."

Any flat light that managed to seep through the torrents of wafting snow left the terrain gray, without shadow, as two-dimensional as a kindergartner's drawing. Where once the snow had lain smooth and crusted, the wind had now winnowed out great empty indentations. Each time they came to one, the sleigh jolted, pitched forward to one side or the other, and sent all three of them stumbling.

They grabbed for each other, for the hay, for the rickety sides of the sleigh. As each runner passed over the wind-carved furrow, the thing righted itself with one mighty, wooden groan. Sometimes, in the midst of it, everything but the horses' rumps seemed to disappear. The sleigh's passengers could see no farther ahead than that.

It was Demi who first shouted, "Look. Here they come! We couldn't find them, but they've found us."

Through the confetti of the snow, great brown phantoms loomed, their heads raised in curiosity, their antlers jutting with virile purpose into the sky. A band of them materialized, appearing in the small circumference of a vision like something thrown into focus on a screen.

"They *have* found us," Rebecca shouted, lifting the first bale victoriously. "They must've heard the horses. Or maybe they smelled us."

"Or the horses smelled *them*, like you said." Demi reminded her of that. "Maybe Mabel and Coney knew where we were going all along."

She dropped the hay onto the floorboards. With cutters, she snipped through the baling wire and rent it open. Even in the fierceness of the storm, the alfalfa hay gave off a scant, lush potpourri of summer grass. Ben speared it with the prongs of the pitchfork and strung it along behind them.

More and more of the elk poured forth from the white obscurity, becoming distinct for moments, then being blotted out by the raging snow. Where for so long they'd searched, now the dark shapes emerged everywhere, ragged sienna hides clumped with ice, spindle-shanked legs fighting to wallow toward them, toward sustenance, survival.

As best she could, Rebecca examined them as they moved past, taking stock of their condition. Once, twice, three times she hollered, "Feed this bunch a little more, Ben. They're older." Or younger. Or haven't been up to pasture in a while. "It looks like they're going downhill some."

They'd unloaded over half the hay when they came upon the first carcass. An assembly of ravens stood nearby, black silhouettes against the ice. The horses startled the huge birds; they arched their wings, beat the air, and were gone, flown off into oblivion by the time Rebecca jumped from the moving sleigh and ran to see.

Through the snow, Ben could see her bending over the downed animal, her face practically to the ground, her hands running along the heavy hide, feeling its thickness with her fingers as if she were blind. When she came back, he reached down and lifted her onto the boards beside him. She shook her head. "He was probably too far gone even before the storm."

"He'd dead, then?" Demi clenched the reins with two fists, her hands sweaty despite the fierce cold, her face wet from snow, wind, tears. Her eyes shone round, innocent, uncomprehending. "He's dead when we might have saved him?"

"We're going to find more of them, Demi. If they've used too much of their body fat when it's still this cold, they don't stay warm enough—" She could say no more. She stood next to Ben, aching, all too aware again of the inevitability against them, of what she'd wagered, all she'd won and lost, because she'd let herself need this man at her side. Be it for one night. Be it for one day. She'd opened something within herself that hadn't been vulnerable before. Something that, like the elk lying prone in the snow, could only die.

She turned to him. "Ben. I'm begging you. You mustn't leave in this weather, not unless you take the truck. You won't make it."

"You're bringing that up again? I told you what I think. If they stop me and trace the truck, they'll know it's been you who has helped me."

"Why leave, then, if you're so certain you'll be caught? Why do it at all?"

She had him there. "If I don't go, Rebecca, everything I've believed in, everything I've risked, will be for nothing. The years I've lost of Demi's life. My home. My livelihood. My marriage." Yes, he'd risked many things and lost many. Other parts of his life, he knew now, he'd simply given away. The only way he could face himself, the only way he could balance the scales of reason, was to follow it to the end, to backtrack, to find himself on Hanna Coal property by tomorrow afternoon.

"Risk." She said the word as if she hated it. She stared out into the storm, defying it. He had to move closer to hear her steady voice. "Maybe nothing's worth anything, if it isn't worth a risk."

"Maybe." He thought, as he watched her, he'd always remember the profile she made, her hair hanging over her ear like a draped curtain, her face turned up to the sky. Snow fell across her cheeks, caught in her lashes, pooled to water the moment—the very instant—the snowflakes touched her warmth.

She wouldn't be swayed from this subject. "Leave the truck somewhere, then," she told him. "If anybody asks, I'll tell them it was stolen."

He had to smile for once. "Rebecca. If I don't agree, what are you going to do? How will you stop me?"

"I'll hold you both hostage." There was a loneliness in her eyes that tore at his very soul. But Demi didn't see it. Demi smiled.

Ben played along for his daughter's sake, for all their sakes. "How do you propose to do that? With the gun?"

Rebecca reached for the farm implement he'd left slanted against the side of the sleigh, thumped the prongs once, twice, against the wood for good measure as the wind howled around her. "No. With the pitchfork." Despite everything—the fear, the certainty of Ben's leaving—a hint of humor appeared in her expression. "I'm good at keeping hostages confined with a pitchfork. But I haven't had to do it in a long time."

"You think that old truck would make it all the way to Hanna?"

"I think that old truck stands a lot better chance than you do."

Truly, the storm and the carcass surrounded by ravens had convinced him. He'd thought once he and Demi made their way out of the mountains on foot, they could hitchhike along the roadway. The possibility lurked, though, that someone could recognize and report them.

Oh, but he hated taking her truck.

Seemed like every time he touched somebody's life, he endangered someone or put them at risk or caused them to be questioned. "I might as well dig it out when we get back to the house. If it makes you happy, Rebecca, we'll take it when we go."

She moved her head to see Ben, then faced the pile of bales again. "That makes me only able to stand it, Ben. Perhaps for now, that should be happiness enough."

"There's only one place Rebecca Woodburn would be in weather like this." Margaret Cox tugged her heavy mail satchel higher onto her shoulder and knocked on the door for the third time. "She's gone out in the sleigh, caring for the elk herd."

"Out? In this?" He hadn't realized it would be so cold up here. He stood looking out over the porch steps and what he could see of the land, his numb hands poked as deep into his suit coat pockets as they would go.

"She goes out every day all winter, as long as snow covers the ground. Her brother used to do it, too. Only he got stars in his eyes and ran off to Hollywood." She squinted off into the white nothingness, pulled strands of hair from her face like seaweed, only to have it blow right back. "The barn's over there, only you can't see it." In this snow they could barely see where she'd parked the jeep, either. "There's hundreds of head of elk out there as well. On a clear day when you can see it all, you'd swear you'd come high enough in the mountains to reach heaven."

"How long are we going to stand out here waiting for nobody to answer the door?" He was freezing. His knees knocked. Oh, but he was glad he hadn't decided to come all the way up here on his own.

"I had hoped she would answer it. It's one reason I didn't leave everything in the box out by the cattleguard. I wanted to check on her." Margaret tried the door by herself, as people in Star Valley were prone to do. The knob turned all the way. She felt the latch give. "Guess I'll just leave Rebecca's mail on the table. She'll find the letters and the newspaper and know I've been here."

"Can I come inside with you? Just to warm up?" Funny, he thought. After all this, he didn't have to connive to get inside. He had a perfectly good reason. He felt like his hands might fall off if he didn't rub them by a fire soon.

"Rebecca wouldn't mind. Her stove's always got a fire in it. This is quite a place, mister. A county landmark. Definitely worth having a look around.

Don't mind if I do, he thought smugly. Don't mind if I do.

"Tell me what Rebecca Woodburn is like," he said. "Seems like an odd way for a woman to live, all alone like this."

"It's an odd way to live all right." Margaret reminded him pointedly, "But no more odd than what you're doing, investigating criminals all over town, saying you've got a personal interest but never giving anybody your name."

"I offered to pay you, didn't I? That's all you need to know." He couldn't let her divert him. He had to keep his focus on the matter at hand. He didn't have much time.

The house smelled old like someone's attic, rich like cured pine and heavy smoke. While Margaret thumbed through the items in her bag, he stood in the middle of the room, uncertain of what he was searching for. Anything to support his hunch, he supposed, anything to prove this Rebecca Woodburn wasn't in the house alone. Anything to suggest she could be hiding someone.

The man ran a hand along the wool tweed of the sofa. He touched the warm, smooth stones of the hearth. Nothing.

Nothing.

His hopes sank. After all, suppose he found nothing. God help him, he had to get to Ben before Ben got to Hanna Coal.

"I'm ready to go," the mail lady said, her voice seeming soft and far away. He glanced at her. Her somber expression belied her words. She watched out the window, peering into the driving snow. "I do wish Rebecca would turn up. Another hour or so of this wet snow and that road's going to be impassable. I'd like to go back to George Peart's place and tell everybody in the barber shop that I've seen her and that she's doing fine."

"What's upstairs?" he asked, seizing the opportunity. "Is there a bathroom up there? I think I need to go."

But Margaret Cox saw through his bluff, which annoyed him. "Go poke your nose in the rooms upstairs, too. Rebecca wouldn't mind. But you won't find a bathroom up there. This house doesn't have indoor plumbing." She gestured toward the window, toward a wall of falling snow outside. "That bathroom's out there."

He checked upstairs quickly. Everything besides Rebecca's room looked uninhabited. He surveyed the outhouse from the upstairs window. "Guess I don't have to go as bad as all that." He came downstairs, straightening a little. "Guess I'll wait until we get back to town."

"We'd best get out of here," she said again. "It's a shame you missed meeting Rebecca. I know you wanted to. You think you should leave her a note or something?"

He perused the room, disappointed. "No. I don't think so."

Margaret stalled one last time. She strode once more to the table, straightened the pile of envelopes, readjusted the angle of the *Star Valley Independent* one last time. "There. She'll be surprised to get her paper today. She won't be expecting that special edition. I'll leave it laying like this. That way she'll see the headline first thing when she walks into the room."

Margaret Cox made one step toward the door. One step. With his eyes, he followed her. And that's when his breath caught in his throat. He spied the evidence he searched for, in plain view, on the floor beside the wall.

He grabbed her arm.

"What?"

"We can't leave yet."

"Why not?" She shrugged away from him. "Mister, is something wrong with you?"

He ignored her question. He stooped beside the pair of worn leather shoes, a black pair that looked as if they'd walked a million miles, institution made.

"What's so important about an old pair of shoes?" she asked.

He picked one up, ran his fingers along the pock-marked sole, the creases where leather had broken with each step. He made note of the water marks, the decrepit curled toes.

Prison shoes.

Ben's shoes.

"Funniest-looking shoes I've ever seen," Margaret commented, doing her best to make conversation with this strange, distracted fellow. "Folks usually wear pac boots around here, not funny-looking things like that. Wonder why Rebecca's got 'em sitting on her living room floor. I wonder if they used to be Howdy's."

He set them back exactly as they'd been, toes aligned along the wall, heels side by side. For a long moment he buried his face in his hand, massaging both temples with one motion. Then, softer than she could hear, he said simply, "I've found him. Ben's here."

The pilot tried three times to land in Jackson Hole.

Even though he couldn't see the ground, Thom knew the approach by heart, knew the throbbing, steady pulsing of the engines as they flew directly over Palisades Reservoir and Teton Pass, the sharp bank to the left as they dropped altitude over the national park and curved to the west around Blacktail Butte. In only moments they'd be headed due south, coming in long and low, trying to touch down on a runway so short that the tourists would swear they were going to land in sagebrush.

Thom leaned against the cold window, his nostrils leaving haze on the glass. The plane bounced again, setting his stomach aloft. Below, all was nothingness. If the sky had been clear, they would've seen the town glittering like a jewel in a cranny between the mountains. They would've seen the Grand Teton to the west, its majestic snow-covered crags towering over them already, even though they weren't on the ground.

He felt the plane begin to rise for the third time, and his throat drew tight with disappointment. They weren't going to make it in. So close, he thought, but still so far away.

The plane banked once more to the east, but this time Thom felt them climbing. The pilot's loud, jovial voice came over the loudspeaker. "Well, folks, we've had a slight change of plans this afternoon." Thom hid his smile beneath his hand. The fellow sounded like an announcer on *The Price Is Right,* not someone who'd just had to make life-and-death decisions about landing a plane in low visibility on a short runway beside towering granite mountains that no one could see. "They are experiencing a snowstorm in northwestern Wyoming today. At Jackson Hole airport, they're reporting crosswinds of up to fifty-three miles per hour. The valley has received over eight inches of fresh snow since midnight, with more in the mountains. The weather service is predicting another six inches to accumulate before nightfall."

People all over the plane looked out the window, looked down, as if they expected to see something that they hadn't seen before. Something other than white.

Yes. A snowstorm, Thom thought. And I know what Rebecca's doing right now. Rebecca's out in it. Rebecca's feeding elk.

He turned to the woman beside him and said, "I've written about this." And won awards for it, too. Academy Awards. "This is where I belong. I've written about it, but I haven't been to see it for a very long time."

She moved slightly away from him and stared at something forward in the aisle. He didn't care. He felt like a little boy, antsy on his seat when something spectacular was about to happen.

"We've been rerouted to Pocatello, Idaho," the pilot continued. "It's snowing there, too, but the visibility is much better."

"What the hell are we supposed to do in Pocatello, Idaho?" an angry man asked from behind him.

"I'm scheduled to be at my grandson's hockey game this afternoon," a distraught woman announced.

But Thom knew where he'd be, what he'd be doing. He was good at this sort of thing. He wouldn't wait for the snow to clear out, and he wouldn't complain. Let the others spend the night in a hotel and try to fly to Wyoming in the morning. Thom would rent a four-wheel drive in Pocatello.

The stranger paid Margaret Cox an extra twenty dollars to drop him off at the Lincoln County Sheriff's Office in Afton. He strolled smugly into the office and found them all there, drinking coffee, eating an assortment of doughnuts, and continuing their dissertations about the sorry state of the weather. Everybody in a uniform had gathered here—Andy Rogers, the state troopers, even Joe Don Manning, the sheriff himself, and Gladys Crates, the dispatcher.

"Why are you all here?" he asked. "We've got a criminal loose in Star Valley. Why aren't some of you out working the roadblocks?"

"Roadblocks? In weather like this?" The state man, the one everybody'd been calling Jarvis, folded his arms before him. "You must be nuts. Nobody travels when it's doing this outside. Nobody does anything except sit around and talk about it."

Gladys backed him up. "Don't have to worry about roadblocks when it's snowing so hard the roads could be closed themselves."

Joe Don held up a half-eaten French cruller and motioned for the stranger to take a chair. "Just suppose you sit down and eat yourself a doughnut, mister. And while you're eating the doughnut, you could tell us a little bit about yourself. You could tell us who you are and why you feel the need to be asking so many questions of these fine folks in Star Valley."

"I don't want a doughnut." He didn't sit down. He smiled down at all of them, felt an odd anticipation well up within him. "I've only stopped by to make a citizen's report."

"Gladys'll get you the papers to fill out," Andy told him. But Gladys sat still on her chair, her coffee mug gripped in both hands, obviously not wanting to move.

"Go ahead, Gladys," Joe Don urged. "Get him the papers so he can fill everything out."

"You won't want me to take the time to fill out papers," he said smugly.

Even Andy Rogers, as easygoing as he was, didn't like this man's attitude. "Just suppose you let us decide that, sir. We'll follow procedure with you the same way we do with everyone else in this office." Yes, have a cup of coffee and a doughnut. "Fill out those papers." Gladys had retrieved everything he needed, a felt-tip pen and the official incident report that would need, before the day was over, to be photocopied in triplicate.

The first thing the report called for was his name and address. Well, he'd leave well enough alone with that. He bypassed that section completely and wrote with the pen, as large and as bold as he could make it: "The escaped convict is at Rebecca Woodburn's place." He held it up high so everyone could see it.

He was right. They all jumped at once. Even Joe Don Manning took his feet off the desk and sat up a little bit.

"No way," Andy said. "You're wrong."

"Prove it."

"We've already been up there. We've already searched the place."

"How thoroughly did you search?"

Andy thought back, hesitated. "Okay. Maybe we could've done more. But we questioned Rebecca Woodburn. She took us through all the outbuildings, showed us all the places a man could hide. We asked her if she'd seen anything. She would've told us if she'd been suspicious—"

The stranger's smile grew broader. "What about the house? Did you search the house, too?"

"Of course we did. Although Rebecca didn't think it would be necessary. When we mentioned searching the house, the entire thought frightened her. I could see it in her eyes. It scared her to death to think that someone might've gotten in without her knowing."

"You're only overlooking one thing."

"What is that?"

"The fear in her eyes. Could it be possible she was afraid you'd find him?"

"You can't be serious."

"Could it be possible she's been harboring him up there of her own free will?"

"No. That's not possible. I know Rebecca. She's . . . she's . . . *trustworthy.*"

But now Joe Don Manning stood up, too. One by one the state troopers and the sheriff's deputies began buckling on their holsters. "We'd better get up there again and check it out, Andy." He turned to the man. "I suppose you have evidence to support this claim?"

"Yes," he said, finally helping himself to a doughnut and biting in. It was raspberry filled, his favorite. "I do. If you'll just let me ride with you, I'll tell you about it on the drive up."

"Come on." The sheriff gestured. Then he turned back to the assorted group of officers standing at attention. "Men. I want to warn you. This is a man arrested and convicted of murder. Consider him armed and dangerous. If we get up there and he tries to run, I'll give orders to shoot on sight. Do you understand?"

The officers nodded. "We understand."

Confidently, they headed to their cars.

18

Because Demi, Rebecca, and Ben desired it so, the day of the elk, of battling the snow, stretched out endless before them. How many times did Demi slap the Belgians' rumps with the reins to keep them at their slow gait, another bale of alfalfa, another group of hungry elk, always at hand? How many carcasses did they find in the snow before they decided, for their own sakes, it would be best not to count?

Their bodies, exhausted and sore, gave testimony to their grueling task. Still, even so, the hours pitching hay had passed like minutes. For once Mabel and Coney were snug in the barn, once the leathers had been unbuckled and hung on each peg, nothing would keep Ben from tromping out to the old Dodge Power Wagon and shoveling out the snow around the tires. Once the truck had been gotten out, nothing would stop the Pershalls from leaving. They'd be better off to go, surely, while the snow still raged. No one would be on the roads. In its own way, this storm would shelter them.

When they got to the barn, Demi brushed both horses, her songs silent. She followed each brush stroke with a caress of her hand, imparting favor and sad benediction with each flowing movement of her arms.

"I'll pack some sandwiches," Rebecca said after she'd finished and they trudged toward the house. As if, in the very bag she would hand them, she could send along a part of herself. "You won't have to stop for food that way. Or risk seeing anyone."

How many times today would they speak of risk?

How many times would they count the cost of providing haven for one another?

Even the short distance from the barn to the house seemed too much to travel. The ice needled their skin. The onslaught of the wind deafened them, made them feel as if they were being consumed by the great walls and circles of the snow. "No matter how long you try to hold your breath out there," Demi gasped as they reached the porch, "the storm holds its longer."

Ben turned at the steps and surveyed all he could see, taking it in the way a child takes in his surroundings, his room, his things, when he leaves them for the first time. "Look," he said. "You can't even see the barn."

Demi went into the house, but Rebecca stopped to stand beside him, looking out. "You wouldn't know it was there, would you, just by looking?"

He took a deep breath, held it, as if he wanted to hold inside everything he'd unearthed here. After a long while, he said, "Many things in this place are that way."

She didn't say anything. She'd folded her arms across her breasts. When he glanced toward her, he saw that she instinctively raised her head higher. She moved her mittened hands slowly up and down her own arms. Shoulder to elbow. Elbow to shoulder.

"Has it been my way of seeing things that's gotten me into this?" he asked. "I haven't been very good at trusting in what I couldn't see."

"Some people say that's what miracles are." She smiled, still staring out to where the barn should be. "Like the barn we've just been inside, like the elk we knew were there but couldn't feed until they appeared through the snow. Miracles aren't some tremendous power coming from far away. They come to us when our perceptions are made finer, when we see everything from a higher place. Perhaps it only comes for a moment, that sight. But that's when our minds can absorb—can hear and see—everything that's surrounded us always."

Her hands were still grasping her own elbows. He took her elbows in his hands, too, and caught all of her there, leaning her against the ice-etched logs of the house so he could kiss her. He kissed her long and hard, as if he wanted to claim her soul with his very tongue. Ice and fire. Unending.

Demi had opened up the doors to the stove when they walked in. The embers glowed red hot. "Oh, look," Rebecca said. "While we were out, Margaret came with the mail. She's brought it all the way into the house." She crossed to the table, had her hands on the envelopes, when she saw the headline on the paper. *The Star Valley Independent*, the masthead read. Then all the way across the top: "Special Edition. Special Edition. Special Edition."

"What's that?"

"The newspaper. It's a special edition of some sort. Angus has—"

As slowly as blood flows back into cold fingers, so flowed the realization, the significance, into Rebecca's mind. She held the paper in two hands. When she read the headline, she had to read it twice to grasp the meaning of it. FUGITIVE PASSES THROUGH STAR VALLEY, the massive headline read. "Convict Serving Life for Murdering His Own Brother."

Convict Serving Life for Murdering His Own Brother.

She said very slowly, very evenly, "Ben? Is this about you?"

He didn't answer. He stood rigid, like a stag caught in a car's headlights, unable to move, unable to disentangle himself.

"Ben?"

"I'm going out to get the shovel," he said. "It's time I started working on the truck." But maybe he shouldn't. Maybe she wouldn't let him take the truck now that she'd read about what had gone on in his past.

She held out the paper flat so he could see. Each time she asked it, her voice grew softer, as if she convinced herself more every time she said it. "Is this about you? Is this about you?"

Without saying anything, he nodded. She sank onto the chair and began to read while all the rest of the world disappeared from around her. *Please*, she railed to herself. *Don't let it be so awful. Don't let it be something that would hurt so much or seem so wrong.*

"Come on, Demi," he said, wrapping one arm around his daughter's shoulder and pulling her to one side, waiting, knowing Rebecca would want them to back away. He thought about getting the gun again, but it was too late for that. She'd given him too much. He'd found too much of himself with her.

Rebecca scanned every article, desperate to understand it, praying that she'd come upon a sudden paragraph that said, "Oops. Gotcha," something that would admit there could be a question, that what he'd done had been an accident or some mistake. But it hadn't been. The facts spoke for themselves. The evidence had been presented, and a jury of his peers had convicted him. It spoke of other horrible things—his brother trapped by a cave-in at the mine . . . indication found that a bomb had been set deliberately.

She remembered the times she'd talked about Thom and Ben had grown quiet. She thought of the day she'd asked about his brother and Ben had said, "There isn't much to tell." Rebecca pointed to the page and whispered the name. "Ben? Are they talking about Billy?"

For the second time, he nodded.

"We were talking about our brothers, mine and yours. And I—" She stopped herself. She bit her lip like a little child, her face gone as white as the snow that covered the meadow. "How did you plead?"

"Innocent."

"Were you innocent, Ben?"

He'd taken enough, had enough of telling the story and having no one believe him. He wanted to die, so great was his pain. She'd read a newspaper and convicted him, too. No matter what she knew of him. No matter the parts of himself he'd let become vulnerable to her.

"What difference does it make, anyway? They found me guilty." In her eyes, he saw their eyes. In her reborn fear, he saw their judgment. In her final tears, he saw Wyllis's betrayal.

"You'd best go shovel out that truck," she said evenly, glancing back and forth between him and Demi. "I think it's best for you to be on your way."

Thom drove the rented Jeep Cherokee as fast as he could on the snowy roads. The airplane pilot had been right about the weather. He'd lived in Star Valley a long time, and he'd never seen Highway 287 as bad off as it seemed now. He'd kept the thing in four-wheel drive ever since he'd left Pocatello.

He turned off the main road and veered to the right past the lone tree. He had the radio tuned to KSGT in Jackson Hole. He sang along with the country music, letting the song guide his mood, alternately happy to be going home and grieving over Jillian.

Because of the storm and frigid temperatures, Greybull Pond was frozen over again. Maybe he'd dig out his old skates. He shrugged to himself. You never knew.

As he climbed higher into the mountains, the road narrowed. It had begun to snow harder, too. Thom could hardly see where to drive. He leaned forward, rubbed the inside of the windshield with his coat sleeve. It didn't help much.

If he had a set of tracks to follow, that might keep him from driving off the road. It looked like maybe only one car had traveled this road today. And that had been a good while ago. The ruts its tires had made were already totally filled in with snow.

He poked around on the dashboard, trying to turn up the defroster. Thom couldn't see at all. He should go slower. But when he pressed down on the brakes and felt the tires lose traction, he realized he'd made a grave error. The Cherokee began its spin almost as if in slow motion. He took his foot off the brakes and tried to steer into the swerve, but it was too late. The rented vehicle sheered off the byway and sank into the deep snow.

Andy Rogers got on his radio and alerted the officers in the cars behind him. "Somebody's gone off the road up here, guys. A red Jeep Cherokee with Idaho plates."

"It's a rental," Joe Don Manning guffawed over the radio. "Some tourist out for a nice spring day's drive."

"It's Thom Woodburn," Andy hollered when he got close enough. "He's come home!"

"What's all the fuss about?" asked the voice of one of the state troopers.

"He's probably on his way up to see Rebecca, too. He's going the same place we are."

Andy pulled to a halt where Thom's vehicle had gone off the road. "Hey, buddy!" he shouted. "What are you doing here?"

"It's time for me to come home," Thom said. "I was on my way up. Guess the L.A. Freeway's got me out of the habit of driving on snowy roads. I've never been so glad to see a bunch of sheriff's officers in all my life."

"Get in," Andy told him. "You can drive up the rest of the way with us. But you may not be so glad to see us when we tell you what's going on."

Ben came back in the door, his shoulders covered with snow again, his eyes sad. "Well, that's about it," he told her. "That old Dodge started right up."

"It always does."

"Got all the snow away from the tires, too. It won't be the safest driving I've ever done, but it oughtta get me and Demi out of here okay."

"It'll be safer than you walking." He finally met her eyes and saw that she'd been crying. "There's plenty of gas in it. You ought to be able to get all the way to

Riverton or Rock Springs, depending on which way you decide to go."

"Thanks."

"Ben, I—" She stopped, tears clogging her throat. She couldn't say more.

"It's okay, Rebecca. Don't say anything. Maybe it's better this way."

She shook her head, desperate to make him understand. "It's awful. I'd always known you were serving life for something. And it doesn't change what I feel or what we've been to each other or how we've talked—"

"You're lying about that," he said. Maybe she didn't mean to. Maybe she just didn't understand yet. "It does change things." He'd seen it in her eyes. Things changed because she'd been with him, known everything he could give her, yet had believed a newspaper. She didn't trust him anymore.

"Good-bye, Rebecca." Dear, sweet heaven, but tears were coming to his eyes, too. "Damn." He turned away, not wanting her to see.

"I've made you the sandwiches." She handed him a brown bag heavy with meat and fruit. Demi wrapped her arms around Rebecca and hugged her so tight, she could scarcely breathe. "I love you, Demi," Rebecca whispered. She raised her eyes to the girl's father. "I love you, Ben," she said. "Please. Take care of yourself."

He was wiping his nose and his streaming eyes with Howdy's shirtsleeve when Demi said, "Sh-h-hh. What was that?"

"What?" Rebecca asked. "I didn't hear anything."

"It sounded like a car door."

Rebecca looked out the window. She gasped. Seven sheriff's cars and state vehicles had filed up the driveway. Men were jumping from them, drawing guns.

"They know you're here!" she shouted.

He glanced around the room, trapped. "What should we—?"

Tears had come to Demi's eyes, too. "We're going to die, aren't we? Dad, I'm scared."

"No." Rebecca took command. "You aren't going to die. You don't have to be scared." She wheeled toward Ben. "I'll keep Demi safe. I promise. No one here need ever know. I'll get her back to Wyllis if need be."

"You'd do that for me?"

"Of course I would. Now, go. They haven't surrounded the house yet. Get out that back window and follow the willows to the pond. The one where you had your bath. The steam will keep you warm while you hide."

He grabbed her, kissed her. "Dear God, Rebecca," he said. "Whatever happens, I love you. Know that. Remember that."

"I will remember it," she promised. "For always."

The officers called out on their bull horns, "Come out! Come out with your hands up!"

She didn't go out. She needed precious seconds to come up with a story, to regain her composure. She hid behind the couch with Demi, trembling, buying Ben as much time as she could. *Please, God*, she prayed. *Please keep him safe*.

From out in the driveway, she heard men shouting. "Don't hold me back, Andy," a familiar voice shouted. "Let me go in and find out what's going on. She's no hardened criminal, Andy. I won't let you hold guns on the house like this."

"You're more trouble than you're worth," Andy told him. "Maybe I'm sorry we stopped to pick you up in the first place. That man in there with her *is* a hardened criminal. There's no telling what he might convince her to do."

But all was over for Rebecca. She'd heard her brother's voice. "Thom!" After making sure Demi stayed hidden, she flung the door wide. "Thom, you're home!"

The others started running behind him. But he stopped, turned around, gave them all a look that froze them in their tracks. "She's my sister. Please. Let me talk to her."

"You've got three minutes to talk," Joe Don said. "Three minutes and that's all. After that, we take matters into our own hands."

He ran to the porch, threw his arms around her, lifted her, and spun. He felt her crying into his shoulder. "Thank heavens you've come," she whispered. He felt her shaking. These men in the driveway had scared her to death. But it was more than that, too. He sensed it.

"Where is he, Rebecca? Where is Ben Pershall?"

"He isn't here anymore."

"But he's been here?"

She nodded, the tears coming in earnest now. "I've taken care of him."

Thom gripped her shoulders. "He's still on the land somewhere, isn't he? You've got him hidden out."

"No . . . he's trying to go. . . . I mean, yes . . . "

"Where is he?"

"I won't tell you."

"You have to, Rebecca. They mean business out there. If you don't, they'll search him out and find him. They've got orders to shoot on sight. If you'll let me bring him in first, at least you stand a chance of saving his life."

"They're going to shoot him?"

"No!" The girl jumped from behind the couch. "Don't let them shoot my dad."

Thom looked from the girl back to Rebecca. He waited.

"Please," Demi wailed. "You've got to help my dad."

"I will," Thom said. "If you'll only let me."

Rebecca closed her eyes and took one deep breath. He won't make it to Hanna, she thought. He won't make to Hanna. But at least he'll still be alive. "He went out the back window."

Thom filled in the blanks. "He went down to the pond, didn't he? He knew he could go down there and stay warm."

"He's there."

Thom took a length of rope from where it hung by the door. He opened the door and bellowed, "You promise not to shoot and I'll bring Ben Pershall to you. Give me ten minutes." He took off running, and, after moments, they couldn't see him anymore. He ran across the meadow, sinking into snow almost to his knees. But he could see where another man had traveled this route, too, not more than a few minutes before. He cupped his hands over his mouth and called out, "Ben? Ben?" But no one answered.

He plundered through into the willows, followed what would be in springtime a pleasant winding of the stream. But today its ice-encrusted banks, eddies, and driftwood barriers seemed ominous.

Suddenly Thom heard someone running in front of him. "Ben? Stop." Together they crashed through the willows. Ben held one hand out as he plunged through the snow and the underbrush. Thom tripped, breathless, reached for the trunk of a giant cottonwood, and seemed to fall toward it. Ben flung branches back in his face. Thom caught himself against them. The limbs gouged into his eyes.

Ben turned, swinging on his pursuer with all the strength he had left. Thom sidestepped, threw a punch of his own. Ben circled, but the snow made him artless. He stumbled, turned his back against the trunk of the tree, fighting to get air into his lungs with a tremendous heave of his chest. "No," he gasped, ready to do battle but incapable. "Don't take . . . me . . . in."

"Have to." Thom bent over, tried to force air into his lungs, too. "To save you." He glanced back over his shoulder at the house. "To save her. If you keep running and they have to track you down, they're going to say she's been hiding you."

Ben shook his head. "I made her take me in. I held the gun on her. I kept guard over her and held her hostage. Then, things got—" He shook his head. "Anybody I end up caring for, I hurt."

"That doesn't have to be." Thom reached out a hand to him. "If you turn yourself in, Rebecca won't get hurt."

Ben bent his head, closed his eyes, remembered all the reasons he'd escaped, all the reasons he had to get to Hanna Coal. "I've got to stop someone. Something horrible's going to happen if I don't."

"Tell the sheriff, Ben. Tell him if you've got a reason for what you've done."

"They didn't believe me the first time. They have no reason to believe me now." It was what he'd meant by believing in things he couldn't see. Good intentions hadn't gotten him anywhere. Tomorrow he'd be locked up in the state pen again, facing the rest of a life term, plus another when they punished him for escaping.

He buried his face in both hands. Maybe Thom was right. Maybe, in the end, none of it was as important as Rebecca. He'd learned it often, and always learned it the hard way. Nothing was more important than the people you loved.

"You're in love with my sister, aren't you?" Thom asked.

Ben Pershall met the other man's gaze and nodded. "Yes."

"You been up here a while?"

"Three days." He wiped the grit and snow from his face with the back of his hand. "So I guess you must be Thom. No one else I can think of would convince me to turn myself in for Rebecca's sake." Ben didn't smile. Instead he held out both of his wrists so they could be bound.

"Here they come!" Joe Don Manning shouted. "Men, hold your fire."

Thom walked with Ben across the meadow, side by side.

"He's got him subdued. He's got his hands tied." Jarvis thumped the hood of his car in a flat-handed move of victory. "Well, I'll be dogged."

Thom led Ben directly to Andy's car. Andy was about the only one in that great frenzied group whom he trusted. "You be good to him," Thom said sadly. "He says he's got good reasons for what he's done."

"Right." The trooper named Jarvis leaned his head back and laughed. "They all have good reasons for robbing banks and murdering their kin. We hear these stories all the time."

Andy Rogers unwound the binding from Ben's wrists. He handed Thom the rope and replaced it with handcuffs. "So," he asked nonchalantly, "has Rebecca Woodburn been harboring you here?"

Ben stared at the toes of the huge old boots she'd let him borrow. "I broke in." And as he told the story to protect her, he never lied. "I held a gun on her. I threatened to kill her or hurt somebody else if she told."

Andy grinned at Joe Don victoriously. "I told you she wouldn't go against the law and hide somebody up here. He made her do it. See, that fellow in the suit was wrong."

They all stopped, stared at each other. "Where'd that man doing all the investigatin' go?" somebody asked. Nobody'd seen the stranger for the longest time.

The officers turned, glanced into all the cars. "Here he is," Joe Don announced. The fellow sat alone, in the backseat of a state car, as if he were hiding from something.

"Why don't you get out and join the party?" Andy asked.

He shook his head. "Rather stay here," he said succinctly.

"Well, you aren't going to be able to stay there," Jarvis Taylor announced, swaggering over to his vehicle and putting his hands on his hips. "This prisoner's going back down the hill in state custody. That means he's gonna ride back down the side of this mountain with me."

The man inched to the far side of the car and waited for Jarvis to open his door. He slipped out, turned his face away from the group, slid behind another officer.

"Okay," Joe Don said, clapping his hands authoritatively. "Let's load Ben Pershall up. Sooner we do that, sooner we call the state pen and let 'em know they've got a wayward son coming home. The sooner we call Rawlins, the sooner we all get to go home and have a hot bath."

A general cheer went up among the officers. "Well, Ben," Andy said, enjoying the victory, "you certainly gave us a run for our money."

Jarvis Taylor directed Ben into his car. One by one the other officers climbed in, too. "Where do I ride?" the man in the suit asked. For a moment he'd been the only one left standing outside. And because Ben had already been loaded, he forgot he was supposed to hide.

Andy gestured. "Over here. You can go back with me."

But Andy heard a voice, a teenage girl's voice, from the porch of the house. "Stop! Don't go yet."

"Who's that?" Joe Don asked out of his window. "I didn't know Rebecca had a kid up here."

No one in the crowd knew, except for Thom. And Thom Woodburn was silent.

The girl began to come forward slowly, gawking as if she'd seen a ghost. She wasn't certain until she got closer. She hadn't seen him in almost six years. She'd been only eight years old last time he'd come to the house and pitched a baseball to her. But she had a good memory. Most fourteen-year-olds do. "Uncle Billy." Then louder, as she got close enough to be certain: "Uncle Billy."

The stranger gaped at the child. His eyes had to be playing tricks on him. *What was Demi doing here*? He ducked below the car, trying to get away from her, but it was too late. He looked one direction, then another, trying to decide which way he could run.

"Dad. Where's my dad?" She stopped at Joe Don's huge stomach and stared straight up. "Dad's got to know that Uncle Billy's here."

"Who's Uncle Billy?" Andy asked.

Rebecca had come running across the snow, waggling Angus's front page for all to see. "*This is Uncle Billy!*" she shouted, pointing at the headline. "Thom. A jury convicted Ben Pershall of killing his brother, Billy." She pointed to the car door behind which the man crouched. "*That* is Billy Pershall."

"The one who's been hanging around church and the barber shop asking questions? He's Ben Pershall's *brother?*"

"Sure looks like it."

"Get Ben out of the car," Joe Don ordered. "I want to see this."

At that precise moment, Billy started running. His suit coat flew open as he wallowed through the snow.

"Get him!" Andy shouted.

"I want that man in custody," Joe Don agreed.

"Uncle Billy!" Demi cried again as the state troopers went after him. In no time they caught and handcuffed him.

Demi clung to Rebecca. Ben stood from the car, his manacles clattering. Two state troopers brought the fellow, each restraining him with an arm behind his back. Joe Don kept a hand on Ben's arm. They brought the stranger close so the two of them eyed each other, nose to nose. "Do you recognize this man, Ben?" Joe Don Manning asked.

Eye to eye. Nose to nose. The whole scene reminded Thom of two dogs meeting each other, sniffing each other, before the fight began.

"Yes," Ben answered softly. "I recognize him."

"Who is he? Can you tell me?"

"His name is William Charles Pershall," Ben said. "He is my brother."

They stared at each other again, while the officers couldn't quite decide what to do.

"All this time, I thought I had to get to Hanna," Ben said. "And look. You've come here instead."

"I know why you escaped from jail, Ben," Billy accused. "You escaped so you could stop me again."

"Somebody had to stop you. You almost killed somebody the first time. And then when I heard in the can that somebody'd come into Wyoming and started buying explosives, I knew it was you."

"The quicker they get you back in jail and out of my way, the better."

Ben glanced around the gathering, wanting them to hear. And hear, they did. "Suppose the owners of Hanna Coal made some mistakes. Suppose they *are* responsible for Dad's death. Two wrongs don't make a right."

"Shut up!" Billy shouted. "You make me sick, trying to do everything right. Sometimes two wrongs make justice."

"I went in there trying to save people. You set me up, Billy. Then you ran away so nobody'd know. You let me go to trial and take the blame. I trusted you, Billy. Trust is important."

Billy Pershall began to shout. He shook his fist. "I didn't *want* you to trust me. I just wanted to be a kid. I just wanted to go off to school like Dad promised."

Joe Don Manning quietly motioned for Andy to hand over his key ring. The sheriff moved to unlock the shackles around Ben's wrists. "Seems to me we've got the wrong brother in handcuffs. I'm going to have to take you in, Ben, to get everything taken care of. But I'm not keeping you restrained." Slowly, purposely, he began to handcuff Billy instead.

"You can't do this!" Billy bellowed. "You can't take me in. You don't have anything to arrest me for."

"Oh, I'm sure the folks down in Hanna can come up with something. Meanwhile, I'm holding you as a material witness. The governor of the great state of Wyoming is going to be mighty interested in meeting you when he starts to consider a pardon for your brother."

By early evening, the snowstorm had at last spent itself over the valley. When it came time to leave, Demi climbed inside the sheriff's car first. The officers got in next, and each slammed shut one door, the sound both final and remote in the late winter air.

Ben gripped Rebecca's shoulders as he searched her face. From behind him, one of the drivers honked. They were anxious, ready to pull out, ready to go home. He turned his face toward the remaining cars and then back to her, not wanting to leave her, wanting never to leave her. "You know what I'm gonna ask, don't you?"

"I think I do." She stood, more alone than ever, pac boots buried to the bows in the fresh drifted powder beside the house. "You've already asked me once," she said. "Remember?"

"I remember." Staring down at her eyes, eyes that trusted him, eyes that had given him the world and more. Eyes that had given him himself again.

"It's the same thing we talked about, isn't it?" And, because in this place he'd known so much, she knew the answer had come for her, too. "The miracles. That I could go and come, trusting what I couldn't see. That I might not have to stay because all this"—she gave an expansive gesture with her hand, one that took in the entire landscape—"stays within me."

"Will you come with me, Rebecca? I don't have a lot to offer or anything, but we could just try—"

Rebecca turned to her brother, lost, torn between all that she'd been and all that she had, even then, set her heart on becoming.

"I'll feed the elk for a while." Thom touched his sister's arm to reassure her. "I haven't forgotten how to drive the sleigh and harness horses. And you all can come home when you're finished in Rawlins. You only have to try this. I'm here, Rebecca. You go on for a while. You *deserve* to go on."

"I've never left before," she whispered.

"Some things are worth leaving for," he told her, "and some things aren't. I'm learning that along with you."

She smiled at her brother with eternal sadness. Perhaps she thought of the baby he'd told her he lost, or of the babies she'd have, of the strong-legged, summer-brown children she'd bring to this place and teach the ways of Timberline. Then she said to Ben and called out to Demi and all the officers who sat fidgeting in the car, "Yes. I'll get my things if you'll wait for me. I'd like to come, too."

Ben whooped and picked her up, spun her around, kissed her while her sadness turned to laughter. Their circling boots sprayed snow and dug down so deep that the hole stayed in the yard for the rest of the winter, not disappearing completely until the last of the ice soaked in and became mud, the promise of spring. Once he set her down, it didn't take her long to fill her bag. She hurried out, heaving Lucille's old tapestry duffel over one shoulder, as she sloughed through the deep snow. Someone opened the trunk from the glove compartment, and Ben helped her pitch it in.

As one engine roared to life, then another, and the official cars picked up speed toward the cattleguard, Thom could see his sister through the glass. She didn't glance with false penitence toward the house. Instead, as they drove away, she raised up in the car to see in the opposite direction, craning her neck, her eyes following the landscape of the rolling snow-covered meadow where the animals would always be when she returned, their dark familiar shapes leading off to the timbered wilderness, eternal, one long, restless string of elk.

Long after the sheriff's cars had driven away and he'd stopped waving, Thom stood in the yard of the old place, remembering, and thinking he'd better get down to work to move in. He wanted to write. Of course, he *would* write! In this old place he felt stories coming on, filling him, healing him. A novel about his sister and Ben, perhaps, instead of another screenplay.

Thom faced the sky, looking high, as high as he dared with his eyes and his heart. Above him, as the twilight grew thicker, an eagle spread wide its pinions and set off from the sheer rock, never once flapping or fluttering, never once struggling, letting the updraft fill its wings, becoming one with the wind.

Harper
Monogram